ALL THE LASTING THINGS

ALL THE LASTING THINGS

a novel

David Hopson

Little
a

Text copyright © 2016 David Hopson
All rights reserved.

Excerpts from *To the Lighthouse* by Virginia Woolf. ©1927 by Houghton Mifflin Harcourt Publishing Company. Copyright renewed 1954 by Leonard Woolf. Reprinted by permission of Houghton Mifflin Harcourt Publishing Company. All rights reserved.

Thank you to the Society of Authors as the Literary Representative of the Estate of Virginia Woolf.

Published by Little A, New York

www.apub.com

Amazon, the Amazon logo, and Little A are trademarks of Amazon.com, Inc., or its affiliates.

ISBN-10 (hardcover): 1503952002
ISBN-13 (hardcover): 9781503952003

ISBN-10 (paperback): 1503951995
ISBN-13 (paperback): 9781503951990

Cover design by Adil Dara

Printed in the United States of America

For Melvin and for my parents

. . . so that the monotonous fall of the waves on the beach, which for the most part beat a measured and soothing tattoo to her thoughts and seemed consolingly to repeat over and over again as she sat with the children the words of some old cradle song, murmured by nature, "I am guarding you—I am your support," but at other times suddenly and unexpectedly, especially when her mind raised itself slightly from the task actually in hand, had no such kindly meaning, but like a ghostly roll of drums remorselessly beat the measure of life, made one think of the destruction of the island and its engulfment in the sea, and warned her whose day had slipped past in one quick doing after another that it was all ephemeral as a rainbow . . .

—Virginia Woolf

ALL THE
LASTING
THINGS

My name will be the last to go. If the doctors are right, if the last memory in is the first one out, then yesterday disappears before anything else. Yesterday, then last week, then, like sandcastles meeting the tide, the months. The years. My wife, my children, my work, even her, even Jane, all of it swallowed and churned. No less gone than if I'd dropped my life into the sea. But Henry. They'll have me in diapers before I forget my name. Henry, they'll say, and up I'll look, not knowing who is speaking or why. Just Henry. Before another wave rolls in and the last castle falls.

I.

There would be no ghost, not tonight.

No "Adieu! Adieu!" Benji thought. No "Remember me."

He stood in front of the mirror, arms spread wide, as a strange man rushed to dress him. Jerry, the man who usually dressed him, had called in with a migraine, which Kay, the Stalinist stage manager / code cracker, immediately deciphered as "too drunk to stand." Now, as inquisitor, she used her considerable hip to hold open the door of the men's dressing room and waited for Benji's bloodshot eyes to meet hers in the mirror.

"Headaches," she mused. "You never know what's going to bring them on. Weather. Bright lights. Caffeine."

"Voices," Benji added. "Certain voices."

The more modest members of the cast shied in their underwear at Kay's appearance, hurrying into their doublets and hosen, but Kay continued, unfazed. "A bottle of Canadian Club. It doesn't bother you that Jerry's in rehab? *Was* in rehab. Who knows how much your little lunch date set him back."

The obvious responses spun through Benji's mind—the bottle belonged to Jerry; Jerry, a scant year away from a senior citizen's discount at the Beverage Barn, was responsible for his own rehab—but the words, as if set on a lazy Susan, were in front of him, then gone before he could choose. He blinked to keep Kay from doubling in the mirror, twin flannel shirts and Elvis pompadours merging fitfully into one. "Too bad you didn't know the kids on *Diff'rent Strokes*," she said.

It was a setup. Of course it was a setup. There Kay stood, unshrinking as Serena at the net, just waiting to smash the ball into Benji's pickled face. "Why's that?" he asked, lobbing the question at her with a slump-shouldered show of fatigue.

"You could have started your own newsletter. Notes from the industry type stuff. Best bars for drinking away your unemployment check. How to make bail. Transition into porn. Too bad they're all dead."

"They're not."

Static burst from the fat walkie-talkie that was all but surgically attached to Kay's hand. "Right. There's Danny Whatshisname."

"That was *The Partridge Family*."

"*The Partridge Family*," Kay repeated. "I bet he'd do a column."

"If he has anything to say about makeovers, I'll pass it along."

Benji felt himself becoming stiffer and heavier with each plate of armor the costume dresser fastened to him, but a sense of spryness, certain as the whiskeyish warmth that spread from his center, took hold of him. He imagined springing through the air and slamming the door in her face.

Weeks ago, when he walked into the theater's small, shabby green room, Benji found Kay among the band of cast members he privately thought of as the Kiss-Ass Crew. Membership was exclusive to those whose disposition soured in direct relation to the number of lines they were given to speak and who, during rehearsals, snuggled up to the director to discuss motivation or deliver lengthy monologues about their "method." Naturally, Hamlet was their leader. Tall, toned, appropriately

Nordic, he regularly invited the cast to join him in breathing exercises. On this day, the Crew stood gathered around their diaphragm coach as he clicked his way through what appeared to be a particularly amusing website. As Benji entered the room, they all looked up in a way that made clear to him that he was the subject of their search. For a bunch of actors, they did a lousy job of hiding their guilt. He grabbed a yogurt from the dorm room refrigerator that shuddered and dripped between two filing cabinets and, eyebrows arched, made a stand. He may have been defeated, but he refused to retreat. The gaggling sputtered to a stop. A blush crept into Ophelia's cheeks, and in awkward, shuffling silence, the meeting of the Crew adjourned.

The computer, a grimy, loudly whirring beige beast, looked like it predated the Internet by at least a decade, but connected it was, and a quick review of the browser's history confirmed that his castmates had, in fact, been laughing at him. Benji pulled up the *Wikipedia* page last visited.

Benjamin Fisher

Benjamin "Benji" Fisher (born October 21, 1972) is an American actor best known for his portrayal of Andy Osgood on the television sitcom *Prodigy*. Soon after a talent scout spotted him in a JCPenney fashion show, Fisher was cast in a few commercials, most memorably as the boy astronaut for Moonflakes cereal. In 1981, he earned his first television appearance in *Little House on the Prairie*. Three years later, he landed the part of the young genius in *Prodigy*. Fisher's trademark line—"That's what *you* think!"—can be heard in almost any *Prodigy* episode and in his cameo appearance in *Dickie Roberts: Former Child Star*. Since *Prodigy* ended in 1987, Fisher has had small roles in four feature films: *Lickety-Split; The Truth About*

Charmaine; *On Comet, On Cupid*; and *Snow Day 2*. He has appeared in VH1's series *I Love the Eighties*; played Arthur Rimbaud's older brother, Frederic, in the never-aired PBS miniseries *Rimbaud*; and also provided the voice of Solomon in the animated feature *A Hamster for Hannah*. His father is the reclusive Pulitzer Prize–winning novelist Henry Fisher.

Kay brought Benji back into the dressing room with a tepid laugh. "All I'm saying is next time you feel like taking my prop master on a bender? Don't."

"Who still says *bender*?" Benji snorted. The same sense of injury and outrage that had seized him as he snapped off the computer and threw his uneaten yogurt into the trash returned to him now, but the idea of leaping across the room and introducing Kay's scolding face to the door withered on the vine.

The costume dresser lifted the gorget into place and asked Benji to tilt his head forward, but Benji could no more comply and forfeit what had become a deadly serious staring contest than admit that, yes, maybe the afternoon's bender had gotten out of hand. Kay made a considerable opponent, obdurate and unflinching, but Benji had an unexpected leg up. It helped that he couldn't actually see her or, more accurately, that he couldn't decide which of several Kays to focus on. The three-hour lunch of Canadian Club shots had reduced Kay's blockish, beflanneled form to a smear of blue-and-green plaid, a trippy fractal of thick rectangular glasses and shiny black hair.

And he would have won. He was sure of it, if only the frustrated dresser hadn't tired of asking an uncooperative actor to cooperate and pushed Benji's head where he wanted it to be. By the time Benji looked up, finally fully dressed, Kay and a tiny (but much needed) victory were gone.

He snatched his helmet with an acidy burp and rattled out the door to find her. The hallway hummed with preshow activity, but it wasn't the melee that pressed Benji flat against the wall. It wasn't the gaffer, Bill Turnbull, hauling his salami-scented bulk at improbable speed in search of a missing cord, or Delores Henderson-Cratch, denizen of regional summer stock and obsessive pacer, who liked Benji almost as much as Kay did and closed her eyes in a show of pained forbearance whenever she saw him. It was the fact that fifteen minutes ago, he hadn't known just how drunk he was. Fifteen minutes ago, before the image of his stage manager had fanned out and filled the doorframe, Benji felt as fine and together as a compromised man of compromising compulsions was likely to feel. But now, like the cartoon coyote that falls into the canyon only after he realizes he's been hanging in midair, he suddenly sensed trouble. Could the awareness of being drunk make him drunker? Maybe. Maybe not. But he did have the distinct impression that the floor listed beneath him.

Delores passed in her state of momentary blindness, worrying the train of her gown and reciting, with something approaching religious fervor, the tongue twisters that loosened her "instrument": *You know New York, unique New York. You know you need unique New York.* Benji's feet moved two quick steps to the right in a reflexive little jig to keep up with the shifting floor. He leaned into the wall and breathed, his helmet dropping to clatter against his boots. A gulp of fresh air and he'd be back in business. A few minutes under the wakening stars, possibly a private moment behind the Dumpster—two fingers down the throat usually found a reliable reset button—and still he'd have time to give Kay a piece of his mind.

He psyched himself up to let go of the wall and plunge into the stream of actors and stagehands rushing for their places, but then she was beside him, making it impossible to move, saying his name.

"Are you all right?"

Ophelia. Catherine. Cat. Although Benji could number the inter-
actions they'd had that strayed beyond niceties and weather reports at
exactly three, she nevertheless remained his favorite person in the cast.
This, he liked to think, had more to do with admiration for her talent, with
her charming and—especially among the Kiss-Ass Crew—refreshing
lack of pretense, than her tight, yoga-built body or disarmingly perfect
ass. The startling green of her eyes reminded him of a marble he used
to carry for luck, and her boyishly short blond hair not only was sexy
in a Mia Farrow circa 1968 sort of way but, more practically, made bear-
able the nightly tussle with an unflattering and complicatedly braided
wig. At twenty-five—which in some people's books placed Benji in a
defamatory chapter on cradle robbing—with a BFA fresh in hand from
Carnegie Mellon and an impressive list of roles already under her belt,
Cat displayed the centeredness and self-possession of a considerably
older woman. At first, with her taste for boldly patterned wrap dresses,
he'd pinned her closer to thirty, which, for a man two months shy of
his fortieth birthday, would have put her just this side of datable. As if
age, Benji admitted, was the hurdle he had to clear.

He hiccupped. "I'm fine."

"You don't look fine."

With a gauntleted hand, he tugged at the immovable collar of his
metal suit. "You want to grab some air?"

"They just called places. Ten minutes."

"Ten minutes," he drawled, as if elongating the words would have
the same effect on time. "Did I ever tell you about Arthur?" he asked,
though he knew perfectly well he never had. He himself hadn't thought
of Arthur Billings in years and wouldn't have been using him as an
opening gambit if 1) the lunchtime tide of liquor had not totally washed
away his inhibitions and 2) Jerry had not brought him to mind earlier
that afternoon. But Jerry had mentioned Tenafly, and it was Tenafly, or
"Ten Swamps," as the Dutch called it—the things Benji remembered!—
that provided the dreary backdrop for young Arthur Billings' boyhood.

Benji could hear Billings now: the melodramatically inclined chair of the Skidmore theater department where Benji had spent all of three semesters liked nothing more than sharing with his students scenes from what he referred to as "his very own eighteen-year-long O'Neill play."

"You must have had a teacher like him," Benji said, without bothering to elaborate on the kind of teacher he was. "He always said you can fit actors into one of two slots. Those who act because they want you to look more closely at yourself. And those who act because they want you to look more closely at them." The weight of the armor made him lean to one side, putting him a conspirator's length from Cat's ear, in the bright, herbal halo of her shampoo. "The first is harder to come by. Most of us—me, I—most of us want a spotlight. We'll eat our mail, if someone will watch us doing it. You smell good."

"Benji."

"But you. Something happens to you out there. I've watched it. You're here, talking to me, okay, maybe you're just being polite and listening to me, but then you're—you're *show me the steep and thorny way to heaven.* You're gone. And all anyone sees is a sister fighting with her brother over whether she's in love with the right guy."

Cat narrowed her eyes. She was gracious and kind, Benji knew, but she wasn't about to be flattered into ignoring the obvious. "You're drunk," she said.

Benji's face broke in a spasm of feigned incomprehension, which Cat good-humoredly mirrored. "Really?" She laughed. "You really want to pretend it's *my* judgment that's impaired? You want to be that guy?"

"No," Benji answered, chastened. "I don't want to make you feel impaired."

Cat bent down and picked up the helmet. She opened and closed the metal visor before passing it into Benji's hands, then turned and walked away.

"Come on. If I can get over you"—he paused, carefully choosing the bait for the end of his line—"you know, laughing at me—"

To his surprise, she stopped and snapped it up. "When did I laugh at you?"

"Really?" Benji parroted. "You really want to be that girl? The day I walked in on everyone in the green room. I know what Hamlet was doing. I get it. It's laughable. *Snow Day 2* isn't exactly—well, it isn't exactly *Hamlet*."

"How do you know I wasn't laughing at Hamlet and his need to laugh at somebody?"

There are more things in heaven and earth, Horatio, than are dreamt of in your philosophy. "You're saying you weren't laughing at me?"

"I'm saying if I was, it wouldn't be for *Snow Day 2*."

With renewed command of his stewed muscles, Benji set the basinet firmly on his head and slapped the visor shut. That Cat might lift the slit plate and plant a tender, mollifying kiss on his mouth was probably too much to ask. Just barely, he saw the white of her dress slipping like a ghost across the narrow field of view. He flipped the visor open in time to see her duck behind a heavy black curtain at the end of the hall. There stood Kay with two of her minions at a waist-high table, guarding the passage like some mythical three-headed beast. They consulted the ponderous binder that held her script, turning the pages thoughtfully, not unlike a small coven poring over their spells. In her smug willingness to lump him together with Bonaduce and Coleman and the burned-out stars of eighties TV—the dangerous, the debauched, the disgraced—Kay lodged like an allergen in Benji's nose. His eyes went teary, as they did before a good sneeze, with the need to expel it. Part of him wanted nothing more than to march forward and tell her where she could stuff her wiki, but a sudden sloshing wave of gastrointestinal distress threatened to carry him off in another direction.

He hadn't time to ponder the question before the visor flipped open to reveal not Cat and her sweet, pillowy lips but a man Benji knew only as Knuckles, the assistant to the sound engineer, whose purple-ringed, slightly bulging eyes and beakish nose gave him the aspect of a baby bird fallen from its nest. Taken aback, Benji registered the intrusion as if he'd discovered someone peeking into his home through the mail slot. "What do you want, Knuckles?"

Knowing the risk he'd taken in approaching an actor after Kay had called places, the man glanced behind him, taking stock of the stage manager's proximity and whether, like some fanged forest animal locked on the scent of a defenseless chick, she had spotted him. "I have a favor to ask." He spoke quickly but quietly, a torrent of words practiced on his approach. "My mom's sixtieth birthday is coming up, and she's a huge fan of your father. She used to teach English and has all of his books. I'm not kidding. All of them."

"That's not so hard to believe, Knuckles. He isn't Trollope."

"Who?" Knuckles asked before shaking off a question he didn't care to have answered and returning to his script. "Anyway. Could you ask him to sign one? It would be great. Happy birthday, Marge." Here, he pressed a hardcover edition of Henry's fourth novel, the seventh book in history to win both the Pulitzer and the National Book Award, into Benji's hands. If the uninvited game of peekaboo was a violation, this equally uninvited game of hot potato was worse. Benji flicked the novel back to Knuckles, but Knuckles had already turned and, quick as a child who believes his every wish will be granted if only he can outrace the word *no*, scurried away uttering a stage whisper of, "Thanks, Brian."

Brian? Benji hammered on the name like a coffin nail as his dulled but not entirely useless reflexes sent him fumbling after the airborne book. He caught it with every intention of hurling it after its owner, but it became, in that instant, heavy as marble. His arm felt like he'd been carrying that stupid book his entire life. Brian. He could die with Brian etched on his tombstone and who—other than his mother and father and sister—would register the mistake?

Benji wilted against the wall in his great metal suit. The lambent red of the exit door shone like a beacon, and his feet, before his mind could tell them to move, ferried him outside. The sudden shot of mid-August air, already crisp and cool as a September night, fueled him past the reeking leviathan of the Dumpster, into which he tossed the birthday present for Knuckles' poor mom. He had no particular destination in mind, but, in what was technically a stolen suit of armor, he began to run. Or at least move as swiftly as he could encased in fifty pounds of metal and mail. The thrill of escape from the thankless chore of playing King Hamlet, from the crushing, mocking, monolithic successes of his own father, from the indignity of being called Brian—fucking Brian!—spurred him forward. That, and the adrenaline that came from being chased.

As he ran, he made ridiculous music that brought to mind a festoon of tin cans rattling behind the newlyweds' car, a sound punctuated by the flat footfall of the homelier of two assistant stage managers, who demanded, sotto voce, that he stop, turn around, and get back here right now. With her shiny Elvis hair and oversized lumberjack shirt that essentially rendered her pear shape shapeless, the woman looked not merely like Kay's assistant but her clone. Even in work boots, she was, compared to Benji, lithe and swift and beginning to gain. Her winded, whispery plea zipped into Benji's ear at such close range he expected her to grab his shoulder and throw his helplessly stiff body to the ground, but at the edge of the parking lot, like a dog who's reached the perimeter of an invisible fence, she stopped. It was eight o'clock. Soon, the Alice Stone Memorial Pavilion's little stage would be aboil with light. The curtain would rise. And Kay No. 1, regardless of the actions of a washed-up child actor and now costume thief, expected outpaced Kay No. 2 to be in her place.

Watching her hurried retreat, Benji stopped running and, hands on knees, struggled to catch his breath. The thought that there would be no ghost, not tonight, curled his mouth into a dark, momentary smile. He hadn't set out to fuck Kay over, or jam up the night's machinery with a wrench big enough to cause even the easy-breathing Judge Tornquist to hyperventilate, but if that was the icing on this particular cake, he wasn't above licking the fork. Then again, maybe fucking them over was exactly the reason he'd run. Imagining the lot of them now, Judge and Delores and sweet, sanctimonious Cat, who one by one had looked across the table on that first day of rehearsal and claimed they'd never heard of him, being either too young to remember any sitcoms older than *Saved by the Bell* or, in Delores' case, too flatulently theatrical to own a television, Benji savored a backstage scene of contagious panic. The very people who'd left him feeling untalented, unsexy, unsung, whose poisonous mockery still rang in his ears, would, as curtain time came and went, want him, *need* him. They would hate him, all their worst suspicions of him confirmed, but a second before that they'd choke on their own superiority and simply wish he were there.

He dropped his helmet and continued on his way.

A road well-tended by the state parks commission snaked for more than a mile down a gently sloping wooded incline. It descended a hill of significant historical note, a trail of blue-and-white signs, ubiquitous in these parts, explaining the role it played, in 1777, in General Burgoyne's surrender. Or something. Quicker, though, a path cut through the trees, a straight shot along the ridge of a craggy ravine, across an old, moss-covered bridge, to the entrance of the park, where a rotating cast of rangers, either committedly mute or annoyingly chipper, sat in a booth handing out maps and parking stubs, making change. And, in the one named Seth's case, selling the surplus from his personal stash of pot, mushrooms, and pain medication.

Over the course of his many pilgrimages, Benji had come to see Seth as the fallen powerhouse of his high school swim team. Seth had had the trophies, the top place on the record boards, the requisite hot swimmer girlfriend and college scholarship, then in about the time it took to tear a rotator cuff, he traded it all, everything he loved in life, for a stiff-brimmed olive-green campaign hat and a drug problem. Good-bye, girlfriend. Good-bye, scholarship. Hello, OxyContin. Ultimately, though, Seth's biography mattered less than the fact that he was an appreciative *Prodigy* fan and, unlike most drug dealers in Benji's experience, willing to extend credit.

Shagged with a shifting carpet of pine needles, the path gave under Benji's feet, and the grade proved steeper than he remembered. Because his time onstage was so brief, the boards he traversed so straight and level, he'd failed to realize the very real difficulties in walking in a metal suit. The more he tried to hurry, the more he moved like he had Parkinson's. He took small, stuttering steps, sliding and clattering between the trees, ricocheting like a silver pinball, before a sunny ray of the obvious cut through the afternoon's whiskey haze: why not take the armor off? He began with the gauntlets. One by one, with little grace and a violent twisting motion that would have given onlookers the impression that he meant to use his armpit to rip off his own hand, he shed his metal mittens.

The rest of the suit proved less cooperative. Benji moved with care, knowing he'd be unable to get up, pathetic as an overturned turtle, if he happened to fall. He really did need a dresser, needed Jerry, to unbuckle the fine leather straps that held in place the leg things and the arm things and the shiny, tiered skirt that covered his crotch. The rain gutter–shaped pieces fastened to his forearms relented after ample struggle, but the buckles of the skirt waged a war on his recently trimmed fingernails, and without removing the skirt, he couldn't get the bend he needed to undo the greave or the cuisse or the little round saucers that covered his knees.

Freed in the end from only a few less cumbersome pieces, Benji left the molted armor on the ground, continuing on through a stand of tall, thin trees that opened, high above, into umbrellas of sparse pine boughs. As he approached the dark bridge, he nearly fell, his feet sliding slapstick style through the dirt and rot of the forest floor. In the light of day, the bridge, built just wide enough for a ranger's jeep, looked barely capable of supporting a ranger. It was a miracle it hadn't fallen into the ravine years ago.

His efforts to stay upright had him panting, and a trickle of sweat, fed by the efficient furnace of the cuirass, rolled maddeningly down his unscratchable back. He took a cautious step, ears trained for the first sigh of splitting planks, but heard nothing. No wind. No traffic from nearby Route 4. Nothing but a drunken blood gush pulsing in his own ears. A few stars winked through the broken lattice of branches, and it was under these fair lights that Benji's stomach staged its revolt. In one great heave, up came what remained of his lunchtime spree. It splashed over the railing and coated with vile chunks the leaves of a small, dry bush.

This was not the life he intended to live.

As quickly as his tuna melt rushed out, a stream of regrets rushed nastily in. Benji had no trouble making himself the subject of his own entertainment television interviews, speaking at length—in the shower, in line at the bank—about the movies he had yet to make, the theater he had yet to do, the awards he had yet to win, the accolades that had yet to be bestowed upon him and that would, by some strange alchemical process associated with fame, be transmuted into contributions to the world that mattered. What would he be remembered for? What would his legacy be? What of him, beyond the movies and performances and awards, would last? Saving the children. Saving the ice caps. Advocating clean, available drinking water across the developing world. Condemning industrial farming. Condemning violence against women. Condemning war. Condemning fossil fuels and marriage inequality and elephant poachers on the Kenyan plains. But here he was—more or less halfway through life's journey, with what to show for it? The question came in his father's voice: *What the hell is your plan?*

Whenever Henry Fisher accused his only son of aimlessness (or worse), Benji's mother swept in with the word "unconventional," brandishing it like a shield to cover him from dragon's fire—Benji isn't flighty or feckless or retarded, he's *unconventional*—but it was exactly the lack of the conventional trappings of adulthood (at least the kind most often clung to by straight, middle-class, white American males) that so often made him feel worthless. He had no wife, no children, no savings account or stock portfolio, no house, no car. He didn't have a BA. He didn't even have a cat. His filmography read like a joke. His credit cards should have melted from overuse. And what had his recent forays into theater, into more serious (and, he'd wrongly thought, more easily had) work, earned him besides two DUIs and, outside a small dinner theater in the Catskills, a charge of disorderly conduct? He could forget about Ophelia kissing him.

Now, with the floodgates of self-pity opened wide, he saw the stupidity in abandoning a show in which he'd gotten a (minor!) part only because his doubtful and already fed-up agent had pulled enough strings to make Pinocchio dance. And even though *Hamlet* offered parts that were more minor, it must be said that no one in the cast was more expendable. Even poor Gary Jeffries, whose Bernardo, according to the arts section of the local *Gazette*, seemed no less wooden than the battlements he stood upon, would be missed more than Benji.

There would be no ghost? On the contrary. By this time, Kay and her clones would have grabbed Benji's concave-chested understudy (a boy half his age and built more like reedy Gertrude than King Hamlet), dusted his face with powder, and, working around the missing armor, cinched him improvisationally into the murdered monarch's nightshirt from act three. And all this before Gary could mumble, "Who's there?" Of course there would be a ghost.

No sooner had these thoughts raced in for another round of pummeling than a second seismic heave doubled him over. This one, though dry, brought Benji to his knees. Tears rolled from his eyes as he retched and spat and wondered at the gaping black space on the other side of the railing. To jump or not to jump, that is the question. He pulled himself upright, stood with his hands on the moss-furred rail, and, hanging his head, allowed himself to sink deeper into the darkening thought. But, no. His aversion to diving off a bridge, like his aversion, in 1988, to swallowing more than two of the handful of Valium he'd stolen from (and, as soon as he woke up, returned to) his father's medicine cabinet, pointed precisely to his capacity for what George Simonson, his former therapist, called self-dramatization. George knew it. Benji knew it. Where was the Hemingway in him? The Freddie Prinze? The Kurt Cobain? He could never check out like a real star, staging a good, old-fashioned, indelible fuck-you of a good-bye.

Maybe the melodrama currently embroiling him made him lift his imploring eyes to heaven; maybe he was merely gauging the time (that is, the likelihood that Seth the Ex-Swimmer would still be manning his drug kiosk) by the dying light. Whatever the cause, Benji looked up. Looked up to see the moon of his most morbid thoughts eclipsed by what appeared to be an apple, hanging just out of reach on the opposite side of the railing. A tree from the right bank of the ravine leaned at a remarkable angle over the gorge, as if stalled in the process of falling. From it dangled a single piece of fruit in silhouette, a black cutout against the darkening sky.

The uncomfortable heat that came from hating himself dissipated in the cool breeze of a gentler memory. It was October. His birthday. 1981. The day before his mother flew him to Los Angeles to play a publicly maligned but essentially loveable humpback opposite young Melissa Gilbert, his father had broken form and proposed a family trip to an apple and pumpkin farm just the other side of the Vermont border. Thanks to Henry Fisher's inflexible writing schedule and the ill-timed arrival of his sister's first period, the family got a ridiculously late start, arriving at the orchard just as all the other families were packing their soon-to-be jack-o'-lanterns and paper-handled apple sacks into their cars.

Living by a clock that had little to do with daylight or other people's watches, Henry grabbed a bushel basket and, despite the protests of a teenaged employee whose lanky frame and protuberant Adam's apple did not escape the writer's critical eye, started down a tractor-rutted track into the orchard.

Benji blanched. "Dad," he pleaded, "we're not supposed to. They're closing."

"If Ichabod Crane wants us," Henry Fisher said, "he can come get us."

Evelyn offered a few words of encouragement to her mortally embarrassed daughter, but Claudia refused to lift or reach or do anything that would either please her mother or raise the knee-length sweater she'd put on as extra protection against a foreign and untrustworthy pad. The basket the women carried—for, though practically paralyzed by her body's pubescent treachery, Claudia reminded everyone that now, officially, she was a woman—rattled with a few sad apples, moodily picked from the ground, while the men's overflowed with Cortlands, Empires, and Ginger Golds.

Benji scurried in his maroon Roos onto the lowest branches, stripped them like a starving child, and dropped the bounty into his father's waiting arms. Only when a tobacco-voiced farmer, trailed by Ichabod's emboldened form, appeared to discuss insurance liability and, worse, call Henry *friend* did Henry relent. Every man had his limits, and false fraternity marked Henry's. He put down his basket and waved the farmer away. Father and son carried the brimming harvest together, straddling a puddley, tire-scored ditch. It was one of the few uncomplicatedly pleasant memories of Henry that Benji could summon for George Simonson. And more than once during those $150 sessions that Benji could no longer afford did he return to that final moment, when, passing under a tree silhouetted against the inky sky, he noticed the day's last apple, almost Edenic in perfection, waiting, it seemed, for Benji to pick it. Which he did, sitting atop his father's shoulders, and promptly, greedily, bit into.

Why, thirty-one years later, Benji found himself back on those thick, powerful shoulders, wanting the apple that hung above him, was a mystery to him. He hated his father. Or claimed to. And it wasn't an apple that now caught his eye. It was a pinecone. But the desire persisted. The desire won. Benji wasn't sauced enough or stupid enough or, as he was currently dressed, flexible enough to climb onto the three-inch-wide railing and stretch to his most harrowing limits. But his veins surged with the dangerous conviction of his own ingenuity. A brief search of the nearby ground turned up a long, tapering branch that, in concert with the suit of armor, looked something like a pronged lance he intended to use to pull in his prize. But lashing the branches together soon seemed as likely as Cat McCarthy falling into him with that slow, soft kiss. He reevaluated. If he wedged his feet between the damp black balusters and stood on the bottom rail, he'd gain another five, maybe six inches and get the height and leverage he needed to knock his prize free with one hand and catch it with the other.

He blinked against the spinning world, waiting until he felt adequately focused, then sliced the lance through the air. He missed. Swung again like a one-armed man attacking a birthday piñata. And missed. He missed and missed and missed and hit too high and sent nothing but a shower of pine needles raining down and then missed again. Leaning out as far as he dared, he ignored the burn that threatened to unhinge his shoulder. His stomach muscles strained with the added weight lashed to his torso, but he steadied himself with a long, stabilizing breath that would have made Hamlet proud and swung his stick through the air.

The branches connected with a dry thwack. The pinecone let go. A thrill of attainment, a little nightbird of joy, soared for a split second through Benji's heart. After that, it became clear that his calculations, compromised by his blood alcohol level and a more general lack of spatial intelligence, were hopelessly off. The pinecone missed his hand by a good two feet and dropped, regardless of his desire, without ceremony, into the waiting maw of the pitch-black ravine. Benji let his lance drop, waiting for the soft sound of its landing far below. He stepped off the railing and, though he knew himself to be alone, looked searchingly into the darkness around him.

How different he might have felt had somebody been there, not the applauding audience he usually imagined as the world's only worthwhile comfort but a single interested person to ask him his trouble. He waited. Like Hardy's Jude, the reckless dreamer and college dropout to whom Henry often compared him, Benji waited for someone to come, but nobody did. Nobody did, because nobody does. Not that another person would have known what to make of Benji's trouble.

Benji stepped back onto the railing. Slowly, he raised his arms from his sides. He looked, he imagined, like Kate Winslet on the prow of the *Titanic*, if Kate Winslet had been dressed for the Thirty Years War, although his stance indicated not an embrace of the world but a challenge to it. *Fuck everybody. Fuck everything.* He leaned against the wooden rail with the full force of his weight, daring the universe to deliver its final insult, daring the banister to break. When it didn't, Benji laughed, a spark of amusement that his quickening breath soon beat into a hot, angry flame. *I can't even do this right.* He brought the mad laughter to a stop with a loud, growling scream. *Fuuuuuck!* The sound, a better purgative than puking, made a violent tear in the quiet of the woods. No one heard it. No one heard the word, or the faint echo of it whispering back through the trees, or—there it was: finally, at last—the splintering rail exploding with a crack so sudden, so extreme, the wood seemed to be voicing some argument it had stifled for far too long. No one heard any of it, including the sound of a man, too stunned to call, falling headlong into the dark.

Jane. Jane: I walk with the others, calling her name through spruces and pines and skeleton trees sleeved with snow. I call until my boots freeze. I call until I can't feel my hands. I call until there's no voice left to call with. I call until I taste pennies in the back of my throat. I call when the sun sets and call again when the sun rises. I call with freezing fists of white jabbing from my mouth to batter the air. I call because nothing is right in the world, because nothing will ever be right again. I call because calling is all that's left. I call after the others go home.

2.

Claudia followed the social worker out of the emergency room. They took the quickest route, braving the gauntlet of wheelchairs and gurneys and beeping, hissing machines, where the challenge for Claudia was finding someplace safe to look. Her eyes were drawn to the tableaux happening on the other side of the dividing curtains—the moaners, the bleeders, the hopelessly bored—and she struggled to keep her attention on the backs of the social worker's shoes.

They walked briskly along, past the buzzing hive of the nurses' station, past radiology, through one set of automatic doors after another, until they came to a lounge at the end of a long, antiseptic hall.

The room was stifling, filled with pressed-wood furniture and the milky-gray light that seeped between crooked blind slats. Crumpled, mostly coverless magazines littered a scuffed coffee table, and the smell of institutional gravy, wafting in from a nearby food cart, clotted the air. The social worker, whose name tag read "Valerie Emerson, CSW," pulled together two chairs and, with a small, placid smile, sat down.

"Now," she said, once Claudia had parked her roll-along bag and settled in beside her, "why impossible?" She folded her large, mannish hands on the stacked folders she held on her lap and looked at Claudia expectantly.

"It's just not something my brother would do."

Valerie, whose Peter Pan–collared blouse and lightweight gray cardigan suggested to Claudia a modern-day nun, looked unconvinced. She tucked an auburn wave behind her ear and patiently, as if she didn't have twenty other cases jockeying for attention, began to explain how jumping into a dry streambed seemed to be exactly what Benji had done.

What if he had done it? What if he had?

"Claudia?"

Claudia blinked back a well of tears and squared her shoulders with renewed focus. "You were saying?"

"People in distress," Valerie began, "sometimes surprise us with their behavior. Do things we wouldn't expect them to do. Has your brother seemed." She closed her eyes for long stretches as she spoke and chose her words so mindfully, with such unhurried care, that her sentences sounded snapped in half by silence. "In distress?"

"Ever?" Claudia asked. The word flashed like a blade.

"Recently."

Two months ago, her brother had given up the one-bedroom apartment in Greenpoint he shared with two other actors and moved three hours north, into a converted toolshed belonging to the assistant director of a ragtag regional theater company. He was thirty-nine years old and brought home $325 a week. Owed MasterCard over $9,000. Owed his sister and mother twice that, easily. Shied from sexual relationships that lasted longer than a hangover. And now had been found, fractured and bruised and drunk, at the bottom of a ravine. He was, in many ways, the definition of distress. Claudia shook her head.

"Has he ever mentioned." Silence. "Harming himself?"

Did chasing a high on a daily basis count as harming himself? "Not seriously."

With this, Valerie's professionally soothing smile disappeared. She turned pink, as if the lightness of the remark embarrassed her. "What your brother did." Ends of that sentence hung like fruit on a tree. She puzzled over which to choose. "Is *very* serious."

"We don't know what my brother did."

Technically, this was true. The small search party that left the theater parking lot shortly after midnight—when the sleuthing stage manager found Benji's helmet at the brink of the woods—had stumbled upon him in a state of drifting consciousness. He knew his name, recognized the few stalwart and morbidly curious castmates whom the director had rallied to scour the grounds, could correctly (although, owing to his severely bitten tongue, almost incomprehensibly) name the day of the week and the current president, but shed no light on how he ended up thirty feet below the peculiarly broken bridge.

Not that anyone asked. The paramedics who towed Benji up the steep wooded slope on a bright-orange backboard, the woman named Cat who called Claudia with the news, this psychiatric social worker who'd picked up his file for the first time an hour ago, all of these people had already solved the mystery of her brother's fall by insisting that it wasn't one. Even the police, who were days away from collecting an official statement, seemed to be sniffing around for form's sake. Only Claudia resisted the race from premise to conclusion. Only she chose to believe that her fucked-up brother wasn't quite that fucked up.

"Has he mentioned suicide?" Valerie pressed, crossing her thick ankles and leaning into the question.

"He's been living in a toolshed. It would be odd if he didn't mention suicide."

Claudia went on to explain, and Valerie went on to write down, why Benji's occasional threats to throw himself in front of the L train or jump from the Williamsburg Bridge were not the serious cries for help one might mistake them for. They weren't flares shot into troubled psychological skies. They weren't even jokes. In asking the fastest route to the Verrazano-Narrows or hiking his leg teasingly over the rail of Claudia's fire escape, what was he doing but opening a release valve, letting go the disappointments of a botched audition or a date that ended disappointingly with a forced hug on the doorstep or a collection letter from an angry creditor? Yes, her brother mentioned suicide. But he was an actor. He could be melodramatic, hyperbolic, hypochondriacal, histrionic, selfish, and self-centered. Sometimes all at once. But he told Claudia everything. And Claudia, who took heart in knowing the dark of Benji's darkest corners, could say with certainty that his selfishness didn't extend to doing himself in.

She meant to make a simple point, but the more she talked, the more trouble she had making it. She mentioned one bridge or another no less than five times, which even a lukewarm Freudian would have found significant. It was only a matter of time, she seemed to be saying, before the man dove off of something.

And maybe he had. Claudia had been resisting the thought of it since the phone rang at five thirty that morning, summoning her. She'd thrown a wall up against the idea, a wall as big and fortified as any that stood in the world and bore her name. Yet here she was, trying to convince herself that Benji had not, could not, would not.

"Is your brother being treated for depression?"

"Not anymore."

"But he was?"

"He was."

"His blood alcohol content was 0.20 when he came in."

"Drunk isn't suicidal."

"Would you say he has a drinking problem?"

"Last night he did."

"Would you say last night was unique?"

"Falling into a gorge in a suit of armor? Yes, that's unique."

"It sounds like he may have been—"

Claudia did all she could to keep her hands from reeling in the hampered word.

"Self-medicating," Valerie eventually offered.

Claudia frowned. A sculptor of conventional beauties would never have paired a nose that slender with such a surprisingly wide mouth, but the components of her face, together, gave stunning proof that the whole was more than the sum of its parts. Her dark eyes were particularly expressive and could no more hide her annoyance with Valerie's prying questions than her fear of failing her brother by mishandling them.

"I don't want to tell you how to do your job," Claudia began in a tone that registered her desire to do exactly that, "but shouldn't we speak with Benji before diagnosing him?" She clung to the idea of her brother speaking for himself like an inner tube on a stormy sea: soon, he would tell them how absurd they were.

"Absolutely," Valerie said. "This," she stressed, indicating the mess of pages on which she'd been scribbling, "isn't diagnostic. But it sometimes helps. In cases like this. To talk with the family. Before meeting the patient."

Claudia crossed her leg and let her attention wander to the heel of her boot. She was being rude, but then she had never mastered (or ever really applied herself to) the art of sparing another's feelings when her own were hurt.

Her mind sought some momentary relief, a distraction, any distraction—the spot (was it blood?) on her sole; a pearly mole on the side of Valerie's neck; even Nick, whom she hadn't seen in over twenty years but who still roused her memory (and her ardor) whenever she touched foot on home soil—but she couldn't get away from the thought of it. Her brother falling through the dark. What if Benji had jumped? What if the darkness she presumed she'd charted was merely the surface of a much deeper, much darker abyss? What if those few Valium all those years ago were a prelude she'd passed off as adolescent attention grabbing and every subsequent allusion to suicide a sign she'd misread, a danger she'd prematurely dismissed? Then again, what if she was right? What if her brother hadn't jumped but had somehow, unintentionally, fallen off the bridge? It meant that Benji's binges had stumbled from the asinine and essentially harmless into the realm of real self-destruction. No matter how she sliced it, the problem looked unmanageably large.

She put her foot back on the floor and once again apologized for her wandering mind. "It's early," she offered, as if the hour of the day proved more difficult than the situation at hand. Had it been up to her when her phone trilled at just after five thirty, she would have thrown the thing under the dresser and burrowed deeper into the sheets. Thank goodness for Oliver. Oliver, who, after ten years of marriage, remained gentle, considerate, generally more interested in people and the reasons they might have for calling at such an hour. He answered on the third ring and said, "Babe. Babe. Something bad."

To her credit, Claudia was in a cab bound for the Port Authority before Benji's ambulance reached the emergency room. At just over three hours, the bus ride proved more reliable than US Air's perpetually delayed shuttle, more responsible than dangerously chasing her panic along busy, northbound highways, though it put her in cramped, unwelcome proximity to men and women who felt comfortable eating Styrofoam cartons of Chinese food more or less on a stranger's lap any time of day or night. Passengers on this morning's bus had been few and far between (and, mercifully, not very hungry), but the experience nevertheless whittled away at Claudia's nerves. She called the hospital no less than six times during her three-hour ride. She'd had her fill of Valerie's dowdy sincerity and the room's niggling aesthetic assaults—she saw the framed still life of pumpkins and autumn leaves that looked like something her mother might paint, and in the murky black mirror of a television mounted overhead, she saw it again. Her patience and generosity were at an end. She loved her brother as much as she loved anyone, but couldn't help feeling a venomous, terrible, toe-curling anger at the inconvenience that, one way or another, he'd caused.

"If you wanted to jump to your death," she said, immediately doubling back on her apology to Valerie and taking up the offensive, "you'd find something higher than thirty feet. You don't necessarily die at thirty feet. You break your neck. You spend the rest of your life in a wheelchair, dribbling onto a bib." This put Claudia in the absurd position of arguing that Benji's injuries, serious as they were, weren't quite serious enough.

"We're lucky neither of those things happened," Valerie said. "Benji didn't die. And the doctors are hopeful that he didn't sustain any permanent injuries. They haven't found any internal bleeding, which is what they were afraid of." She fished these sentences up whole from the deep, her need for deliberation suddenly gone, as if all her voice required to find its pace was a bit of genuine nonsense to drive away. "In my experience, most suicides want to send a message more than they want to die."

Claudia widened her eyes against another sting of tears. "A message."

"Maybe this is Benji's way of asking for help."

"There's no need for smoke signals," Claudia said with a short, bitter laugh. "My brother's never had a problem asking for help." She felt a momentary urge to shame him, to parrot the list of delusions and offenses that Henry had no trouble rattling off but that she, Claudia, usually did her brother the favor of swallowing. The things she could have said, if the words hadn't caught in her throat. He'd taken her money. He'd refused her advice. He'd quit more jobs in a year than she had in her entire life, all in the name of a dream from which everyone, everyone except Benji himself, had woken long ago. He was a disappointment. Why not say it? A failure. She sat frozen. The realization that she was about to be shattered by a sob, that tears would fall the minute she opened her mouth, struck her dumb. She didn't breathe. Valerie, slow in speech but apparently not in understanding, brought the interview to a charitable end. She shuffled her papers away, handed

Claudia her card, and left with more courtesy than Claudia expected from a woman who, thanks to her, had gotten nowhere.

❖ ❖ ❖

Evelyn no longer woke to the sounds, but in anticipation of them. A box of Christmas ornaments crashed to the floor or he left the bathroom faucet to run or hollered for a dog that drowned in 1986. These were the bells that called Evelyn Fisher into the ring. She heard her husband rise and, now that they no longer slept in the same bed, shuffle into the tiny bathroom that connected their rooms.

"Henry," she called, sliding into her slippers and pulling on a light, flower-printed robe as she approached from behind.

He glared at her over his shoulder, as if she were a stranger interrupting his private business at a public urinal. As she stepped toward him, he gathered into himself, hunching his back like a shy, red-faced boy. Never in their forty-three years of marriage had he lost this comical, almost perverse, sense of modesty. Not that he had anything to be ashamed of. His once daily regimen—a five-mile walk to the Episcopalian cemetery, two hundred push-ups on his office floor—rewarded him with a trim waist and powerful chest, charms that only recently, in the last two or three years, when he could no longer keep count of his exercises or be trusted to find his way home, had begun to fade. But unlike so many men his age, men with sagging breasts and beach ball bellies who took a kind of defiant pride in their bodies (or, at the very least, at the town's Fourth of July picnic, showed a shirtless indifference to them), never did he flaunt what he had. He stayed fully dressed on the most sweltering days. Emerged from the shower only after snugging a towel around his middle. Refused to pee with her anywhere in the vicinity. The walls she'd encountered in the handsome, promising young writer, despite the corrosives of age and illness and murderous familiarity, still stood strong.

Henry inched into the corner where, like the plunger or the rusty-bristled toilet brush, he could be most inconspicuous, and tucked himself away. "I have to call Roger," he said, forgetting his own fastidiousness as he bypassed the sink and pushed brusquely past her.

The house had five bedrooms. Henry and Evelyn no longer used the master suite, which took up the entire third floor. As they'd entered stage five, the doctors thought it safer to trim the extra flight of stairs from Henry's routine, and Evelyn, to be closer to him in the guest bedroom, moved into Claudia's old room. Claudia, who couldn't have cared less about the fate of a bedspread she'd left behind twenty-five years ago, nevertheless relished the opportunity to imagine a slight.

"What about Benji's room?" she asked.

"Your brother's room is at the other end of the hall."

"My brother's room is a shrine."

Evelyn let this fly buzz about her ears without bothering to swat it.

"What about the *library?*" Now that Claudia equated printed books with an unforgivable assault on trees, on her tenets of urban planning, and so on the planet as a whole, the space the Fishers required to house them had become a fresh source of contention.

"Your father's office?"

"You say that like it's inviolable space. Daddy doesn't work in there anymore."

Again Evelyn was silent.

"Fine. Then let the library be."

Into this large room with its salvaged army surplus desk and tufted leather sofa, Evelyn followed her husband. The worn walnut stenographer's chair in which Henry had written five novels, two collections of short stories, and a book of essays creaked under the familiar weight. His fingers dove into the hooded desk lamp's pool of light and started racing through his Rolodex.

"Henry," Evelyn said. Then, sharper: "Henry!"

Without looking up, he snatched a card from the file and began tapping it on the desk. "I have to call Roger." Between his shoulder and ear he jabbed the handset of a heavy, corded, black rotary phone that neither lit up nor folded into his pocket nor plotted the route to the nearest Walmart. His Rolodex, his phone, his weathered blue Olivetti: long before he'd gotten sick, these museum pieces (as Benji called them) stood like beloved ports in an endless technological storm. Henry had preached sermon after sermon about the evils of the electronic revolution. Since the day he allowed the children their first Commodore 64, he'd been ranting about the dumbing down of an already dumb culture. The death of privacy. The rise of surveillance. And, thanks to every armchair journalist with an unwelcome opinion and a blog, the democratizing and devaluation of the written word. Of course, the children were right: he sounded like a kook, like an angry messenger from the Amish, like a snob, but he preferred living life without a sleek silver laptop, without a promotional video on YouTube or a website for his bio and bibliography, without even so much as an e-mail address. Happily would Henry Fisher die a Luddite.

"You're not calling Roger."

He started to dial.

Evelyn followed a worn path across the rug and put her finger on the switch hook. "It's three o'clock in the morning."

He puzzled the darkness in the window, tapping the card faster and faster. "The book is done," he said emphatically. "He needs to read the book."

Whether he meant the abandoned manuscript locked in the safe behind him or one of the books he published years ago, Evelyn didn't know. And better, really, not to ask. She'd learned strategies for getting her husband back to bed, for taking his hand when he got lost in the fog. In the doctor's office, in the caregiver guides that sat beside her own bed, in her talks with Sandra, the day nurse, these tactics made perfect sense. Speak in a clear, reassuring voice. Respond to the emotion, not the confusion. Never argue. She might have said, "You sound anxious about work." Or, "Are you missing Roger?" The proper volley was easily imagined, but Evelyn played better in practice than she did in the game.

"Stop being silly. He's read the books. All the books. Except the one you didn't finish."

It took an hour of pulling and corralling and repeating herself to get him out of the room. The more she pressed him to calm down or tried luring him into the sanctuary she'd set up in the living room, the angrier and more agitated he became. He didn't want to go sit in his chair. He didn't want to listen to music. He'd sooner drink bathwater than a goddamned cup of chamomile tea. She tried toggling the light, as if it were intermission at the theater and flashes of darkness might quiet the crowd, but Henry and, with him, the specter of Roger Fitch refused to leave. Tonight, it was Roger. But it could have been anyone: Claudia, Benjamin, his mother or father, the sister he'd stopped talking to two decades ago. Even she, Evelyn, thirty years younger, fresh from packing the kids off for school, had haunted Henry's nights. Only Jane was missing. He had yet to see her, which surprised and, it would be lying to say otherwise, pleased Evelyn deeply.

The hour-long tussle, which ended with Henry throwing his wedding ring in the trash, left them defeated and spent, but Evelyn, with her still-sharp mind and unwavering purpose, emerged the victor every time. She may have been seventy-eight, but other than a touch of arthritis in her hip, she moved like a woman a good deal younger. With bowed head and shuffling feet, Henry followed her downstairs. He allowed her to deposit him in his easy chair. Suffered the radio she'd tuned to Brahms. And there he sat, a frightened boy left to find his way through a dark, dark thicket and reach the clearing (that may or may not exist) on the other side.

Exhausted, Evelyn went into the kitchen. With its white cabinets and white tiles, it struck her as a canvas she'd never gotten around to painting. She'd always intended to add more color, to paint a great garland of flowers that ran around the room rather than the solitary swag with a cabbage and a bird's nest that decorated the wooden valance above the sink. But then—well, but then: life.

She picked up her husband's socks where he dropped them, had dinner on the table the same time each night, painted almost every day without a scrap of ambition to have her work seen. She was a certain type of woman who lived a certain type of life that most girls of Claudia's generation regarded as a disease they'd been lucky or wily or smart enough never to catch. Where Evelyn felt contentment, Claudia felt claustrophobic. Where Evelyn saw a home she could take pride in, Claudia saw a swamp to sink in. Through Claudia's acrimonious filter, the prioritizing of family became the death of imagination. Care became sacrifice. Fidelity, a chain. But Evelyn *had* wanted a family. More than anything, she *had* wanted children. And it saddened her to no end to think that she and her daughter were at odds over both. Claudia's approach to marriage had been as slow and trepidatious as her rejection of motherhood had been decisive and swift. They gave to different charities, went to different movies, spoke of the past as though it wasn't one they shared. Inch by inch the differences added up until the two stood on opposite sides of a great gulf. It broke Evelyn's heart.

Gathering herself in the kitchen in the dawn's dove-gray light, Evelyn hit the button on the coffeemaker, *her* coffeemaker, which sat alongside a much larger and more evolved cousin. The cappuccino machine docked like a shiny silver barge on the kitchen counter, ready to brew double shots of espresso or froth milk, should she suddenly, at nearly eighty, develop a taste for lattes. It had arrived on her last birthday, with a card from Claudia and the unwritten purpose, Evelyn believed, of making her feel simple, unsophisticated, less than. Benji, on the other hand, had given her nothing, his usual gift for any giving occasion, and Evelyn couldn't help wondering (more than once while the morning coffee brewed) whether it was worse to be forgotten or to be so profoundly unknown. She put a kettle on the stove for Henry's tea—the tea, the chair, the music, all recommended by her piled books—and raided the refrigerator for something to paint. She found a head of Boston lettuce, a few white-tipped radishes, a lemon she decided to halve, and carried what would soon become the day's composition into her studio. Otherwise known as the mudroom off the kitchen.

With the tea steeped, she brought a mug to Henry and sat beside him, sipping her first cup of coffee. In these quiet hours, they rarely spoke. Speaking, she found, tended to muddy the waters that settled near dawn. A half hour later, before Henry finally dozed off, Evelyn took him by the hand and, with the same assurances she used to whisper to the children after bad dreams shook them, led him back to bed. *You're fine, you're fine. I'm right here. Now go to sleep.* She pulled the covers up to Henry's waist, drew the curtains, and was halfway out the door when she remembered the ring in her pocket. A strip of light from the hallway fell across her husband's face as she crept back to the bed, but he was already asleep. She had no trouble slipping the heavy gold band onto his finger, where it belonged.

In some people's books—Dr. Bell's, for instance, or Claudia's— Evelyn was a fool for not hiring a night nurse to supplement Sandra's daytime visits. Worse than a fool, in her daughter's estimation. Irresponsible. "You're putting Daddy's health in jeopardy," the lecture went, "not to mention your own. You can't stand guard twenty-four hours a day. I don't care what you say: you can't get by on four hours of sleep. You're wearing yourself out. And then we're going to have two sick parents to deal with. I know you think you're being selfless in all of this, in putting Daddy's needs before your own, but Daddy's not getting the care he deserves, and neither are you. It's actually very selfish."

Evelyn hadn't the heart or, frankly, the stomach to follow Claudia's logic, the bread crumb trails whereby every fault led more or less directly to her. And besides, Evelyn didn't agree. She didn't agree that a stranger could do better by Henry. They were lucky—*she* was lucky—to have Sandra, yes, but a second aide at this point would have created more problems than it solved. First, Henry wouldn't accept it. He grew more suspicious, more paranoid of people he'd known for years, most recently accusing Chip Hanehan, their legally blind neighbor of thirty years, of various and random acts of thievery; how could he be expected to open his arms to a complete stranger? Second, another nurse wouldn't come free, and though they weren't exactly in financial jeopardy, Benjamin required more pocket money than most forty-year-olds, and Evelyn couldn't, wouldn't, no matter how many times Henry called her an *enabler*, let her son starve.

Claudia thought otherwise. But what task did Evelyn have, what was there to safeguard, what was there to hold together, but *this*? Her *family*? She painted, and painting was nice, but it wasn't her work. Not in the way writing was Henry's or architecture Claudia's. They may have thought she'd done a mediocre job (if they thought at all about the job she'd done), but she'd go to the grave swearing she couldn't have done better. Let them say what they would. In the meantime, she liked retiring to her "studio" after tucking Henry into bed, where she dabbed away at her lettuce and lemons, at the blushing pinks of her radishes until ten o'clock, when Sandra arrived.

It was nine thirty when the phone rang. She rushed for the kitchen extension with brush in hand, incensed that such a careless caller might wake Henry, but paused before answering it. Claudia's number on the caller ID. Claudia, who imposed uncharitable restrictions on the hours she allowed Evelyn to call her, could apparently phone Evelyn whenever she wished. Evelyn felt a delicious retaliatory impulse to let the call go to voice mail, but picked up the handset before it could ring again.

"Mom?"

Someone, Evelyn thought by her daughter's tone, is dead. "What's the matter?"

"Calm, Mom, calm down. I haven't said anything yet." Claudia spoke in an unusually soft, coaxing voice that was anything but calming.

"What's the matter? Where are you?"

"I'm at the hospital."

"The hospital? Are you okay?"

"I'm fine."

"Is Oliver?"

"It's Benji."

Evelyn dropped the paintbrush, its moist tip kissing the top of her slippered foot.

"He's okay. They're pretty sure he's going to be okay."

"Claudia, tell me right now."

"I can't tell you if you don't calm down. And I can't stay on the phone long."

Cast helplessly into silence, Evelyn bit into her bottom lip and listened.

"There was an accident. Or. They won't say it was an accident. But there was a fall."

"Benji? Benji fell? Where are you? I'm coming."

"Mom, no. No. Not until we know what's happening. You're better off there, with Daddy."

"Sandra can stay with your father."

"There's nothing for you to do. There's nothing for *me* to do. I'm sitting here. The doctors are still with him."

"But what *happened?*" Evelyn pressed Claudia on the how, the why, the where, and Claudia, never dropping her mask of calm, answered with maddening composure. "Saratoga!" Evelyn cried. "What is he doing in Saratoga?"

"A play."

"He never told me he was doing a play! As if I wouldn't have gone to—"

"Well, now's not the time to get upset about that." Evelyn hushed, chastened. "Mom? Are you there?"

"What do you mean they won't say it's an accident?" Evelyn heard Claudia take a breath, a deep, shuddering breath, as if she were going underwater for a long time.

"They think he may have jumped."

Evelyn put a hand to her heart. "Who thinks that?"

"I'm telling you what they told me."

"Who is they?"

"The people who found him. The police. Everybody." The tremor in Claudia's voice, comforting.

"Why would they say that? He wouldn't do that. He would never do that."

More silence.

"I talked to him last week," Evelyn insisted.

"So did I."

"Why would they say he jumped?"

"I know as much as you do, Mom."

Evelyn shook her head vigorously, as if she could loosen the idea of her son choosing to plummet to his death and send it flying out of her head. "Your brother's not unstable." Then, tuned to the possibility of some waspish response, "Not unstable like *that*."

"There is precedence," Claudia said softly.

The word *precedence* irked Evelyn, as if they were arraigning Benji in a court of law. "What? The pills? I wish you wouldn't bring that up. It was twenty-five years ago. And he did that for attention. He barely took enough to put himself to sleep."

"I don't want to believe it either, but who's to say he's not looking for attention now. We're talking about Benji."

"That's how you talk about your brother? At a time like—?" Evelyn's voice crumbled under the weight of the sentence. She put her hand against the wall, as if she, too, might fall, and cried.

"I don't know what to think. But the more I think about it—I wouldn't exactly say Benji is happy."

Happy? Evelyn thought. *Who is?*

"Mom," Claudia began, but confusion and sadness and a sickening tide of outrage had doused Evelyn's circuits. She shut down. Hung up the phone. Cried until Sandra came, when she insisted she needed to be alone, climbed the stairs to her bedroom, and cried some more. She was no longer a religious woman, but even when she had been, in her casual, noncommittal way, it never would have occurred to her to bring beads into it. Still, she clutched her hands and moved her fingers as if worrying an invisible rosary. *He wouldn't do that,* she repeated. *No, no, never. He would never do that.* Again and again, like a prayer. Until it no longer sounded true.

I know what they're going to say before I open the door. They're going to say they found her. They're going to say she's dead. That's what men in uniforms with faces like that come to say. Sir, do you know a Jane Mueller? I'm sorry to have to say this, sir. But Ms. Mueller. I invite them in. Evelyn offers to make coffee like the church deacons have come for a visit. I don't blame her: some part of her, some part she may not even recognize, must feel like serving cake. When the cops say no thank you, ma'am, she picks up Claudia and the baby, hugging them tight, and carries them into the other room. They ask me the questions they need to ask. How long has it been since you've seen her? Two years. Almost two years. Were you married? No. One gunshot wound, they say, apparently self-inflicted. Does that surprise you? they ask. No. Was it her gun? It was mine. Did you know she'd taken your gun? Isn't that in your report? It is, sir. Wouldn't you know if someone had taken your gun? They listen to what I say, but listen closer to what I don't. Maybe there, in the silence somewhere, is my hand in it. Do they expect me to cry? I could tell them I've cried all I can. I could tell them about the way the world works, but I suspect they of all people already know. A man can cry himself to dust if he lets himself. And then the dust carries on.

3.

You're one lucky guy. The chattier nurses reminded him of this on a regular basis, prompted to point out the small daily wonders of life to a man who had so recently tried bringing his own to an end. He'd nearly bitten off the tip of his tongue, had fractured an elbow, broken a leg, and sustained a serious scrape along his left cheek, but these were no worse than the damages done by people falling from stepladders or tripping down stairs. His roommate, a retired, emphysemic schoolteacher recuperating unsociably on the opposite side of the partition, had done as much when he spilled a bucket of patching tar and tumbled off his son's roof. The more the nurses warmed to Benji, the more they looked to fate or karma or good, blind luck to explain the miracle of his relatively minor injuries. Zelda, the night nurse who woke him at two each morning with the benediction of Percocet, asked the name of his guardian angel, but the real reason he'd been spared the cracked pelvis and pierced organs everyone expected to find had a more earthly origin.

The doctor who reminded him of this was a young black man named Malek with a perfectly bald head, a square face, and an overall stiffness that would have served him well in saluting. Accusingly, he'd asked if Benji knew the best defense in a car accident. "Better than a seat belt. Better than an air bag. Give up? Being drunk. It never fails. Drunk driver runs into Mom in her minivan. Who walks away? Not Mom. She sees it coming. She tenses up. That's when bones break. But the drunk guy, he's relaxed. He's a rag doll. Did you ever try to break a rag doll? You know where he ends up? Sitting on the curb scratching his head. Give the jerk a Band-Aid and call it a night."

But once this sour exchange was over, Benji's prospects turned unexpectedly sweet. He clearly saw that the drunken state in which he'd been found might easily be read as the final flourish of a desperate man, and there were perks to being a desperate man, undeniable and welcome perks that, perkless as his life had been lately, he had no intention of surrendering so soon. His perceived psychological trauma required a longer stay at St. Anthony's than anything he'd done to his body, but even these slight physical impairments lay beyond the psych ward's parameters of care. His immobilized elbow and leg pardoned him from a frightful stay on the fifth floor, where his imagination, fed by visions of Jack Nicholson and Louise Fletcher, furnished a frightening cast of cuckoo characters, loud and volatile and charismatically crazy. Instead, the nurses assigned him to a comfortable room among the generally infirm where they served up an adjustable bed, cable television, and a steady supply of pills that would have been murder to procure from Seth. Excepting his wheezing and annoyingly tight-lipped roommate, he might have been in an indulgent, if not terribly well-appointed, hotel.

Of course, Benji could have corrected them by now. Whatever happened on the bridge lacked the unambiguous intent of Madame Bovary gobbling up her arsenic or Inspector Javert flinging himself into the Seine. Benji's recklessness may have bordered on a death wish, but he knew he'd been enjoying the fruits of a lie, as if he'd been feasting on a basket of sympathy and concern addressed to someone with a much more serious illness. Even with his tongue stitched and swollen, he could have scribbled on the pad his nurses provided him and told

Claudia or his tearful and tiptoeing mother or the nice doughy social worker who looked in on him every other morning that they had it all wrong. But he'd spent two weeks tucked in a warm nest of communal misunderstanding, and, corrupt as it may have been, that, for the moment, was where he wanted to stay.

Which isn't to say Benji didn't feel guilty. How could he not? But whatever guilt his deceit stirred up, his store of ancient resentments quickly helped to settle. There were his father's magniloquent speeches about the virtues of holding a job, a *real* job, a job that, unlike pet or apartment sitting, required the payment of taxes. The wan, worn admonition to "leave Benji alone" that counted as his mother's primary defense, the eye-rolling impatience with which Claudia dismissed his career: he resented these things almost as much as he resented the career itself. *A Hamster for Hannah*, for God's sake!

He took the D-list movies and bit roles in crappy regional reps in stride, with the sort of self-mocking humor common to men whose failures may in fact be their greatest success, but he hated the substantial scripts that passed him by. His greatest achievement (or at least the one with the most gravitas)—the miniseries in which he played Rimbaud's brother—had had its plug pulled and sat collecting dust in some crypt-like vault under PBS, never to be seen. He hated the agents and directors who failed to see in him what he occasionally saw in himself. He hated the audiences who'd never heard of him or, worse, treating him like a trained monkey they happened upon in their favorite restaurants, bullied him into putting down his salad fork and saying the only four words they thought he knew—*That's what* you *think!* The more slights Benji counted, the more forgivable, even justified, his lie seemed. To right a cosmic imbalance didn't necessarily square with committing a great wrong.

Besides, his distress brought out Claudia's kinder side, and he liked Claudia's kinder side. The hospital allowed him, like the rest of the patients under psychiatric care, two one-hour visits of no more than two people per day, and he sank more comfortably into his stiff, pancake-thin pillows knowing that Claudia would be one of them. She brought him frozen fruit bars and thick, cold smoothies, the only forms of nourishment his poor tongue could take, and refreshed with tabloid and fashion industry trash the pile of mindless magazines that grew to teetering heights on his nightstand. And though she, too, wasn't above urging him to take a job waiting tables or giving him a hard time for the few hundred dollars he borrowed here or there, she would quietly make sure that his uninsured fingers never touched a bill.

That all this eventually had to end came as no surprise to Benji. Who knew better than a childhood star the proverbial fate of all good things?

"We have a problem," Claudia said, stepping into the room with a look that told him somehow, overnight, the honeyed spring that so satisfyingly flowed his way had run dry. No more magazines. No more smoothies. "They're not willing to release you on your own." She pushed a high-backed vinyl chair closer to the bed but stayed standing behind it, the coming pronouncements apparently wanting the severity of a podium, even a makeshift one. "I spoke with Dr. Malek. Agreeing to see a therapist isn't enough. He's not convinced you're not a danger to yourself. He wants you supervised."

The day before, the same Dr. Malek had dangled the promise of freedom like a hypnotist's charm, so to have the spell broken now, with such callous sibling economy, brought an angry flush to Benji's face. He reached for the pad he used to keep up his side of the conversation and wrote, *Supervised?!*

"That's what he said."

Benji grimaced. Of course, the only thing better than being in the hospital would be getting out of it, and he'd been looking forward to doing just that. He considered this unexpected twist in the road, trying to figure the best way around it. *I'll stay w/u,* he wrote.

"And do what?" Claudia asked impatiently. "Wander off to find the next bridge?" She sat down in the chair as if suddenly very tired. "He's right. We can't let you hobble on back to the toolshed like nothing happened. Things don't snap back to normal like that. I don't know why I thought they would."

He hadn't planned beyond the toolshed—she had him there—but the thought of prolonging their afternoons together, of milking every last drop of Claudia's kindness, brought the curl of a selfish smile to his lips. To spend the day drifting in the shallows of reality TV, sipping berry blasts on his sister's calfskin couch: an unemployed actor could find worse ways to recuperate.

"Damn it, Benji." She covered her eyes with her hands and rocked forward, elbows on knees. He watched a shudder move along her back and grinned against the pain in his mouth. He was such a problem, wasn't he? What trouble would he get into next? He was ready to have a good laugh with her. Even if he ended up being the punch line, he'd laugh his way onto that calfskin couch.

But then the sniffling began, and he realized that his sister wasn't laughing. He dropped his pad in his lap, helpless to help her, miserable to see how thoroughly he'd cracked her shell. Her sadness, maybe because she so rarely showed it, demolished him. "Caw-da," he said, his tongue moving like a speared fish. She didn't look up for a long minute, not until she wiped the last tears away. Rarely did she give anyone the privilege of seeing her cry, and now she looked embarrassed, flushed red beyond her breakdown and angry for having succumbed to it.

"You're such an asshole," she said, her voice still shaky but unwilling to yield. "Why are you doing this to us? I know this isn't about us, but fuck you, Benji, this is about us too. It's about Mom and Dad. It's about me. You were going to leave me alone. With *them*. What were you thinking?"

Benji hung his head and answered as best he could, "E oth oo soopid hings. Ow."

Claudia gave him an exasperated look: she didn't speak Bitten Tongue.

We both do stupid things, he wrote.

Claudia looked doubtful.

We pick each other up. It's what we do.

"I've never done anything this stupid," she said.

His pen was poised to write *Nick!* Forget writing *Hello?! Baby!* The name of her ex-boyfriend would have been enough of a reprimand, but he put his pen down and sighed.

She looked from her brother's eyes into her own hands, as if their emptiness might comfort her in ways he could not.

"How could you do it?" He couldn't count the number of times she'd come back to that question. And still he had no answer for it. "I spend every second I'm not here worrying about you. Wondering if you're ever going to be okay. How any of us can ever trust you again. And I spend every second here wanting to strangle you. I do, Benji. I'm sick about it, and I hate you for it." She ruminated over her cup of coffee, sipped at it as though it imparted bitter wisdom. "You didn't end up on that bridge alone. I know that. I helped you get there. Or I didn't stop you from getting there. I wasn't enough to stop you, which amounts to the same thing."

It had nothing to do w/u, Benji wrote.

"I wasn't opening a discussion." Claudia shifted in her seat, wiped her eyes one last time. Everything about her now said *business.* "I didn't help you then, but I'm helping you now," she said, reaching into her trendy bag and producing a colorful trifold brochure with two smiling octogenarians on the front, their heads touching tenderly under a flowering tree. "Treadwell Acres." She tossed it on his lap.

Benji gave it the once-over, flipped to a new page in his pad, and drew a big *?*.

"Dr. Malek gave it to me," she explained. "It's one of the best rehab facilities around. They have a fantastic mental health unit." She mustered a hopeful but hollow smile, as if presenting a child with a secondhand toy she meant to pass off as new. Benji responded with a dubious look and began bouncing his pen along the thin and pulpy page. *I can stay w/u.* He placed a dot under each word as if leading Claudia through a sing-along.

"You can't stay with me." Claudia broke the news a bit too cheerfully, Benji thought. "I'm sorry, Benj, but you can't. I start teaching next week and haven't read half the books on my syllabus. I'm behind on the Selkirk place. I don't have time to babysit."

Benji didn't like to sulk, but he wasn't above it either. *I don't need a babysitter!*

"Your doctor disagrees. So does your social worker. So does your therapist. So do I."

Treadwell Acres?! I'm not 80, he scribbled, then drew a series of mad lines under and through each word until the message looked thoroughly redacted.

Claudia opened the brochure to show him another picture, this of a freckled young woman staring out a sunny window with a stock photography glaze of hope in her eyes. "Look. Not everyone is eighty."

It failed to make him feel better. *I'll find someplace,* he wrote, flashing his notepad with a petulant shrug.

"Where?" Claudia asked. "Where will you find?"

To be fair to Claudia, most of Benji's friends *were* poorly equipped to play Florence Nightingale. They spent their days hiking from one audition to the next and their nights telemarketing or tending bar or offering certified (but not necessarily chaste) massage, which left little time for developing a bedside manner. His nursiest friend, a straitlaced chorus boy currently making his way across Washington state as a flying monkey in the traveling company of *Wicked*, could no sooner swoop down and tend to him than his former roommate, who'd sublet Benji's room to a couple of cater waiters with dreams of becoming Alvin Ailey dancers, could offer him his old bed.

Rhonda & Jim, he wrote defiantly, desperate to prove his sister wrong and satisfied that he'd found two of the most decent, responsible, bulletproof people either of them knew.

"Rhonda?" Claudia's eyes widened in disbelief. "Who has thyroid cancer?"

He caught a brief, stinging glimpse of his own narcissism—what kind of friend forgets a friend's thyroid cancer?—but his mind refused to pause. He suggested Thom and Guyang and several strategically unnamed "good friends" he claimed Claudia didn't know, but she shot each of them down with marksman's skill. Thom lived in a sixth-floor walk-up. Guyang already had a baby. And friends she'd never heard of? How good could they possibly be?

"There's nothing wrong with Treadwell," said Claudia, resolute.

Benji uttered as emphatic a "No!" as his throbbing tongue would allow. It was a howl more than a word and spurred his roommate to raise the volume on his TV to an unneighborly pitch. "I wava say ear," Benji cried in pain, his Sharpie shaking as he translated, *I'd rather stay here!*

"I'm sure you would. But here isn't an option." Claudia pulled a sleek silver thermos from her bag and, her still-red eyes finding him over a capful of steaming coffee, continued in a harsher tone. "Not that you get a vote. You surrendered that right the minute you decided to play Billy Joe McAllister. You turned your ballot over to me."

I'll stay with Mom.

"Mom is nearly eighty, Benji, and already has enough patients," Claudia answered. "Her hands are full."

U think Mom will let me end up in a nursing home?

"It's not a nursing home. For God's sake."

He tossed the brochure back at her. *Looks like one.*

What, he wondered, *if I tell the truth?* It was impossible to know whether an alteration to the story of his fall would spare him the torture of his sister's good intentions. But what had once felt like a pardonable omission of a key detail now, in the fiery light of Claudia's grief (not to mention the shadowy threat of waking in a rehabilitation facility for the aging), felt like a hoax. A hoax he was about to be punished for.

"You realize sharing a house with Mom means sharing a house with Dad?" Claudia asked.

True, he hadn't thought of that. How could he possibly share a house with Henry? How, when nobody knew how to push Benji's buttons better than his father, who many years ago, like an architect charged with building a young boy from the ground up, had helped install them? Henry called actors "mountebanks" and maddeningly, purposefully, added the word "the" to every title on his son's filmography—*The Prodigy*, *The Hamster for Hannah*. And though age and illness had considerably dulled Henry's sharpest edges, his belittling commentary continued to play in Benji's mind, as a radio plays on even after the power's been cut. It was Henry who Benji now heard. A cruel and cacophonous litany that rose above Claudia's sorrow and chastening, above the blare of the clumsy roof patcher's TV. True, he would come clean to avoid his father.

"This could be exactly what you need," Claudia persisted, flapping the brochure in front of him like a fan. "Time to relax. Regroup."

But Benji had stopped listening. His brain busied itself composing a confession that his sister wouldn't automatically reject as a ploy to steer past their father on one hand, a convalescent home on the other. *What to say? What to say?*

Facebook! he wrote, adding the exclamation point with a flourish of relief. Why hadn't he thought of it before? He had 658 friends on Facebook. Certainly one of them, or a friend or acquaintance of one of them, or a friend or acquaintance of one of *them*, would cast a pitying eye on what could be billed a meagerly famous near-suicide. He was, after all, the answer to a Trivial Pursuit question ('80s edition). A little fame, like a pinch of spice, still clung to him. Certainly someone on Facebook would be willing to season their stew with it.

Claudia's face collapsed with disdain. "Facebook."

He'd forgotten his audience. His sister wasn't quite the technophobe their father was, but she subscribed to a philosophy of social media that easily made her look as dated as an Atari.

"Is Ashton Kutcher going to come to your rescue? What? You're one of his four million friends. Or maybe your prom date? She was a nice girl. Or someone else you haven't spoken to in twenty years."

"Yur tho mean."

"And you're ridiculous. If you died tomorrow, how many of those friends would be at your funeral?" This was a favorite question, one that present circumstance rendered completely inappropriate but habit and passion spurred her to ask anyway.

Benji managed a look of shock that Stella Adler would have been proud of.

"Sorry. That was a shitty thing to say. But we've talked about this, Benji. Relationships are like trees."

"Ot the twee!"

"Yes, the twee. If we're lucky, we get a few that feed a lifetime. One. Maybe two. They're strong, substantial. They put down roots. But most of them, most friendships, are leaves. They're here. A nice little blossom for a time. A bit of color. Then they fade. We shed them. It's *natural* that we shed them. You're not supposed to know what the girl you took to the prom does with her day. Joanna Goverski is eating at IHOP! Who cares?"

"'Who cares?'" The echo came from the opposite side of the biscuit-colored curtain, followed a moment later by their mother. "Who cares about what?" Evelyn lacked the bearing and attitude to be called regal, but she had the face for it. She was tall and trim, with a fine, upturned nose, lips drawn thin by perpetual sufferance, and a helmet of immaculate silver curls. "Come on," she called, glancing irritably over her shoulder at Henry as he shuffled into view.

"Tone," Henry warned. "I'm not a dog."

Ignoring this, she stepped to the far side of the bed and bent to kiss Benji. A tightness around the mouth let him know he hadn't been forgiven. Not for nearly dying. That offense proved so mountainous, so impossible to scale, she could do nothing but overlook it. Benji knew: her anger burned for another reason, for the fact that he had lived so close for nearly two months—a half hour away!—without telling her. He hadn't visited. Hadn't told her where he was staying or invited her to see the show. As if she, of all people, wouldn't have welcomed a night out. Not, as Claudia reminded her, that she would have taken it. "Who cares about what?" Evelyn asked her daughter in lieu of a hello.

Claudia got up and, hugging Henry, steered him into her chair. "They're discharging Benji, but he needs somewhere to go."

Perplexed, Evelyn stared across the gulf of the bed and asked, "What do you mean 'somewhere to go'?"

"He needs supervision."

"Why would he need supervision?" Evelyn asked, smoothing a wrinkle out of the bedspread.

"He tried to kill himself, Mother. That's why."

"I told you to stop saying that."

"She'd rather admit I wet myself last week," said Henry with a rattling struggle to clear a plug of phlegm from his throat. He swallowed "And we all know how willing she's been to do that."

"Henry." Evelyn reached for the plastic pitcher sitting on Benji's nightstand and filled a cup with water. "Take a drink instead of sitting there hacking."

"Henry come. Henry drink. Henry roll over and play dead."

Like a conductor bringing his orchestra to attention, Benji tapped the baton of his marker on his pad and, with large, wounded eyes, held up the paper for Evelyn to see.

She wants me to go to a nursing home.

"It's not a nursing home, drama queen!" Claudia jabbed the promotional pamphlet into her mother's hand and watched as Evelyn pored over it. "He thinks he should stay with a friend."

"What friend?"

"He doesn't know. Someone on Facebook."

"Facebook?" Evelyn grimaced. "That's nonsense. He'll stay with us." Evelyn dropped Treadwell Acre's best pitch into the trash as if it were a bill she had no intention of paying, then surveyed the flower arrangements next to Benji's bed. She snapped off a daisy's browning head. "Your room is ready for you."

"His room is the Shrine of Guadalupe." Henry laughed. "Let me see that. What you just threw away."

Evelyn stopped pruning the flowers long enough to retrieve the brochure and deliver it to Henry.

"She's starting her very own assisted living community." He considered the hazily happy invalid on the cover and said, "You move home. I'll move here. At least they wouldn't talk to me like they're training a Saint—a Saint . . . Jesus fucking—what's the name of it?"

"Saint who? How would I know?" Evelyn answered. "We're not Catholic."

"The dog, the name of the dog!"

It was onto this battlefield that Benji was about to pitch himself. He saw a week into the future, waking in his childhood bed under the watchful eyes of his *Star Wars* figurines. The sound of his parents' latest skirmish would rise with the smell of coffee from the kitchen, and Benji, hobbling downstairs as if he'd had a bull's-eye painted on his chest, would become his father's newest target.

"Bernard, Daddy," said Claudia, rubbing Henry's back. "Saint Bernard." She turned to Evelyn and, packing away her lullaby voice, asked, "You plan to take care of Benji and Daddy by yourself? At the same time?"

"I'm not by myself. I have Sandra."

"For six hours a day. That leaves eighteen."

"You make it seem like I'm about to climb Mount Kilimanjaro."

"Either way you'll be running around until you break your hip."

"You and your broken hip."

"You and *your* broken hip, Mom. And who will have to take care of you then?"

"Don't worry. I know better than to ask you."

"Stop it!" Henry called out. "Both of you."

Benji's marker moved across a fresh sheet of paper with the high-pitched sound of a hungry mouse. *I have something to tell you.* He flipped the page: *I*

Henry pointed and snapped, "Philomela's trying to tell you something."

New page: *DIDN'T*

Oblivious, Claudia still faced her mother. "Benji and I agreed that he's not going to put that kind of strain on you. Didn't we, Benji?"

Now that he had stepped up to the edge of the cliff, Benji stopped. Jump. He was one word away—a few sharp little mouse squeaks, a simple J-U-M-P—from the truth, one syllable with the power to allay his family's fears, to free himself from an untenable tenancy. Or would he simply be convincing everyone that his primary problem wasn't a suicidal tendency but a psychopathic one? If his family thought he was troubled before, what would they think when he pulled the curtain back on his latest charade? They'd call him psychotic. Alcoholic. Nutcase. He'd be spared the unthinkable stay at 34 Palmer Street, but roundly delivered into a sequestered twelve-step program in the remotest Adirondack woods.

He took a deep breath before placing pen to paper, but before he could finish his sentence, he heard a voice—*that* voice—that made it impossible to go on. "Knock, knock." He turned to see Cat McCarthy standing there shyly, half obscured by the curtain, smiling a smile of uncertain provenance. She'd traded her stylish dress for ragged jeans and a boxy yellow (but still unaccountably sexy) T-shirt emblazoned with the words "Save Compton's Mound." She took a hesitant step toward the bed, but managed by the time she reached him to shed all signs of apprehension. The smile surprised him with its tenderness. Even if this was a performance, even if Cat was slipping comfortably, convincingly, into another skin as he'd seen her do five nights a week for the last two months, Benji didn't mind.

As she leaned over to kiss King Hamlet on his unbandaged cheek, Henry made a sharp warning sound, as if she were about to step off a curb into a puddle.

"Careful," he said, the tone of his voice traveling two orbits closer to congenial. "You'll catch a cold."

Cat stopped, uncertain. She looked to Benji, who shook his head to erase the interruption and ready himself for that long-deferred kiss— delivered at last—while Claudia, hands on knees, bent toward Henry with the loving indulgence of a nanny. "Daddy, you know where you are, don't you?"

"Why wouldn't I? We're in the hospital."

"And you know why we're in a hospital?"

"Benjamin's sick."

"He is. But not with a cold."

Cat extended her hand to the rest of the family, explaining who she was as if they already might know. Benji breathed in the scent she brought with her, that shampoo smell he'd been so sure he'd never smell again, with an exhilarating sense of confusion. Why in the world was she here? He expected visits from Jerry and stoner Bill and maybe even Kay, whose overly ornate get-well bouquet practically reeked of schadenfreude, but never Cat. Her appearance was a puzzle, one that couldn't be solved—not by him, not now—but one he would enjoy piecing together in his happy haze of Percocet.

She gave him a beautiful used copy of *To the Lighthouse* wrapped in newsprint and dove with Henry, whose clarity returned to him as quickly as it departed, into an animated discussion of its merits. Benji fumbled through the opening pages while Cat spoke with his father. Henry's reading lists, which as a teen Benji tended to find joyless and demanding, had largely turned him off serious novels, but he rallied unexpectedly to these opening pages. How bad could a book be when a young boy sits ready to stab his father through the heart with a pair of scissors? But after five minutes the day nurse wandered in with her blood pressure cuff and broke up the fun. Cat, ready, it seemed, for a hasty retreat, kissed him again—a softer, more lingering kiss—or did he imagine it? He set the book down and scrambled for his pad. *Come back!* he wrote.

She laughed as if the idea hadn't occurred to her. "If I can."

Wait. I won't be here. They're discharging me.

"That's good news."

I'll be with my parents for a while. U can read to me.

"Read to you," Claudia said, incredulous. She leaned in close to his ear, whispered, "We're not done with the Treadwell conversation," and, before he could protest, offered to walk out with Cat.

Benji shot her a Medusa's stare but grabbed Cat's hand and persevered. "Pwomise?"

"Okay," she said with a rising blush, "I promise."

When Cat and Claudia had left, Evelyn finished beheading the last few dying flowers before taking her spot on Benji's bed. She placed a hand lightly on his arm and said, "Your sister loves to stir things up."

Still savoring the delicious smoke of Cat's promise, Benji didn't breathe. He held his breath, as if compounding his high. He hardly noticed Henry get up from his chair, but then he felt the weight on him, extraordinary and rare. His father stood over the bed like a priest, eyes closed, head bent, one hand pressed to his son's forehead as if to bless him. "No fever, Ev. You check."

Evelyn shooed Henry's hand out of the way and went through the motions of taking Benji's temperature with supreme indulgence. "No fever," she said, then, having ushered Henry back to his seat, turned to Benji. "What were you saying? Before your friend—" Evelyn paused at the word, turning it over like a teacup in a china shop, curious to know the price. "Before your friend came in?" She picked up his pad and turned back the page to where he'd written *DIDN'T.*

"You didn't what?" She wagged a finger at him as if to say he couldn't get away with anything, not on her watch. "See?" she said confidentially, taking his hand. "Some of us still remember around here."

Held by his mother, watched by his father in an attitude of strange and attendant warmth, Benji took a head-clearing breath and shook his head. His fingers fluttered at his temples to show that the thought, whatever it was, had flown away, before picking up his pen. *I forget.*

Evelyn is afraid. It's her first time, though no one can know it's her first time. This is important to her. The neighbors are one thing, there's no getting around what they've seen, but the doctors, the nurses: it's none of their business, she says. She has to pray the neighbors will keep their mouths shut. And remarkably they do. Forty years later, somehow, miraculously, Claudia does not know. But at this moment, Claudia is barely four. She is in my arms. She wears a green gingham dress and wants to climb onto the gurney with her. I stoop to where she can reach and say, Give Mama a kiss. Claudia fidgets and cries; she doesn't want her mama to go. Evelyn puts her hand in mine. I give it a squeeze before they wheel her off. It's morning. By the time they come back, it's night. She's in the recovery room, they tell me, asleep. We go to the nursery. Claudia passes out on my shoulder on the elevator ride up. There are other fathers at the window, men in loosened ties with their hands pressed against the glass, staring. The nurse waves to me in her starched whites, then wheels a glass bassinet to where I can see. A boy, says the man next to me. He claps me on the back like it's the best thing in the world. A boy, he says. What do you know about that?

4.

Three weeks on Palmer Street put Benji in a mood. He liked the nubbled blue blanket from his boyhood bed and the almost arctic setting of the air conditioner he favored even in mild mid-September. He liked the season's last tomatoes pulled warm and dusty from his mother's garden and the sweating, fat-bellied pitcher from which she poured a heavenly homemade lemonade squeezed especially for him. After nearly a month, though, even these pleasantries had lost their charm, dulled by repetition, tarnished by daily tussles with Henry. And every time he complained to Claudia, trying to convince her that a modestly priced hotel was a better place to stage his recuperation, if only he could borrow a little cash, she said, "Forget it."

"But all this bickering," said Benji, unafraid to ring the same bell more than once. "It isn't good for either of us."

"So stop bickering."

"Easy for you to say. He's not on you all the time."

But Henry's being on him wasn't the problem. He'd had forty years to get used to the taste of his father's vinegary disposition, and he had. More than the arid plains of his father's foul moods, it was the march over the peaks and valleys of Henry's illness that scared and exhausted

Benji, that made him long for the Motel 6. He had no interest in watching the slow, disconcerting descent or measuring the degrees by which illness reduced the literary lion to a shadow of his former self.

Maybe Claudia was right: he had no right to complain. Evelyn made Benji's lemonade and picked up the potato chip bags he left in his wake. With a few generous checks, she kept his creditors at bay. He didn't have to worry about evading his roommates on rent day or making his share of the electric bill. His thankless run as Hamlet's dead father had come to an early end. And perhaps best of all, he'd won the sudden interest of a girl who, before his fall, barely gave him the time of day. He had no clue why, but falling from the bridge had set a flame dancing over his head, and Cat, quick as a moth, headed straight for it. Maybe it made him tragic in a sexy sort of way. Maybe it reminded her of her brother, who, a few years after their parents' awful death (airplane crash), finished a bottle of Jack Daniel's and (accidentally or not) drove himself into a highway divider. Maybe she wanted someone to rescue.

Whatever the case, she showed up daily to take him on the short walks he could manage in his big black boot cast or lull him to sleep with Molly Bloom's soliloquy or, lately, late at night after his parents had gone to bed, gently jerk him off while riding the fingers of his one good hand. He was thirty-nine; she was twenty-five; and they were, out of fear of being discovered or uncertainty over what they were doing or perhaps merely in deference to the immobilizing silicone and plaster encasing two of Benji's limbs, having sex like unschooled pubescent teens, but these sweet, relatively chaste tumblings were unexpectedly taking root, touching Benji in ways countless other carnal encounters had not. Nothing in his life became him like almost leaving it.

He hesitated to use the word *love*. Where, except in the great, shattering romances of Britain and Russia and France, did anyone fall in love so fast? Still, toying with the idea, Benji thought *I love you, I love you* as he kissed Cat's fluttering eyelids and practiced an increasingly deft, one-handed maneuver to unfasten her bra. Twice a week, Benji reported to Ernest Salter, whose parades down some of psychotherapy's mustier corridors were a condition of the patient's release, and agreed with the good doctor's diagnosis: a budding romance would be . . . improvident. The idea of submitting to any therapist had terrified Benji, who doubted his ability to play before a professional the part of the emotionally unhinged bridge jumper. How to sustain the illusion that he'd meant to do what he'd done for anyone beyond his family (who, with the exception of Claudia, was only too happy to let him forget it)? But Salter's inquisitive stare proved more kindly than penetrating, and soon Benji relaxed the need to temper his enthusiasm. "I think I love her," he offered one day as an astonished non sequitur to a dream about a drowning elephant. To which Dr. Salter replied, in an unapologetic moment of Freudian devotion, "What does your mother make of this?"—*this* being the love, not the elephant.

Evelyn, six years her husband's senior, congratulated herself for overlooking the couple's considerable difference in age, unwilling to deprive her son the happiness that recent events convinced her he so seriously needed. Henry also approved, volubly and wholeheartedly, though his endorsement had little to do with Benji's happiness. His radio had never really tuned to that channel, but he was glad to see Benji smitten with someone whose future promised more than a starring role in an exercise video.

"Don't muck it up," Henry said one morning, stabbing a piece of toast into an egg yolk and leveling the dripping point at his son. "I know you're used to women with a higher nonsense-to-substance ratio, but this one has something to offer."

"And what's that?" Benji asked, glib but genuinely curious.

"She reads beyond the ingredient list on a Luna bar, for starters."

"She's an actor, Dad. You don't like actors."

"I don't like disillusionment. There's a difference." He rapped his fork on the rim of his plate like a judge bringing his court to order.

"We're not starting down that road. I'm done with career counseling. I said she's a keeper."

Benji had the distinct impression that Cat could cut out his kidneys, sell them on eBay, and (as long as she could quote from *Ulysses*) remain a keeper in Henry's book. Not that it mattered. Cat *was* a keeper, though Benji's reason for thinking so had nothing to do with Joyce.

He loved Cat's passion. The way she'd swoon for a tulip but took lilies as a personal affront. Or how, in one breath, she'd condemn the "incarceration of the underclass" and then, in the next, devise cruel, practically medieval punishments for anyone caught answering his cell phone in a restaurant or wearing sunglasses indoors. "Unless you're blind," she reasoned, "or just coming from the ophthalmologist, there's no excuse." He loved her weakness for buttermilk biscuits, the diplomatic ease with which she handled his parents, and how, before kissing him good-bye, she grabbed a fistful of his hair and ungently pulled. He loved that she hated words that ended in *y*, that she made exceptions for adverbs but refused to say *tasty* even when something was. He loved her eyes. And the line of Whitman tattooed in typewriter font on the inside of her wrist. And the sudden, shocking devotion he'd won by false means.

She'd rented all four seasons of *Prodigy* while he was in the hospital, all five of his films, even *A Hamster for Hannah*, and discussed them without mockery, seriously, as a body of (her word) *work* that might one day have him thanking Uta Hagen from the dais. He plugged her into his Oscar speech, his Tony speech, his Vague but Meaningful Lifetime Achievement Award speech—the monologues he should have stopped rehearsing in his twenties but hadn't—and she fit. *I'd like to thank the members of the academy and all the people who helped put me here. Mom and, ahem, Dad and Blah and Blah and Blah. And Cat. My beautiful Cat. Ma chère Catherine. My Catchenka.* No matter how he said it, she fit perfectly.

Part of Claudia's refusal to play ATM and provide him with funds for a stay at the Motel 6 was her disapproval of how he'd spend his time. "Vicodin and *Voluptuous Vixens*," she quipped.

She wasn't wrong. (He'd once left the third installment of his favorite XXX franchise on a laptop he borrowed from her.) But Benji's dream of making off to a hotel had as much to do with hoarding Cat for himself as it did with painkillers and porn. There, he imagined, they'd lie on a quilted coverlet and, day passing into night passing into day, float far beyond a sex life suitable for airing on a moderately racy *Afterschool Special*. If they didn't have to worry about a sundowning Henry calling Cat by the name of his sixth-grade teacher, they might finally lose themselves and, carried away by something stronger than the polite little eddies of frottage and finger banging, discover one another. They'd be two explorers on a great, unsinkable raft, and nothing, not his incapacitating casts or the germiness and decidedly French fry smell of the bedspread, would hold them back.

But the dream of the hotel had evaporated with Claudia's unequivocal "Forget it!" and every increasingly emphatic "No!" since. Benji withheld his disappointment from Cat, concerned that what he could only describe as his sister's selfishness would glaringly expose his own, but he held out hope on another front: she'd leased the cottage on Saratoga Lake through the end of September, and although Benji had never stepped foot in it, her tour through the "Summer 2012" album on her smartphone convinced him that here was the perfect place to wall up with Ophelia and finally get down to "country matters."

"We have two weeks before you have to be in New York. Two weeks without my parents hanging around."

"Hanging around? Benji, it's their house." She moved her hand from his zipper and rapped a knuckle on the hard plastic casing that covered his leg. "Besides. You're supposed to stay put."

He stopped short of insisting. Already he'd sailed further with Cat than he once thought possible. Why press his luck and risk running aground the ambivalence that kept her from making an invitation in the first place? But the time for pressing his luck had come. It was Monday. If Benji wanted to play lord of Cat's castle, he had to stop behaving as if rejection were a virus he feared catching and simply ask if he could move in.

He stood at the living room window, waiting for her to come. Now that the trial of lunch was over, now that Henry had convicted him of wearing his hair too long or never having read Montaigne, he could take up his afternoon post. He parted the curtain and looked out at the street. One of the prettiest Alluvia had to offer, the tall maples and gently sagging Queen Annes of the town's forefathers, but quiet on a morning like this, everything still as a painted backdrop. Benji waited, watched. His mind lingered over the sight of a silver Mercedes parked across the street, a rare curbside flower not indigenous to these parts, but before he could bother to guess its origins, *Judge Judy* called him away. He hobbled back to the couch. The copy of *To the Lighthouse* that Cat had given him lay butterflied on the armrest. He tried ignoring "The Case of the Dented Bumper" and opened it to where he'd left off: Mr. Ramsay stalked across the lawn with the notion that a truly splendid mind could tackle the range of human thought, from A to Z, while his own mind, splendid enough but nevertheless limited, would never get farther than Q. Benji read,

How many men in a thousand million . . . reach Z after all? Surely the leader of a forlorn hope may ask himself that, and answer, without treachery to the expedition behind him, 'One perhaps.' One in a generation. Is he to be blamed then if he is not that one? provided he has toiled honestly, given to the best of his power, and till he has no more left to give? And his fame lasts how long? It is permissible even for a dying hero to think before he dies how man will speak of him hereafter.

But reading, at least in front of the doily-collared Judge Sheindlin, was a losing battle. He watched two more cases with a vacant stare, as pleasantly glazed-eyed as fledgling sobriety allowed, and made it halfway through a third—inept wedding planner, deplorable bride—when the doorbell rang. From the kitchen, Evelyn called out that she'd get it, but Benji shouted back, thunking across the tasseled carpet as quickly as he could and throwing open the door. The man standing on the mat lunged forward without so much as a hello and took Benji into his arms.

"Roger?" Benji croaked.

Roger Fitch held on to his godson for a good minute, too grateful (to judge from the crush of his embrace) that Benji was actually there to hold on to. When the hug wound down, he stepped back, taking Benji by the shoulders, assessing him. "Benji, my boy," he said brightly, "you look like I popped your balloon."

Roger was a small man, daintily built, with a pronounced gap between his front teeth and ears that stuck out from his immaculately shorn head with elfin prominence. Physically, he looked less suited to building the careers of literary giants than to cobbling their shoes or tinkering with their watches, but Henry (and, according to Henry's math, at least five other decorated scribblers) would have been digging ditches without him. His writers called him Leo or, when they felt like driving the point home, Napoleon, for though he stood barely tall enough to ride most roller coasters, there was something undeniably magisterial about this son of a grocer from Canarsie, the product of public schools and city colleges, who, despite (or maybe because of) his humble origins, understood the appeal of world domination. To see Roger hammering out the details of a subrights contract or poaching an author from an agency twice the size of his own was to watch him grow a foot before your eyes.

"You were expecting someone prettier," Roger said, cutting off Benji's apology with a solid, avuncular pat on the back. At least once a year, in the heyday of Henry Fisher's career, Roger could be counted on to materialize at this very door, contracts for Henry in one hand, Zabars for the rest of the Fishers in the other. He made it known that it wasn't a trip he enjoyed making—the few charms of upstate New York that he could name (camping, cow tipping) held no appeal for him—but Benji, who used to race to his car like a bounding dog, ranked high among its consolations. He dropped his bags at his feet and gave his godson another hug.

Roger was, like many a well-heeled Manhattanite, hopelessly provincial; everything he could ever want ranged on an island thirteen miles long. Should he ever need a face-to-face with one of the few non–New York–based writers he represented, he insisted they bring their business to him, the indignities of traveling beyond Brooklyn being a form of penance for living in Eugene or Princeton or some other godforsaken land. To this rule, he made two exceptions. In 1965, at the age of thirty, Roger Fitch packed up his desk at one of the country's leading literary agencies and took with him two young writers nobody at Curtis Brown thought to miss. The first was E. Pritchett Moon; the second, a twenty-seven-year-old construction worker who'd written his first novel in a tiny apartment alongside his boss's garage. Edwin, author of what turned out to be an endlessly proliferating saga of randy warlocks, earned him money, vast sums of it. Henry, who continued hanging drywall until his third novel won him the National Book Critics Circle Award, earned him respect.

"Did my father know you were coming?" Benji asked.

"You know me, Benji. I don't leave the fortress unless I'm summoned."

"Yeah, but does he remember summoning you?"

"He remembers fine," Henry said, suddenly behind them, surprisingly stealthy on his stocking feet.

"There's nothing wrong with his hearing." Roger winked before walking off to clasp his old friend's hand.

The buzz finally drew Evelyn out of the kitchen. She hurried down the hallway, wiping dish suds on her flowered robe. "Roger? What on earth?" She opened her mouth and laughed, somewhere between charmed and offended by the surprise. "Henry didn't," she began, then, reconsidering, leaned in for a conspirative hug. "I could kill him. Look at this place. Look at my hair." She pulled her robe more tightly around her and sourly cinched the belt.

"He's not here to check if the pillows are fluffed," Henry said, starting back toward the kitchen. "Let's go, Leo."

Roger offered Evelyn his arm and followed along. "Don't worry about your hair, Ev," he said, polishing his shining head like Aladdin's lamp. "Look at mine."

Evelyn carved the babka and set it on the table with a stack of small plates, while the men poured the morning's leftover coffee—Roger insisted that Evelyn go to no trouble—and settled into opposite chairs. Benji, more curious than hungry, lingered in the doorway, picking lazily at a slab of sugar-tarred dough.

"You're wondering why I called you here."

Roger spread a napkin over his knee and smiled at the lack of grace he'd come to see as the larger part of Henry's appeal. "Nary a hello," he said, laughing. "Henry, my friend, nowadays doctors would place you on a spectrum of some sort. Is it a mild form of Asperger's or a signature brand of cantankerousness that makes small talk so unthinkable?"

"Well, tell your doctors to get in line behind mine, who have plenty of diagnoses of their own."

"Which you're absolutely going to tell me all about," Roger answered. "But first"—he turned an empty chair in Benji's direction and motioned for Benji to sit—"I want to hear from this one."

"Benji?" Henry balked. "Benji's fine." But Roger's level stare proved too much for even Henry's obdurate nature, and he waved his agent on like a man who'd ignored his sound warning and insisted on driving down a dead-end street.

They waded into the conversation slowly, between sips of coffee and observations about a Republican senator's crush on Ayn Rand, but as soon as Leo asked the inevitable question—"What was going through your mind?"—Benji's monologue started up. It now played like a song from a jukebox, easily, automatically, drop a quarter in the slot and out it came. In the constant retelling, he'd worked the blur of that strange August night into a finely focused tale of drunken desperation, the climax of which had been years in coming. He fashioned himself as more determined than mere accident allowed, showing them his damage but also something that he himself had lost sight of long ago: his depth. What else was he hiding if he could hide such despair? Each retelling of the story poured like molten steel into this new mold, into a new Benji, whose form was more impressive, whose qualities—the despondency that pulled him down, the strength of will that lifted him up—gave rise to a more monumental man.

Evelyn, still unable to contemplate the state of mind that led her son to attempt a suicidal leap, turned back to busy herself with the dishes while Henry sat quietly by. At the end of Benji's monologue, Roger reached for his godson's hand and squeezed.

"Life will always be disappointing," he said with pressing emotion. "Even if everything looked exactly as you thought it would, even then, there would be disappointments. Deep, even ruinous disappointments. Compromises we think we can't possibly live with. But we do. We do because we must. It's the contract we sign for being here. We have to treat life like it's precious. Even when we think it's not. Especially then. Because then we see how easily it can be thrown away. Do you understand? We can't have you doing anything like that ever again, Benji. Ever." The few quiet tears that rolled down his face as he spoke surprised everyone, which was perhaps why he was in no hurry to wipe them away. They made a point that, in this family, whose silences and evasions Roger knew so well, needed making.

Benji felt a dull throb of remorse, but he'd padded himself well against the knowledge that his lie was often a source of great pain, and the shame at causing it failed to reach him where he lived. He sat like a statue, unmoving.

"We all have our to-be-or-not-to-be moment at one point or another," Henry interrupted irascibly.

"Henry," Roger warned.

"He's here! Look, Leo, he's sitting right here. With no complaints, except for me. Can we move on now?" Henry looked from his son to his wife to his oldest friend imploringly, as abashed as his character allowed him to be, which wasn't very abashed at all. "Give me a break," he said. "My watch is ticking twice as fast as everyone else's; I don't have the luxury of navel gazing." But when no one answered, when no one so much as blinked, the sound of his fist coming down on the table rang out like cannon fire.

"It's done!" he shouted. There was a salvaged air of lordliness in the pronouncement, the imperious brevity of it, the missing antecedent, the pause. "It's done. It's done, and I want you to read it."

The stoical mask fell from Roger's face first to reveal eyes ignited by the news, mouth agape. Neither he nor Evelyn nor Benji needed to be told what *it* was. *It* had lived among them, between them, sometimes on top of them, for the last eight years. "You said you'd given up on it."

"And it was true. True enough: I never thought I'd finish. This last year, I've been lucky to get an hour a day when I feel sharp enough. When my mind feels like mine. One, maybe two hours a day. I couldn't spend it listening to you claw at the door. I worked better when everyone thought I wasn't working. No offense."

Roger toasted Henry with his coffee mug.

"I had to finish. I couldn't reconcile myself to the thought that you'd find three different drafts after I died and cobble them together with one of those awful forewords. The book he might have written, if only he had more time."

"You know me better than that."

"I would have haunted you if you did."

"You finished the book, Henry. Christ!"

"Said the Jewish atheist."

Roger clapped his hands together and bubbled over. "I'm thrilled. I couldn't be happier. I'll have it read by tomorrow. We'll get Fanton on the phone. We'll take care of the book. But, my God, man. I haven't heard from you in months. I want to know how you are."

"I just told you how I am."

"You told me how the book is, Henry. You understand those are two different things? I'm asking about *you*."

"Me." Henry nodded gamely. "I'm in what they call 'moderately severe cognitive decline.' I love that 'moderately severe.' Like 'passionately indifferent' or 'blithely miserable.' My long, last march into the dark. What this means exactly varies with the hour. The other day the doctor asked me to count backward from twenty by twos. I looked at him like he wanted proof of Planck's constant. I might lose track of the days of the week. Maybe I've forgotten my address. I can quote George Eliot but a minute later turn around and forget the word for 'fork.' Meaning 'moderately severe.' Meaning I've pissed myself, but I don't need help wiping my ass. Yet. But that day's coming. Is that what you had in mind?"

Roger's eyes widened at the challenge as he sipped from his mug.

"And I never said anything about Bill Fanton. We're not publishing it. Not while I'm here. Not now," Henry continued. "I want you to read it. You, Leo. It goes no further than that."

Roger leaned in with his left ear, as if he'd heard wrong. "You've lost me."

"I need you to read it, to make it real. You. It goes no further than that."

"Henry," Roger began.

But Henry cut him off. "Publish it when I'm dead. Publish it *as is* when I'm dead. I can't edit it. I don't *want* to edit it. Or get drawn into which goddamn picture they pick for the cover. Or wake up even once in the night and wonder what the hell they're saying about it."

"You've never cared what critics have to say."

"I'm not talking about critics."

"Who then?"

Henry's hand made a circle describing the room, the house, everything beyond. "How much time do I have, Leo? A few months? A year?"

"He still has his good days," Evelyn interjected from the sink, where she scoured a skillet with renewed vigor.

"Only because she keeps lowering the bar," Henry said coolly. "If I remember my phone number, it's a banner day. No, Leo. The sun is going down. I feel it. Every day is a little bit hazier than the last. Soon there won't be anything left to burn off the fog. Life in a cloud. I don't get any say about that. But how I spend the few moments of clarity I have left, the scenery I opt to take in on my moderately severe descent, *that* I get to choose." He shook his head and lowered his eyes. "I'm done, Leo. I've spent enough time wondering if this or that book is the one I was meant to write. Is this the one that will last, the one that will outlast me, or is it just another blip? The awards, the reviews, all the crap that every writer says he doesn't care about? Well, we care. I care. And now I want a break." At this, Henry reached into his shirt pocket and pulled out a stack of index cards. Some were blank. Some were filled with his tight, cramped script. He set off shuffling through them.

"What are those?" Leo asked.

When Henry didn't answer, Evelyn did. "The death of me. He writes on them so he doesn't forget. They're like petals off the cherry tree. Everywhere you look. The other day, I slipped on one and nearly fell down the stairs."

"Nobody fell down the stairs," Henry reported, flipping through the cards with failing restraint. "Damn it. I know I put it in here."

Midway through his second pass, he found what he was looking for: a scrap of torn paper, ruled with thin blue lines and ragged on one side from the wire rings of a notebook. Henry trapped it between two fingers and held it out to Roger, shaking it like bait.

It read: *11-8-21-9*.

"What's this?" Roger asked.

"The combination."

"For the *safe*? Henry. You promised me."

"I never did."

"What about the computer I bought you?"

"For my birthday," Henry said, visibly proud of the memory.

"You told me you were using it."

"I do use it. It's a very nice place to tape my notes."

"Dad likes being the only middle-class American without an e-mail address," Benji chimed in. "It's a point of honor."

"You're telling me you have one copy of the book?"

"Which you'll read. And put back. And retrieve sometime in the not too distant future. When I'm gone."

"I'm sorry, Henry, but you do know how stupid that is? In this day and age? Forget about the ease of writing. Forget that you can edit without blackening your fingers on typewriter ribbon. *Typewriter ribbon!* It's plain reckless. You're honestly telling me you have one copy of eight years' work?"

Henry shrugged. "What do I need with more than one copy?"

"Flood. Fire. Theft."

"You sound like an insurance salesman, Leo. What do you think the safe is for?"

Jane said never ask too much. But I'm not thinking of this as I stand on the porch. It's Christmas Eve. When I find Jane gone, I stand on the porch and ask Evelyn to watch the baby. She calls the police. Each morning, I leave to join the men in padded navy jackets and fur hats from which their badges shine. We trudge deep into the snow-buried woods, climbing fallen branches and cracking through the ice-jagged streams. Maybe she ran away, they say. Maybe the baby was too much. But I know. I know. I go out before the sun is up, and Evelyn is at the door, waiting for me to put the baby in her arms. Claudia, washed and fed by the time I get home, snuggles in a pink blanket and smells softly of soap. There isn't a day she isn't ready for me. And then it's spring. And then it's the day I go to the door to find Evelyn waiting in the bright, early light. She wears a white dress with cherries on it, and there's the smell of grass that already needs cutting, but instead of handing Claudia to her, I reach out and take her hand, but the words won't come. She doesn't let go of my hand. When I can speak, I say, Will you? But my tongue is a weight, and the rest of the sentence is trapped under it. It doesn't matter. She doesn't need anything more. Yes, she says, yes.

5.

Because the widow couldn't bear to sell the house, she rented it out. It was a grand cottage, situated on a superior stretch of lakefront, Adirondack chairs as red as candied apples and a lawn just large enough for croquet. Her husband had been a photographer who'd done a residency at Yaddo as a young man and found at the nearby racetrack the subject that established his name. There wasn't a room that wasn't filled with large black-and-white photos of mud-spattered jockeys and thundering horses, that wasn't decorated to suggest the artful artlessness of equestrian chic. The worn leather club chairs, the tartan wallpaper and silver candlestick lamps, the shelves and shelves of leather-bound books that only the dourest of summer renters would dare pick up. *Gargantua and Pantagruel? The Wealth of Nations?* Benji limped through his first tour in a state of consumerist wonder. "Ralph Lauren had a wet dream," he said, fingering the camel-colored cashmere blanket draped casually over the foot of the bed.

But after three blissful days of residency, he had proven himself a perfect specimen of human adaptability. He put aside all envy and derision and met the morning like a king, propped against a mountain of jacquard pillows in the gigantic sleigh bed, ready to receive his breakfast on a tray, if only he could find someone to bring it. He listened to Cat in the shower—the beat of falling water, a snippet of song—and felt, finally, at peace. He had a view of the lake, the sky, the flawless blue of a mid-September morning that seemed to mirror the clarity of his mind. Keeping what his friends in recovery called a "day count" had always made him feel more like an alcoholic than falling asleep holding the bourbon bottle, but secretly scarcely an hour passed when he didn't add up the time since his last drink. Three days. Seventeen. Thirty-six. The only chemicals to pass his lips now were prescribed by his general practitioner, and every milligram he took he took according to the letter. His respect for Dr. Gratin's dosing requirements may have started with Evelyn, with a worried mother's silent pledge to be the Percocet bottle's childproof top, but as the weeks passed, with Cat more and more by his side, Benji felt the weight, the responsibility of his sobriety shift to his own shoulders. He ticked off the days like mileposts on a marathon, with the swelling pride of a challenge met.

Of course Cat McCarthy wasn't the first girl to inspire Benji to cork the wine. He'd dried out for Marisol Alvarez and her macrobiotic diet. And Daphne Chu, whose own commitment to conquering step seven spurred her to fill two notebooks with the names of people she once wronged. And Angelica Tottencourt, self-professed psychic, whose inner spiritual guide failed to inform her that Benji's teetotaling, like their relationship, had an expiration date. But to compare Cat to Angelica or Daphne or Marisol or anyone else who came before her was to hold a birthday candle to a bonfire. Others simply vanished in the heat.

Benji didn't want to spend his mornings barely conscious or let another afternoon pass in a blear, not when he could open his eyes to the easterly sun and see Cat sleeping beside him. Before Hank, an ex–competitive rower and neighbor to the north, zipped across the square of placid pewter lake framed by the bedroom window, Benji's arm had journeyed across the mattress, reaching for the sweet, warm hillocks that Cat made under the sheet. He moved more like an old man than the svelte, steel-shouldered, septuagenarian neighbor—still slow and sore, encumbered—but closer he came, closer, until he fit himself to Cat's curved and slumbering shape like a puzzle piece. His hand found her hip. His lips brushed the downy fringe on the back of her neck. He practically vibrated with the competing urges to wake her up and let her sleep. As he nestled against her he felt her swim up from the depths, pause before surfacing completely. She let him suffer. But the louder his breath sounded in her ear, the harder he grew against the small of her back, the dearer, he could tell, she found his agony. She'd roll over and look up at him, laughing through a yawn. There was no sour breath. No crust sealing shut the corners of her eyes. No cowlicked hair. In time, the faults that made her human would assert themselves, but in the poetically sealed vault of their three-day tryst, Benji sensed only her perfection.

He'd gone to the cottage with a rough sketch of Cat's life, but the long conversations on the splintered gray dock, the dreamy postcoital confessions, allowed him to start filling in the lines with color. She was the daughter of a high school guidance counselor and a Joyce scholar whose monograph on micturition in Irish literature had been shortlisted for the James Russell Lowell Prize, a big deal in certain small circles. She'd told Benji in their first days together that her parents had "died in a plane crash," but it wasn't until she was half asleep in a lounge chair by the lake, offering her back to be slathered in sunscreen, that she admitted that rescue workers had discovered her father, still strapped to his seat, in an old woman's garden. Her mother's body had never been found.

Cat, who was only a year old at the time, remembered nothing of her parents or their tragic end, but Molly, her older sister and self-appointed surrogate mom, provided a store of painful memories for Cat's most private monologues. She talked about her mother's struggle with depression and her father's rigorously managed drinking problem, but most of Cat's memories focused on Molly or their brother, Dennis, or the decent but unpalatably Republican aunt and uncle who dutifully stepped in to raise them. Cat was less inclined to shine the spotlight on herself—an odd trait, Benji noted, for an actor—but he listened attentively to the tales she felt like telling, waiting for the moments when Cat appeared, when she, the secondary character in so many of her tales, stepped to the front of the stage. Then he caught a glimpse of the girl he was beginning to love.

And then there was the sex.

He'd imagined their days away from Palmer Street and the chaperoning eyes of his parents would be a time of discovery. And they were. They were, first, a lesson in what could and couldn't be done with two of four extremities in casts. Without both arms to support his weight, the missionary position was out. As was anything that required standing for too long. He couldn't cup her firm, young ass and pin her to the wall or take her in a handstand, holding on to her legs like the handles of a wheelbarrow. He tried standing behind her, his good hand braced on her back as she planted forward into downward dog, but soon the pain elbowed in like a bothersome third who wanted a piece of the action, and he had to lie down. He was best sitting or on his back, with Cat riding his lap or rising above him with calisthenic abandon or holding on to the headboard with a grip wide enough for motorcycle handlebars and lowering herself—ever so teasingly—onto his face.

It had been years since he'd paid attention to the subtle emotional tremors that attended sex, since he had cared enough for his partner to see her so vulnerably exposed, but the aftershocks of their lovemaking registered once again on the heart's delicate apparatus. He saw the ways in which Cat could be generous or selfish or self-conscious or scared. He saw the peaks of her happiness. Shadows of a remoter grief. And for the first time in a long time, he wasn't the first one to let go, roll to the other side of the bed, and fall asleep.

He might have been thirteen again, for the frequency and firmness of his hard-ons. Now, letting his mind wander across the pages of their compromised *Kama Sutra*, he slipped his hand under the tented sheet to treat himself to a few vigorous tugs. He trained an ear on Cat in the shower, trying to gauge when the water might shut off, if he could finish before she did, and had fallen halfway into a serious rhythm when the phone rang. The smooth glass face of Cat's phone lit up. It chirped like a cricket atop the neatly stacked books on her nightstand. Benji fumbled for it. He'd never seen a picture of Molly, but the one displayed beneath her caller ID fit well enough with his preconception. Her curly, shoulder-length red hair, riotous freckles, and severe mirrored sunglasses squared with her willingness to meddle and, on occasion, make Cat cry. His fingers, two mischievous steps ahead of his brain, swiped across the screen and brought the phone to his ear.

"Molly?"

There was a pause. "Who's this?" she asked, unwilling to give him the satisfaction of knowing.

"It's Benji," he said, unwilling to give her the satisfaction of having to say more.

"Is my sister there?"

"She is, but she's in the shower."

Another pause. "What's wrong with her voice mail?"

"Nothing," he said cheerfully. "I just wanted to say hi. Introduce myself."

"Oh. Hi." She sounded deflated, as if the pleasantry, insincere though it was, had punched a hole in her peevish mood. But she recovered in no time. "Actually, now that we're talking, I want to ask you something."

"Shoot."

"What's going on up there?"

"What do you mean?"

"I mean, in Xanadu. You *do* know she was supposed to be in New York a week ago, don't you?" She had the thick, sinusy voice of an unrepentant smoker and cleared her throat from time to time with a rough, bronchial bark. "I've been trying to figure it out. But, honestly, I'm at a loss."

"She doesn't have to be in New York until the end of the month."

"I mean, who passes up an opportunity like that?" Molly asked, barreling over Benji's protest like a professional linebacker taking on the JV team. "A Broadway play."

Benji scoffed. "Where'd you get Broadway?"

"She didn't tell you?" Molly sighed, softening toward the philosophical. "A thousand actors would kill for a chance like that. To be invited to an audition in New York City. By. A. Director." She nailed his ignorance to a cross with each hammered word. "He saw *Hamlet* and asked to hear her read. She didn't mention that either, hunh? I told her things like that don't happen every day. She forgets how lucky she is. She doesn't have to wait tables or tend bar or do half the unappealing things most actors have to do. You know what I'm talking about. Am I wrong? She rents a three-bedroom house on a lake while the rest of the cast is sleeping three to a room in some sad motel. I just hate to think of her passing up the opportunity of a lifetime to make sure the Civil War dead get their due. Or to play house. Or whatever it is she's doing up there."

Cat turned off the water and pulled back the shower curtain, brass rings zipping across the rod with the clarity of little bells. Benji, not knowing what else to say, said, "Revolutionary War."

"Sorry?"

"The dead. Compton's Mound? Revolutionary War, not Civil War."

Molly managed to condense her skepticism, her utter lack of interest, into a single syllable, a hard little pellet of sound dropped displeasingly between them. "Hmph." Then: "Tell her I called."

Benji tossed the phone into the dunes of the down comforter without a good-bye and waited for Cat to open the door.

"What's wrong?" she asked as soon as she saw his face. She stood in the doorway wrapping a towel tightly around her as the surrounding cloak of steam tattered into the room and disappeared.

"Your sister called."

"And by the look of it worked her charms on you. I could have told you that was going to happen. Why did you answer the phone?"

"To piss her off, I guess."

"Mission accomplished?"

"You didn't say anything about Broadway," Benji said, hurt. "Or needing to be in New York last week. You said you weren't due there for another—"

"Molly." She said the name apprehensively, as though it were a curse best not spoken, then explained, "I left that whole thing very open-ended. And it wasn't Broadway. I don't know where she gets half the—Broadway by way of Weehawken, maybe."

"Opportunity of a lifetime. That's what she said."

Cat sat on the side of the bed and pumped a few pearls of lotion onto her water-beaded legs. "*Oleanna* in a church basement is hardly the opportunity of a lifetime," she said flatly, rubbing the skin to a high, fragrant sheen.

"So why didn't you go?"

She shrugged. "Maybe I don't like David Mamet."

"I don't think that's it."

She questioned his certainty with a wry grin before returning to her moisturizer. "Okay. Maybe I like what I'm doing here more," she said.

The idea that he himself might be the reason beneath this vague answer broke like sunrays into a recess of dim hope. He'd been so occupied with whether he was falling in love with Cat that he hadn't stopped to consider whether she might be falling in love with him. "And what's that?" he asked. "What are you doing?"

She turned to indulge the other leg while Benji, prick stiffening anew, further indulged this fantasy of reciprocation. As if the thought of Cat's devotion weren't alluring enough, he found the performance of her morning skin care ritual hopelessly erotic.

"I'm fighting evil robber barons," she said.

Benji sighed. This wasn't the answer he wanted to hear. Not only because it had nothing to do with him but because he'd already gone to considerable lengths to clear an old acquaintance's name. "I told you. Nick Amato is not a robber baron. He's a real estate developer."

"Who happens to be developing what should be historically protected land. It's a cemetery, Benji. For war heroes."

"Who no one has visited in a hundred years."

"So that means we should go and dig them up? Who digs up a cemetery?"

"That doesn't make him an evil robber baron," Benji repeated.

"What does it make him then?"

It was a lure, playfully dangled, but Benji gave it a serious snap. "He was my sister's boyfriend," he said. "They probably would have gotten married."

"Probably? Intriguing. What stopped them?"

He could have started down that bump-riddled road to a pretty good story, but the sight of Cat, gilded by the light that shimmered off the lake, had him sinking into the pillows with dreamy satisfaction. She looked like one of Degas' bathers, all golds and irresistible pinks. He retrieved Cat's phone from the jumbled bedding and snapped a quick photo. She turned at the sound of the old-fashioned shutter click and, with a clowning moue, held out her palm. Unapproved photos were not part of her contract. With a frown of his own, Benji surrendered the phone and said, "Your sister thinks we're playing house."

"I love my sister," answered Cat, pausing as one does before equivocating the unequivocal, "but she can be a bitter, bitter pill."

"She said you don't know how lucky you are."

"Because I'm not a waitress, right? I'm so lucky. What she calls luck, I call the death of my parents." Cat gave Benji a dispirited smile and started on her elbows. "She acts like she doesn't know where that money comes from. How did I pay for the BFA or the summerhouse or any of the other things she thinks I'm so lucky to have? The same way she paid for a Range Rover and two divorces. A big fucking insurance policy."

Benji breathed deeply. The perfume of Cat's soap and body lotion worked its way into his system, rocketing every available drop of blood between his legs. He felt light-headed, ashamed to be fully erect in such close proximity to Cat's dead parents, but undeniably ready to fuck all the same. He folded his hands over his lap and did his best to look attentive and grave.

"She has dreams for me," Cat went on. "Mama Rose dreams. Which makes me either June or Gypsy. It's unclear which. I haven't tried stripping yet."

"If ever you want to practice."

She gave him a quick, teasing kiss and hopped off the bed. Shimmying across the room, she danced an impromptu burlesque behind her towel before dropping it to the floor and stepping into a pair of striped cotton panties.

"Molly wanted to be an actor?"

"No, but she was always the one bound for the spotlight. Or so everyone thought. Or my dad, at least."

"And what was Molly's talent?"

"Resentment? She won the science fair one year, and that was it: she was going to be a doctor. Find the cure for cancer. That kind of thing." Cat pulled on torn jeans and a fitted sweater with flared sleeves while she talked, then sized herself up in the standing mirror.

"She's a rich biotech researcher. What does she have to complain about?"

"Her money's pretty much gone. And she tells people she's a biotech researcher. She's an assistant, actually. She isn't curing cancer. She's watching bacteria bloom." Cat ran a wand of colorless gloss over her lips and pressed them together, more or less satisfied with the result.

"She told me she could have won the Nobel Prize if only my parents hadn't died."

"No pressure there."

"Right? My parents' dying is all she ever needed to explain why her life has been so—I don't know what she'd call it. Ordinary."

Benji understood completely where Molly was coming from but, because this was a fledgling nemesis they were talking about, felt compelled to set his camp on the other side of the fence. "Like winning the Nobel Prize is the only way of making a name for yourself."

Cat turned to Benji with an arched brow. "Like you never feel that compulsion?"

"What?" he answered innocently. "I don't want to win a Nobel Prize."

"No, just all the other ones." She batted her eyelashes and, with a southern accent, drawled, "If only I were famous."

Benji supposed she meant to imitate him, but, seeing that he wasn't gay or Blanche DuBois, he thought she fell short of the mark. "But you—you actually belong in a spotlight."

"At least my sister thinks so. Which is why I need to be pushed. And punished."

Benji got out of bed at Cat's clapping command. He pulled on his clothes, brushed his teeth, readied himself to plunge into the day. A knot of dread tightened in his stomach at the thought of parting ways. He didn't want to let go. Not even for the few hours Cat needed to run errands and rally to save the graves of the long-forgotten dead. Benji had, for a moment, broken free of time, lost track of the world and his place in it. He delighted in not being certain whether it was Sunday or Monday, and he paused now before opening the door to the wider world. He didn't want to end this rare honeymoon, to leave his horse-filled hermitage. He didn't want to step back into time. He didn't want to step back into himself.

Carefully, Cat eased the car out of a gravel drive with a treacherous blind spot. The first hints of fall dusted the leaves, streaming, moth-eaten banners flecked with red, yellow, and ochre in the bright-blue air. Benji fed his Wilco CD into the stereo slot, flipped to his favorite song. He leaned his head against the window and drummed a finger absently on the door handle. He wanted to say he'd seen some new possibility, that Cat had shown him a new possibility. He wanted to say something about light. About Cat being the light. What he said was, "We should do a sex tape."

She glanced at him through narrowed eyes before turning back to the road. "Sweet talker."

"Look what it did for the Kardashians. We're at least as talented as they are."

"You think comparing me to a Kardashian is the best way to seduce me?"

They passed a prim white farmhouse with two huge barns and a line of dairy cows chewing drowsily in the muck.

"It could be my comeback," Benji said. "No pun intended."

Cat rolled her eyes. "Gross."

"The guy from *Saved by the Bell* did one."

"Mario Lopez?" She perked up.

"The other one. The one you'd least want to see in a sex tape. Whatshisname? At the end, he does a dirty Sanchez."

"I seriously hope that's not referring to a person. Actually, I don't want to know what that is."

Benji laughed. "If nothing else, it would be another feather in my father's cap. One more thing to prove him right about me." He knew how dreary this line of conversation was, how decidedly unappealing self-deprecation could be, but he couldn't stop himself. It was as painful as scratching a rash but also as satisfying. And besides, leaving the house, bursting that bright little bubble of Edenic seclusion, left him feeling embattled, in want of a target, even if he was the one locked in his sights.

"Crackpot theory?" Cat asked.

It made him smile, the lingo developing between them, their own little dictionary and standing invitation to amateur psychoanalysis. "Please."

"I think you like proving your father right. You get off on it." She turned down the music and tightened her grip on the wheel, her shoulders, her entire upper body gone rigid with conviction. "It's more than just pissing him off. It's your way of staying connected. The antagonism. The impasse. It's how you stay close." He considered her profile, her creased forehead, the straight line of her small nose, the pale down above her upper lip turned to gold by the sun. "Maybe it's why you take these jobs that. That."

Benji watched her teeter on a ledge, not knowing how to finish her sentence without falling off. "Suck," he offered.

"That's your word. I was going to say that are less than what you're capable of."

"How do you know what I'm capable of?"

Cat shrugged. "You act interested when I read to you from *Middlemarch*. You can be very convincing when you want to be." She pulled the car to a stop at a deserted intersection and turned onto the pocked rural road that would deposit them in downtown Alluvia. "What would it mean if you were Hamlet?" she asked. "Not the Ghost. Not the understudy for Horatio. Not the butt of your own joke. But Hamlet. You'd have to change your entire worldview."

"I'd have to memorize a lot more lines."

"You'd have to live with proving your father wrong. And who would you be then? If you weren't failing Henry Fisher?"

Benji plucked a bottle of warm, flat soda from the cup holder and took a swig. "It wouldn't matter. I could be Hamlet. I could be Ralph fucking Fiennes. My father's totally unimpressed by fame."

"That's easy for him to say. You could sink a boat with the awards he's won. But I'm not talking about *fame*," Cat said. She sounded like a schoolteacher saddled with some incorrigibly dull kid. "I'm not talking about being famous. I'm talking about being—I don't know. What am I talking about?"

"Happy?" Benji tried.

"Happy is overrated. Happy comes and goes." She put a hand on his knee and looked at him longer than a person behind the wheel of a moving vehicle should. "Is that really what you want? In the end? To be famous?"

It was. Of course it was. He'd had a taste of it, the largest possible dose a boy could squeeze from a second-tier sitcom in the days before the Internet. The giggling requests for autographs, usually made by moonfaced, acne-prone girls, as he walked through the mall. The jean-jacketed spread in *Teen Beat*. Strangers doing double takes and tugging each other's sleeves as they passed him by. That's what *you* think! That's what *you* think! Hell yes, he wanted to be famous.

"No. That's not what I want. Not the only thing."

The grassy fields gave way to more or less tended lawns, clusters of cheap, vinyl-sided split-level ranches, and cul-de-sac developments named with the puzzlingly idyllic optimism of mental health facilities. *Echo Valley. Windview Fields.* They passed the tennis courts, the Elks Lodge, the municipal swimming pool (closed for the season) before crossing the town line and crawling down Main Street, past the post office, hardware store, hair salon, gas mart, past the pizza parlor and the library and the steepled Presbyterian church that comprised Alluvia's business district. Cat turned right onto School Street, then left onto Palmer, then left again into the Fishers' drive.

And there it was. As soon as Benji saw it, his foot began pumping the imaginary brake that provides comfort to so many frazzled mothers when driving with their lead-footed teenage sons. "Whoa," he said. "Whoa."

The silver Mercedes he'd noticed three days earlier sat under the elm at the curb in a dappled pool of light. He'd assumed the car belonged to Roger, but Roger Fitch would no sooner spend three days in Alluvia than in Al Anbar, and someone, someone of size, someone with hair, someone decidedly not Roger, was sitting in the front seat.

"Back up," Benji said. "Back up to that car."

"Who is it?" Cat asked with a tinge of alarm, letting the car roll slowly down the sloped blacktop.

Benji saw a silhouette, nothing more, but he could tell from the rigid, upright shape that the person was considering whether to flee. He rolled down his window and waved. "Hey," he called. "You. Hey."

In the largest, most fundamentally solipsistic region of his mind, Benji assumed the car was somehow there for him. He entertained the idea that the car belonged to a fan. An enthusiast of eighties television, come to ask for his autograph or to wish him well or, more darkly, to stalk and possibly shoot him. Or did he owe somebody money? Had he fucked (or fucked over) somebody's sister? Was he about to get his other leg broken? There were, of course, more realistic possibilities—perhaps the man (it seemed to be a man) numbered among the doctoral candidates who appeared every so often, like pilgrims at a holy site, journeying to meet the esteemed author, the subject of a dissertation on rural ennui or imploding masculinity.

The door of the Mercedes swung open and, after a minute, a boy climbed out of the car. He was less handsome than pretty, possessed of a pale, waxen beauty that, were it not for the shadow of stubble on his cheeks and a small silver barbell piercing the upper curve of his ear, belonged to a porcelain doll. He was tall and thin with big, staring blue eyes, a slender nose, and a perfect Cupid's bow for a mouth. His dark hair, oiled to a high, almost plastic sheen, was pushed back. He wore black camouflage pants, cut off at the knee, and a lilac shirt with a deep V-neck that exposed the taut and, despite his otherwise androgynous mien, surprisingly hairy plates of his chest. He was eighteen, Benji guessed. Or twenty-five. It was hard to tell. The only thing Benji could say with certainty was that the kid had never seen *Prodigy*.

"I'm sorry," the boy said.

"Can I help you?"

"I'm just sitting here."

"You've been sitting there for three days."

"Not the whole time."

"And not because you like the block."

The boy considered his car, flicked a rock at the tire with a shy sweep of his boot. "No," he answered.

Benji leaned out the window and waited for what followed, waited for more, but nothing came. "What can I do for you?" he asked.

The boy stared up at the house, the pleasant picture made by the dormers and chimneys and pillared porticos, the pearl-gray paint that was almost the same color as his car. "Do the Fishers live here?"

"Pull around back," he said to Cat, feeling mildly heroic in his promise to handle this. He swung his door open and gruntingly heaved himself out of the car, tapped the sun-warmed roof to make Cat go, then took a few wobbly steps closer to the boy. "Who's asking?"

"Me? I'm Max. Max Davis." He swiped the hair out of his eyes and for the first time met Benji's gaze head-on. Had they met before? "What happened to you?"

"Long story."

The boy blinked. "I'm looking for Claudia?"

"Claudia's my sister."

"You're?"

"Her brother." Benji felt entitled to give the kid a hard time until he stated his business.

"Is she here?"

"You're about twenty years too late. She hasn't lived her since, ah, you do the math."

"1990." Max nodded, plunging his hands into his commodious pockets to play an anxious, rattling song of keys and change. "I figured she wouldn't be here, but this was the address they had on file. And there are about sixteen million Claudia Fishers on Google. I wasn't even sure Fisher was still her last name."

Twenty-two years. No sooner had Max uttered the year than Benji, with the startling suddenness of having a blindfold pulled from his eyes, could plainly see. 1990. It was the only number Benji needed to solve the equation. He didn't need Max to tell him who "they" were or what their files contained. He didn't need to summon the memory of the year Claudia disappeared between college and grad school, the entire year she refused to come home. The variables fell ineradicably into place in front of him. Max's eyes, Max's mouth. He hadn't met the boy before, but nevertheless Benji had seen him. He knew that mouth. He *had* that mouth. The same as Claudia's. The same as their father's.

"Oh my God," Benji whispered.

"Yeah. Oh my God." Max swallowed. "I'm."

"I know. I know who you are."

He was, among other things, the reason Nick Amato had proposed, the reason Claudia's first love had ended in a fit of flames, the reason Benji drove her to the most discreet clinic she could find and then, when she couldn't go through with it, the reason she refused to show herself to her parents for an entire year.

"What did you say your name is?" the boy eventually asked.

"Mine?" Benji answered from far away. "Benjamin."

"Benjamin," the boy repeated, then, through a winsome but not yet certain smile, "Uncle Ben?"

Benji's laugh started slowly, warming up like a motor on a cold morning. "Benji," he said.

"Benji." Only then did Max step forward, ignoring his uncle's outstretched hand and pulling him into a tight and pleading hug. "Benji," he said. "I can work with that."

Moonlight paints the room. I stare out at the rain. The water that streaks the windows is mirrored by mercurial little rivers running over the floor. She is out there. Somewhere, like Lear, Jane is out in the storm. What would she do to find me at this window, her daughter in this bed? Claudia stirs. She cries for her mother, but already Jane is not who she means. If Jane came back now, Claudia would not know her. What are you doing up? Evelyn asks, as if she, too, has been up for some time. She tucks the blanket round the girl and struggles to prop herself with a pillow. She isn't yet used to her new size and puts a hand on her round belly as she tells me to come back to bed. She doesn't ask why I'm out of bed in the first place. I climb under the covers and look across at her. We are carved in marble in the moonlight, none of us moving for a long time. Eventually, she reaches out to put her hand on my chest. She's not coming back, she says. The weight of her hand is impossible, but still I nod. There is a saying about the love of a good woman. And Evelyn is good, but she needs something I carry inside of me to die. There is not enough room for it here. She sees it circling above us like a hawk, casting shadows, never letting us out of its sight.

6.

She let the call go to voice mail. Benji. Flying his war flag against their father. Or surrendering his pride to ask for more funds. *Not this morning,* Claudia thought. It wasn't yet ten o'clock, but the day seemed half over, leached away by one distraction after another. She woke at six, determined to review her designs for the downtown outpost of Selkirk and Sons Funeral Home, but already she'd lost two hours to a scrimmage with her contractor who tried unloading on her a shipment of substandard glass. Then there was Oliver. Oliver, retreating to the gym for a cold shower since she turned her back on his morning advances. "It's been five weeks," he whined. "I'll settle for a hand job." But what made a man less fuckable than settling? And it couldn't have been five weeks. Could it?

The Selkirks had awarded her the commission because she had no intention of transplanting their safe (read: stale) Upper East Side mortuary to a hipper zip code and instead insisted on a sweeping glass atrium atop a midrise of multimillion-dollar lofts. Strange placement perhaps, but the obscenely rich died south of Fourteenth Street, too, and when they did, Claudia convinced her clients, they'd want a less stuffy stage for their final departure. They would appreciate her soaring chapel of torqued Serra-esque steel, set under a pristine dome of Manhattan sky. Metal and light. Body and air. Permanence and something as ephemeral as a passing cloud. Her drawings spread beneath her on her dining/drafting table; she stood like a sea captain studying her maps, trying to decide the best course, when the phone rang again. Benji's third call in thirty minutes.

She could turn it off, but why should she have to? Why couldn't the world simply leave her alone?

"What?" she said, jamming the phone to her ear and tossing off her thick, geometric glasses in defeat.

"Why haven't you picked up?"

"I don't know, Benji. I guess I have nothing to do today but annoy you."

"It's working," he snarked before shifting gears. "We have to talk."

"Now's really not—"

"There is no good time for this."

She felt a real pulse of unease under the drama of his pronouncement. And Benji loved a dramatic pronouncement.

"What's the matter? Is it Mom?"

"They're fine. They're them. This isn't about them."

"Then what's it about? I'm working."

"I'm just going to come out and say it."

"Good."

"I mean, it's nothing I can prepare you for."

"Benji!"

"It's him," he said.

"Who?"

"Him, Claude. It's him!" He might have been using his voice to punch a hole in the wall, the jabbing fury of that one word.

She stepped backward, hoping a chair was there to meet her, and sat down hard. A silence wove itself between them, hundreds of miles away from each other yet caught in the same stifling cocoon.

"You there?" Benji asked.

She took her hand away from her mouth and asked, "How do you know?"

"Why would he pretend? We're not Rockefellers. Plus, you'll see. There's no mistaking this kid. He looks just like you. Us."

"Oh, Benji." She felt as if she'd been slapped awake to find herself in the middle of a daredevil stunt, a sudden circle of fire surrounding her, her terror, her outright inability to jump through it. "What does he want? What am I supposed to do? I can't."

"Claudia. Breathe. You have to breathe. Breathe and shut up. Let me talk."

She sank back in her chair and tried to hear what her brother had to say. It wasn't much. The kid, as Benji called him, had a name. Max Davis. Max Davis who was a musician, who grew up in Rochester, who'd started looking for her when he was seventeen but who realized his desire was only half the equation, who acknowledged maybe Claudia would rather eat glass than meet him, which would suck but which he realized was a possibility before he began his search.

"I don't want to be somebody's mother."

"He has a mother."

"So what am I supposed to do?"

"How about you start with 'hello'? One step at a time."

"Where are you? Is he there with you?"

"He's been sitting outside the house for three days, building up the courage."

"But where is he?"

"On the porch, with Cat."

"He's with you *now*? Has Mom seen him?"

"She's inside. Probably painting."

"You have to get him out of there before she sees."

"Like put him in the trunk and drive away?"

"Do you think this is funny? I'm serious. I can't handle her hysterics."

"*Her* hysterics?"

"I swear, Benji. I'll kill you if you make this worse."

She remembered waking in the hospital, twenty-two years old, the bright lights and crisp sheets and a pack of ice slowly melting between her legs, Benji asleep in a chair in the corner while the woman in the bed next to her, breasts mapped with arresting blue veins, tried stuffing her nipple into her wailing baby's mouth. The relief Claudia felt at that moment. The freedom. She had a train of visitors—nurses, her caseworker from the adoption agency, even a priest who didn't mind shepherding non-Catholic sheep—and registered in their piteous looks what each of them expected her to feel. They believed they would find her crushed, a girl so young, bathed in regretful, Madonna-like tears, perhaps even ready to pull out of the deal and demand that the baby—her baby—be delivered into her arms. But that wasn't what Claudia felt. If any regret coursed through her blood, it was regret that she *didn't* feel these things that she was supposedly supposed to feel.

"I want you to talk to him." She heard Benji on the move, a slight susurration of wind, other voices reaching her ears.

"Absolutely not," Claudia whispered fiercely.

This, Benji ignored. The voices grew louder, and before she could say more, a strange, unexpectedly deep "hello?" stopped her racing mind in its tracks.

He sounded like he'd stuck his head in a darkened room, uncertain if anyone would answer, while she felt stuck in a child's game, tagged *It* before she even had the chance to hide. She froze.

"Hello?" the voice repeated.

"Hello," Claudia echoed.

"Hi. Wow. Claudia?" Silence. "This is so weird."

"It is." More silence. "Weird."

"I'm Max. I guess Benji told you that already."

"He did."

"And you're Claudia."

The easy relief she'd felt in the weeks after the hospital had long ago hardened into a sense of the rightness of her decision. She lived, protected, in its shell. But sometimes, not often, but sometimes a feeling of dread crept in. Where was he? What was he doing? Was he smart or skinny or perpetually scared? Was he loved? Very occasionally, she walked the city streets fearful that a child on the sidewalk would tug her coat sleeve and call her Mommy. Once, three years after the fact, she bought a birthday card with a baby giraffe on the front, but having no place to send it, fed it to the paper shredder with a stack of canceled checks.

"I'd love the chance to talk to you," Max said.

"Yes. Yes."

"In person? Do you think we could meet in person?"

"Mm-hmm. I was about to say."

"Cool." A short, satisfied laugh came at her like a siren. He asked her a few other questions, as if trying to make chat at a cocktail party with a committed mute, then said, "When do you think?"

"Soon. I have a few things here," she said, standing and returning to her sketches. A shaking hand smoothed the paper as if to display the enormity of her task, the real and blameless unlikelihood of making time. "But soon."

"When?"

"Tomorrow," came Benji's voice. She could have reached through the phone and snuffed him out like a candle, in good conscience.

"Tomorrow?" Claudia repeated, transformed, it seemed, into the most hapless of parrots.

"Cool," he said smilingly. "Great."

"Can I talk to Benji?" Claudia asked, applying a steady pressure to her voice to keep the murderousness from seeping into it.

"Sure."

She heard Max calling him, heard the phone being passed into her brother's hands, and then the sound of the line going dead.

❖　❖　❖

The call touched a match to Claudia's fuse. She didn't know this yet, not fully. In the front office of her mind, her business was simply getting to the boy, but in the back, in the windowless dark, she sat watching a spark dance up to a powder keg, uncertain exactly what part of her life was about to go up in smoke, but too fascinated to pinch it out.

After hanging up, she collapsed on the couch on the eastern side of the apartment and watched what was left of the morning sun spool across the room in a gauzy strip. Fiery, golden, imperative, the light rolled out like a carpet that led to the bedroom, where her suitcase awaited packing. When Oliver got home from his workout, freshly showered but still sulking, she pushed him onto the bed and, tearing his clothes from him, fucked him without fully removing hers. When it was over, she rolled onto her side, facing away from him, and doubled up her pillow.

"I got a phone call," she said.

He rested his chin on her shoulder as she spoke, listened without interruption, which was Oliver's virtue as much as his downfall. She couldn't help wondering if it mattered whether she chose to discuss the child who turned up out of nowhere or the review of the newest restaurant on the block. If he registered the difference.

"Max Davis?" The first words out of his mouth.

"That's his name."

"Max Davis, the cellist Max Davis?"

Claudia turned. "Benji said he's a musician."

"You know Max Davis."

"I do not know Max Davis. Did you hear anything I just said?"

He did, he assured her. He did. He pulled her onto her back so she was looking up at him. "The Bach cello suites? The recording I gave you last Christmas? That's Max Davis! How cool is that?"

"Cool?" Claudia asked.

"I missed seeing him the last time he was in town."

She kicked herself off the bed and went to the closet to retrieve her bag.

"What? Are you mad?"

"Am I mad?" She posed the question calmly, like a Buddhist sending a quest for insight out into the universe, not expecting an answer.

"I'm so many things at this moment, Oliver. It's hard to pick just one."

"I'm sorry."

"I tell you what I just told you and you're—what?—jonesing for comp tickets to the philharmonic."

"I wasn't."

"Thinking? No, you weren't."

"But this isn't a total shock, is it? I mean, we knew this day might come. It was always a possibility, right?"

"It's a pretty big fucking shock to me." She flipped open the top of her weekender and said, "Grab me my gray sweater?"

"Take the big bag," Oliver said. "I'm coming with you."

"No. No. I'm doing this alone."

He said her name as if she were a toddler and he, cowed, afraid of a coming tantrum.

"You stay here and listen to Bach."

He got up and got the sweater. "Don't be like that. Let me come. I want to be with you. And not because I want to meet."

"No."

She often wondered what formed the foundation of her husband's reliable cluelessness. He loved her so, and yet could life be that mystifying? Could she? What was she to make of the fact that Oliver had forgotten four of her last ten birthdays or his habit of talking ball scores with the bartender while other men sidled up and offered to buy her a drink? More than once, Benji had assumed the role of his brother-in-law's apologist. He praised Oliver's lack of jealousy as a rare and covetable evolutionary step, suggested that addle-mindedness was sometimes nothing more than that, and Claudia took heart. She found it more convenient to let her troops be called back from the battlefront, to let her temper be cooled, even if she never completely lost sight of the red flags that troubled the horizon.

She passed the baton of packing to Oliver, knowing that he could run that leg of the race better than she, and retreated to the other side of the apartment with her laptop. She pulled up the Hertz website, but in that moment rental cars might have been the theory of relativity: they were nowhere on her mind.

Oliver stood over the suitcase, considering its insides like a diagnostician as he shucked a blouse from its hanger and folded it atop the others.

"I'm only staying for a day or two," Claudia called.

He moved to the dresser for a stack of underwear. "You never know what you'll need."

True, she didn't know what she'd need. But she knew, with arresting clarity, for the first time in a long time, what she wanted. How long had it been since she'd thought his name? She pulled up a new window as her fingers raced ahead of her priorities and typed *Nick Amato*. Google yielded over three million results, with top honors going to a self-styled tween idol filling up YouTube with covers from the Justin Bieber catalog.

As she clicked from page to page, looking for the ghost of the Nick she knew, guilt snaked around her heart like a thorny vine. Why wasn't Max her first priority? Shouldn't he be? At some point, didn't the boy deserve to win out above all else? It pained her to think how disastrously she'd behaved on the phone. Stricken and speechless, she'd done little more than stretch two minutes to their most torturous length, agreeing to meet him simply to get him off the phone. It wasn't that atonement and tenderness were beyond her, but the apology she felt she needed to make, like a form stepping darkly out of a mist, had its sights set on Nick, not Max.

Claudia scrolled through several pages of YouTube videos of pre-pubescent homage to a prepubescent Canadian before coming upon a link to Amato & Sons, Contractors Inc. She clicked it, and up popped a functional, utterly frill-less website for the company that Nick Amato Sr. had started years before Nick Jr. was born. Assuming the attractions of a business dedicated to house painting couldn't possibly seduce an accomplished lawyer from a well-heeled life in the Pacific Northwest (or so rumor had it), Claudia hoped to find an e-mail address for one of Nick's loyal but less ambitious brothers, but when she clicked "About Us," she sat face to face with Nick himself, who'd walked out of her life with the steely promise never to enter it again. "Nicholas Amato Jr., President." He hadn't lost that easy, affable handsomeness that still had the power to set her heart pounding, though he'd traded in his lanky frame and shoulder-length locks for a brawny body and a salt-and-pepper burr cut. She e-mailed herself the company's address and quickly closed the window as Oliver, having carried her zippered bag to the door, came forward for a conciliatory kiss. She shut the window on Nick and pulled up a list of links to Max's name.

"I don't know where to start."

"I can help you go through it."

But even as Claudia clicked dutifully on Alex Ross' *New Yorker* profile, her mind continued to feel its way down darkened but thrilling alleys she'd made herself avoid for the last twenty years. Somewhere, somewhere in the murk of the past, lay the body of the man she'd left broken by her attempt to spare him pain. The year she delivered the baby had been spent in the anonymous thrall of New York City. She hid from her parents, who feared that she, like her brother, had developed a drug problem; she hid from Nick, who returned from Stanford to track her down only to find that she'd changed addresses and effectively disappeared.

"You just gave him away." Nick wept the night he finally found her, when she finally explained, three months after she'd placed the baby into strangers' arms. "I didn't deserve a say in that?"

"You would have wanted to get married. Which means I would have left school and probably you would too."

"We can still get married. We can get the baby back."

"No, we can't. I don't want to get married, Nick." She reached out to him and took his hand. "Say we did. Say we got married and had the baby and the three of us moved back to Alluvia tomorrow. How long do you think it would take before I hated you for that? How long before I hated the baby?"

"You've got it all figured out. You have that little faith?"

"In us? I did this for us."

"There is no us!"

At the end of that conversation, he hadn't slammed the door between them, but shut it with such quiet resolve she felt sure it would never open again. Nick denied her the opportunity for penitence, which she knew she didn't deserve. He vowed to fight her, to fight for custody of their son, but in the end, he didn't. He disappeared as decisively as she had. And that, it seemed, was that.

Two decades later, Claudia could still be shaken awake by the sickening feeling that she'd not only turned over her only child but also returned an entire life like a piece of misaddressed mail. She'd set Max and Nick out to sea in separate little boats, but who was to say that if they'd stayed together things would have ended up the way she thought? Maybe she and Nick wouldn't have quit school or retreated to the soggy solace of their childhood homes. She had no way to tell. All she could say with certainty was that she'd always regretted one decision more than the other: she wanted Nick's forgiveness most of all.

But what about Max's forgiveness? Was it not another failure not to ask for that too? On one hand, she'd failed to walk into that abortion clinic and end his troubles before they started. On the other, she'd failed to offer him a mother's love—even a mother who assumed she had little love to give—and placed him instead in the care of a beleaguered social worker whose guarantee that everything would be as it should be sounded hollow as a drum. She failed to seek out her son. Failed to let him know that even though she seemed like a woman forever moving forward, she sometimes, with doubt and sadness, looked back. Even now that Max had found her, she'd failed to return the balls of easy banter he had rolled so generously to her feet during their quick phone call. Did she like living in New York? How long had she been an architect? If she couldn't answer this first round of questions, how could she possibly field the next?

She stared at the Leibovitz photo—"Look," Oliver said with wonder, "I never noticed before how much he looks like you"—and started reading the Ross article from the top: *In 2002, at the age of twelve, the son of a violin teacher and a novice inventor from a small city in upstate New York convinced a packed house at Carnegie Hall that they'd just witnessed the second coming of Pablo Casals.*

By six forty-five the next morning, just as the tenebrous sky began brightening toward dawn, she sped past the old weatherworn sign that stood at the side of the road: "Welcome to Alluvia." She slowed the car to a crawl as she passed the tennis courts, slowed even more as the post office and pizza parlor and library receded one after the other in the rearview mirror. A fist battered inside of her, the knocking so furious that by the time she turned onto School Street, she actually thought she was coming apart. Her breath shuddered. Her hands shook. She gripped the wheel in a stranglehold and rolled to a stop at the corner of Palmer and School.

Expecting, hoping, to find her parents' house as still and dark as the rest of the street, she stared at the boy on the top step of the porch with terror, awe, and a childish attachment to her own pain. He was real. He was *real*. But why was he here? Why was he doing this to *her*?

From the distant corner where she sat, she couldn't make out the face that mirrored her own. She saw only a boy in an oversized black hoodie, head bent, worrying scabs of paint from her parents' porch stairs. In this casual, slightly monastic pose of self-absorption, he was identical to countless boys she saw camped on the college greens. A standard-issue teenager.

No, she couldn't do it.

When she took her foot off the brake, she had no solidly formed idea of where she was going. She simply wanted to get away. Bypassing the house, she continued along the sleeping, leaf-strewn curve of School Street until she came to the Anselmans', a once picture-perfect but now woefully shabby Queen Anne that had belonged to the ancient organist at the Presbyterian church and his spinster sister. Claudia stopped. The cracked paint job and crooked basketball hoop that hung over the garage door made clear that the new owners were younger and less fastidious than their predecessors, but as a child, this had been Claudia's favorite house in all of Alluvia. Its fairy tale tower, pastel fancy butt shingles, and gingerbread detailing had fed a little girl's fantasy of trapped princesses and the deceptively pretty homes of the witches who preyed upon them.

She remembered sitting on the verdant strip of the Anselmans' lawn, sixteen years old, sunning herself like Sue Lyon with her skimpy bikini top and cat eye sunglasses, as Nick painted the flourishing scrollwork of the gables. His father had left him to finish the job with a winking admonishment that Nick didn't appreciate.

"I wasn't making moon eyes at you," Nick called sullenly from his ladder perch. "Does anyone under fifty even know what that means?"

"Come on, Moonbeam," Claudia called back. "The faster you finish, the faster we can leave."

Nick unhooked his bucket and began climbing down. "Screw it," he said once his feet hit the ground. "I'm finished." His rebelliousness was both more decisive and more vulgar now that his father wasn't there to witness it, but Claudia didn't mind. She liked the rare occasion when the scorpion that slept inside this mild-mannered boy scuttled out into the open with its tail raised. She egged him on, lifting her glasses to stare up at his handiwork, and said, "You missed a spot."

He laughed a temperate laugh as he set the paint bucket at his feet, then, taking the brush in hand, leapt at her like a madman with a knife.

"Truce!" Claudia screamed, jumping to her feet.

"Oh. Now she wants a truce." He grinned, forcing her retreat with every jab.

"Look what you're doing to the grass," she said with real alarm in her voice. She pointed to the Pollocky dribs of pink paint, running thick to thin, that threaded the green. "Nice job."

Chastened, Nick held his palm under the dripping bristles and returned the brush to the bucket. He wiped his hand on his already motley jeans and dragged his foot across the vandalized lawn. Frowning at his sneaker, the lousy eraser, he said, "You think he's a pill about his lawn. You should see his house."

"I know," Claudia answered, before correcting herself. "I mean I don't. He used to buy Girl Scout cookies from me, but he never let me inside."

"Really?" The scorpion hadn't crawled back under its rock quite yet. "Come on," he said, starting toward the back of the house. "We're going."

She didn't move. "Going where?"

"Where do you think? He leaves the cellar door unlocked so the plebs can use his subterranean toilet." Nick, already studying ardently for the SATs, enjoyed taking his new vocabulary out for a spin. "We can go up that way."

"No," she said firmly. The house had by that time lost much of its candy-coated appeal, but it had been a strong magnet for a long time: it still pulled. "How do you know he won't come back?"

"I saw them leave."

"Them? Alice never leaves."

"She left today. They went all the way to Lake George to visit their older sister. Can you imagine how old their older sister must be?"

Seeing he'd won, that Claudia's song-and-dance protest was exactly that, he took her by the hand and led her to the cellar's wooden hatch. Five rickety steps and they stood wrapped in the cool, loam-scented dark. Nick took a knowing step and pulled a chain on a hanging bulb, which recast the room in swaying shades of long-shadowed, saffron-colored light. Even underground, the place was immaculate. The hot water heater looked more like a finely tuned instrument capable of space travel than the cobweb-shagged behemoth in her basement that Claudia occasionally witnessed Henry beating with a wrench. Shelves lined the walls on which sat jars and jars of preserves: peaches, tomatoes, asparagus, beans. The light ambered the liquid and made the contents swim like nascent life forms collected for scientific study.

At the foot of the stairs, Nick ordered her to take off her shoes as he flicked off his own. She shed her Keds obediently, then spun around to assess herself in a mercury glass mirror. Her outfit disappointed her—short jean shorts, a slouchy, off-the-shoulder shirt the color of a blueberry Icee that she'd pulled over her swimsuit. Nick stole a quick kiss and reminded her, "We're not getting our pictures taken. Nobody's here." With that, he unbuckled his jeans and dropped them to the floor.

"Um. What are you doing?" she asked, grinning at him in the blousy blue boxers on which little fish swam.

"I don't want to track paint," he answered, as if she'd asked the dumbest question in the world, and turned to climb the stairs. They entered the kitchen first. The small but sunny room was somehow cleaner than the dustless basement, with starched, lace-trimmed curtains in the windows and a family of four porcelain rabbits ranged along the counter: flour, sugar, coffee, salt. Drawn to these, Claudia trembled slightly at the crime they were committing as she ran a finger along the brightly glazed ears of the largest one.

"If you pet every rabbit you see, we're going to be here all day," Nick warned.

From the kitchen, they climbed the back staircase to a warren of clustered and oddly shaped bedrooms. One had sloping ceilings that made it impossible to stand upright without hitting your head. Another was so small the only way to climb into the giant four-poster bed was to scramble over the footboard. All were filled with dark, impressively carved woodwork. All were clean and ordered as museum displays. And all were scattered with rabbits. Rabbits on the nightstands. Rabbits on the dressers. Rabbits on the hand towels in the guest bath. There were rabbits nibbling carrots, rabbits angling in a stream, rabbits riding big-wheeled Victorian bicycles, sleeping rabbits, standing rabbits, rabbits wearing brightly flowered hats. Some were plush and propped on pillows or painted on canvases that hung above the beds, but most were ceramic, lean and leaping cottontails and delicate, droopy-eared dwarves

"Somebody likes rabbits," Claudia said, moving toward a table to pick one up.

"I wouldn't touch that. I get the feeling he's like Felix Unger. Very anal retentive. He knows exactly where everything goes." He approached her then, the veil of his ostensible purpose—a harmless house tour—tearing to shed light on what he'd really come for. He grabbed her around the waist and pulled her to him; his boner lifted the light fabric of his boxers.

"Cut it out," Claudia said. His penis was still a novelty to her, but she had started to enjoy the mastery she seemed to hold over it: making it stand, making it fall. Still, she had the sense that the rabbits were watching her and pushed him away.

A gentleman in matters of thwarted seduction, Nick wrapped up his expedition of the upper floors, then led them down the front stairs with its wonderfully polished banister and considerable newel posts. At the landing, he instructed Claudia to close her eyes. Taking her by the hand, he led her across a floor that loosed a haunted cry under her weight. Her bare feet felt the cool hardwood give way to a soft expanse of rug. She dug her toes into the woolly fibers.

"Okay," Nick said. "Open."

The parlor—a mortuary stiffness in the room's décor stopped Claudia from thinking of it as a living room—bore the stamp of high Victorian style. The furniture crouched heavy and ornate under lamps shaded in tasseled silk; there was even a harp in one corner, ready to sing the deceased to their final rest. All that separated this room from the receiving room at Dunn's Funeral Home were the rabbits. Compared to here, the figures scattered throughout the house seemed like outliers. Here was the warren. Here, the richly appointed burrows. Nearly every surface, literally every shelf on every massive hutch, filled with rabbits.

Claudia clasped her hands together and laughed. Astonished and a little spooked, as if the figurines might twitch alive at any moment and come bounding toward her, she said, "I did a report on rabbits in fifth grade."

"Who did you have?"

"Mrs. Vonstitina."

"Native American Week?"

"You had her too?"

"My brother did. He chose a hedgehog. Not a lion or a wolf or even a deer. His spirit guide was a hedgehog." He tapped his forehead sharply and said, "That should have been our first clue."

"Rabbits symbolize luck. Obviously. And longevity, because they have a million babies. You know, like a long family line. And rebirth."

Nick tightened the sharklike circle he made around her. "I don't believe in rebirth," he said. "When you're dead, you're dead. But I do believe in longevity. In a long family line. And I definitely believe in what gets you there." He was close enough to her now that she could smell the day's work on him, paint and sun and sweet, oniony sweat.

"Predictable," she muttered.

Zeroing in from behind, he grabbed her tightly around the waist, put his lips to her ear, and asked, "What was that?"

"I said you're predictable."

His dick, hard again, was the only response he offered, rocking her back and forth against it as if their bodies were sticks that might catch fire.

"Just like a rabbit."

He pulled back the sizeable mass of her hair and kissed her neck, then moved his hands, a bit mechanically, as if he were rehearsing each move in his head before he made it, to her breasts. Their lovemaking was more academic than passionate in those early days, as if they were trying to please Monsieur Prendergast with their conjugation of French verbs, but they were committed students and seized almost any opportunity to practice.

"What if they come home?" she whispered, realizing as soon as the words were out of her mouth that she'd made her concession.

"Lake George is fifty miles away," Nick crooned. "Mr. Anselman drives, like, fifteen miles an hour."

Claudia turned to face him, her mouth declaring that no matter how slowly he drove, Mr. Anselman would eagle eye their every fingerprint, even while her hand was plunging past the elastic band of his underwear to grab hold of what stabbed her. Luckily, Nick didn't mind mixed signals. As he got down on his knees on the wine-colored floral rug, Claudia followed. They were out of their clothes in minutes, rolling back and forth across a field of finely woven gold primrose with a hundred inscrutable rabbits silently looking on.

Claudia shook herself back into the idling car. She slipped into gear and drove on, trailing behind her the memory of that afternoon—rutting among the glass menagerie—until she hit the main thoroughfare out of town. The road followed the great, iron-colored vein of the river, where houses that had seen better days looked as though they might at any moment abandon their foundations and slide into the water. Eventually, as the houses grew more derelict and the yards more dirt than grass, Claudia came to Alluvia's only stoplight. Here the village proper, which was not without its charm, met the more sprawling town, in which one was hard pressed to find anything like it. To travelers on Route 4, the light was a Cyclops' eye forever blinking yellow, a warning to those passing through, Claudia and Benji joked, not to stop, to keep going no matter what, but on this morning, Claudia stopped. Ahead was Saratoga and Bemis Heights, the sites of bloody historical interest her teachers had taught her to revere as a child. To the left, across a camelback bridge painted an apocalyptic shade of gray, lay open country. Dairy farms, an abandoned drive-in theater now used to store fireworks, and, beyond that, the offices of Amato & Sons.

She made the turn. Fifteen minutes later, oblivious to the paint-by-numbers beauty of green fields rolling gently under a pink, post-storm sky, she turned into a large paved lot. A low, unassuming building marked "Office" stood surrounded by a compound of garages and warehouses enclosed by a chain-link fence. Other than the sign that sat atop the roof, the *A* in Amato topped with a jaunty hard hat, the place had all the appeal of a military barracks: dreary, anonymous, beige. The puddled lot was empty, but she chose a space close to the front door and turned off the car. At rest at last, a safe distance away from Max and her uncertain but unshakable responsibility to him, she felt the tension that had seized her over the last day suddenly release. A giant cable that ran through her body and pulled every muscle to the point of snapping suddenly went slack. She sensed the relief, but the relief was too much to bear, and she startled herself with a terrible, shaking sob. But crying inside the car proved impossible. How could she cry when she couldn't breathe?

Shouldering open the door, Claudia jumped out and paced the blacktop, up and down, restoring herself to order with a few greedy mouthfuls of air. There was time to turn back. She could do so now, and Nick would be none the wiser. Wiping the tears from her face, she took her place behind the wheel. She turned the key in the ignition but couldn't bring herself to shut the door. The alarm, a vexing ding, ding, ding, that drill, drill, drilled its way into her brain's last reserve of equanimity, let loose a torrent of anger and enmity that swept her poise, her polish away. Grabbing the door handle as though she meant to strangle it, she pulled the door shut with such force she thought the window might break, an idea that held a certain and sudden appeal. To feel it shattered by her hands! Claudia opened the door and slammed it again. She smashed it shut as quickly and forcefully as she could, again and again, like a woman caught in some malign meme, like a woman gone mad, until an unignorable pop in her shoulder made her stop. She whimpered, rubbing the knot with a pathetic gaze into the rearview mirror. "Ow!" she cried.

The reverend doesn't know what to make of it. He stands before us in the modest luxury of George Newland's living room, looking at the woman who one day long ago he held over the baptismal font. He has watched her childhood pass in the patent leathers and pastels of Easter. He has pinned the confirmation cross to her dress. Though she is thirty-five, to him she will always be a child of God, and though God had not yet made manifest what she should be, the reverend cannot imagine that this is it. She is too old to be a hippie, to stand before him in a ragtag dress with flowers in her hair and a new, self-selected name. But the road she travels seems to have led to the same place, the very place it would have if she'd christened herself Starshine or China Rose, to the side of a man six years her junior and a baby that (Evelyn admitted to him in confidence) belongs to a woman who's disappeared. He looks on her with his sad, worried eyes and sees that she loves me as if I'm the only man left to love. He sees that she loves me though I love another. That she loves me out of all proportion to what I deserve. He sees it, as I see it. Though, for this, he alone is inclined to forgive.

7.

Max sat on the top step of the porch, peeling paint from the board beneath his feet. He told himself to stop, but no sooner had he flicked away the evidence of his petty vandalism than his jangly and sleep-deprived nerves sent him back for another. And another. At this rate, he'd have the porch picked clean as bone by the time Evelyn appeared to refill his coffee. He took a deep breath and dug his phone from the pocket of his hoodie to check the time. Ten o'clock. She was, according to the schedule that she laid out, an hour late. But the thought of dialing her, of bothering her with his "where-are-yous," withered under the memory of yesterday's call. He had the feeling he'd offered her a prize to a sweepstakes she hadn't entered.

He unlocked his touch screen with a laughably simple code and tapped a hasty message to Arnav.

She's latte. Then: Late.

Patience came the immediate reply. A pale white talk bubble blossomed silently under Max's apple-green one. He couldn't stand the packaged noises that alerted him to incoming calls or, with the sound of a speeding jet, escorted outgoing e-mail, but he appreciated the tiny vibration, the heartbeat, that pulsed in his palm as Navi's words appeared. She'll be there.

Behind him the screen door croaked open, and out stepped Benji, debuting an ivory-handled cane he'd rescued from a box intended for the church tag sale. He wore gray sweatpants and a torn Radiohead T-shirt, over which he'd pulled a silk robe of navy-and-gold paisley raided from his father's closet. If the robe, an ancient gift from Roger that Henry would neither wear nor throw away, made an absurd statement, the cane was its exclamation mark. "G'morning, Nephew," he said, aiming with his best British accent for upstairs *Downton Abbey* but landing somewhere closer to Eliza Doolittle.

"G'morning, Uncle," answered Max.

Benji planted the cane's rubber tip and lowered himself gingerly, as if by lever, onto the step next to Max. "How did you sleep?" he asked.

It seemed more polite than deceitful to lie, to not mention how he'd tossed and turned, running a finger over the blistered minutes of conversation with Claudia. Like pulling teeth, he'd told Arnav, who enjoyed trumping one clichéd phrase with another. Like getting blood from a stone. Like rolling a rock uphill. Unsettled first by Benji's insistence that everything would be fine, then by Evelyn's endless shock and weeping, then by the rising din of a confounded Henry being chased through the house, Max had whispered a play-by-play into Arnav's ear, until, finally, at three, he'd taken a pill to fall asleep. Three hours later, he'd taken another to wake up. Along with the lithium, Neurontin, Zyban, and quarter tab of Klonopin. "Fine," he said.

"Did you eat? Are you hungry? Did my mom give you breakfast?"

Max patted his stomach and made a sour face. "Let's give your mom a break. Besides, I'd hurl. My nerves this morning? I'm a Chihuahua."

Benji said there was nothing to be nervous about, returning to yesterday's mantra that everything would be fine, but his assurance sounded halfhearted, his mind clearly elsewhere. Parting the robe, he freed a crushed scroll of paper from the elastic waistband of his pants and flattened it on his lap. "Speaking of concerts," he said with a sudden turn toward solemnity, "I see you've given quite a few."

Max laughed, angling for a look. "That's not a mystery, Encyclopedia Brown. I told you yesterday I started performing when I was twelve."

"You did. You said you gave your first concert when you were twelve. What you didn't say"—Benji spoke with the rising passion of a prosecutor unveiling his key piece of evidence—"was that your first concert was at *Carnegie Hall.*"

"What is that? A dossier?"

Benji flipped through pages of curling biography he'd cherry-picked from the web, past a radiant profile from the *New York Times Magazine* and an Annie Leibovitz photo in which one of Max's eyes was obscured by the question mark of his cello's scroll. "*Wikipedia,* mostly. Some Facebook. This thing with Terry Gross."

"I told you about Terry Gross."

"You never said Terry Gross. You said you were on the radio. I was thinking WKRP in Cincinnati. Not NPR."

"What's the problem?"

"Did you know that fifty-two thousand people like you on Facebook? Fifty-two thousand," Benji repeated, fully committed to this new way of measuring his own misery. "Guess how many people like me? Six hundred fifty-eight. I've got twenty years on you, and I still can't break a thousand."

"There's a video on YouTube of a dog nursing a kitten. That's been liked, like, two million times. We're both in line behind that. Way behind." Max wanted to talk more about Claudia—not about himself, not about his Facebook followers—but he could see no way of reaching that station without first meandering along whatever tracks pleased his host.

Benji shook his head. "Why didn't you tell us?"

"Tell you what?"

"That you're fucking Mozart."

"*Fucking* him? I don't even *know* him." He waited for the joke to land, as only a bad, borscht belt joke can, but the smile on Benji's face remained spiritless and wan. "First," Max said, "I'm not Mozart." He snatched the papers out of Benji's hand and, shuffling through the patchwork of printed web pages—"Max Davis at Disney Hall" (timeout.com/los-angeles); "Max Davis at the White House" (whitehouse.gov); "Marvelous Max Conquers Kodály" (npr.org)—added, "I can't stand when people say that."

"But people *do* say it. What does that tell you?"

"That they have no idea what they're talking about." He waited for the simple truth of this to sink in, eyes wide, as if he'd just explained to a child that two plus two is four or yellow and blue make green. "What did you think I meant by professional?"

"I thought you were doing what everybody does: exaggerating. I thought maybe you picked up a few bucks playing wedding receptions or bar mitzvahs."

"Because nothing gets thirteen-year-old boys going like a cello solo."

"Carnegie Hall? The New York Philharmonic. The Berlin Philharmonic. The Leningrad Philharmonic." Benji ticked off as many global symphonies and concert halls as he had fingers to count them on. "We talked for hours last night and you never—you just let me go on and on, talking about myself like an idiot. Talking about *Prodigy* and *Little House on the* goddamn *Prairie*. And you never? I don't get it. How do you sit there and not, not—"

Max reached delicately into the tangled knot of Benji's rant and tried to pull free a coherent thread. "Not what?"

"Brag!" Benji pounced. "My God, you won a motherfucking Grammy. Talk about burying the lede. A Grammy!"

Max demurred with a lopsided smile. "So did Milli Vanilli."

"Don't do that. Don't be self-effacing. It's annoying to those of us who have no hope of winning a Grammy. Or anything else, for that matter."

Max could practically see the circuits of Benji's mind light up with the accomplishments of a boy half his age, with what Benji took to be a real and glitteringly incomprehensible lack of vainglory, surging with data that didn't compute. Benji closed his eyes and rubbed his temples as if fending off a headache. "Do you know what I'd do if I won a Grammy? I'd solder a pin to it and wear it as a brooch. Who leaves that out?"

"Should I have said that before or after, 'Hey, we've never met, but guess what? I'm your nephew!'? You'd think what a douche bag."

"Are you kidding? You come out of the gates on a Thoroughbred, you don't run the race like you're riding a donkey. Trust me: I have the opposite problem. I've spent my life riding a donkey like it's Secretariat." Benji scratched his head as his own metaphor sunk in. "Now I see why your mother got so worked up."

The night before, with Evelyn finally calmed, if still undone by her "spiteful, hateful, lying children," Max painted a portrait of Jim and Amanda Davis that was as vivid as it was unflattering. Jim, an inventor by trade whose greatest contribution to date—a coffee mug that displays the temperature of the liquid inside it—had yet to find a public wider than SkyMall shoppers, spent the bulk of his days in the family's basement, waiting for inspiration to pave the way to an idea as necessary and immortal as the light bulb. Amanda, on the other hand, made her name as the most exacting violin teacher between Buffalo and Syracuse. She had all the pedagogical subtlety of a Russian figure skating coach who had been forced off the ice in recent years by an ever-worsening case of rheumatoid arthritis. Where Jim was scattered and removed, Amanda was focused as a despot. Ever since Max could remember, his mother-cum-manager had set her son's priorities, apportioned his time, ruled his life with all the rigor of a totalitarian regime. Until finally, at the age of twenty-two, he packed up his cello and said, "Enough."

The Fishers were sympathetic when he revealed that Amanda had not only kicked him out of the house but also thrown gravel at his car as he drove away.

"Because you wanted to come here?" Evelyn asked.

"Because I wanted to come here. Because of a lot of things. Because I'm taking a break from playing for a while. Because I said I'm gay in a national magazine. Because I took her Mercedes. I don't know what she found more unforgiveable. My career suicide, as she calls it, or her stolen car."

A whining Nissan turned onto Palmer Street, breaking the morning quiet and putting past in a plume of toxic exhaust. Max and Benji looked up. It was the color of dried blood, beat up and toaster shaped, with illegally dark windows and a decal of a delinquent Calvin peeing on the rear windshield.

"I don't suppose that's her?" Max asked.

"She'll be here," Benji answered.

"What were you saying? About my mother?"

"I can see, I said. Now that I know everything you're giving up, I can see why she's having a fit."

"I'm not giving up anything. I get to keep the Grammy," Max said, but Benji, who had seemed so game over guacamole and virgin margaritas the night before, was no longer in a kidding mood. "I'm giving up being a bear on a unicycle," Max added more pointedly. "That's what I'm giving up."

Another car, a serviceable white sedan, approached the house and passed it by. Max watched it coast to a stop at the end of the street, disappointed, relieved.

"Why a bear on a—"

"The main attraction at the circus," Max answered absently, his attention still fixed on the taillights burning like the red eyes of some mythical and retreating beast. "I'm tired."

"Tired of the king of Denmark throwing roses at your feet?"

This Max ignored. "I'd like to see my boyfriend for more than three days a month. I'd like to conduct. I want to do something that's my own. Like write music of my own. That's what I'd like to do. Write music of my own instead of spending my entire life playing somebody else's."

"As if that's the worst thing in the world."

The warming sun wrung the smell of last night's rain from the air. The eaves, dripping loudly, pit-a-patted into beds of hostas that bordered the front of the house, while across the beaded lawn, like a scarf dropped during the storm, a ragged knit of fallen orange leaves. "I don't mean to give you a hard time," Benji said, throwing an arm around his nephew and pulling him close. "It's just hard for me to imagine walking away from anything I was so good at. I can't walk away from acting, and I'm not very good at it at all."

"I'm not giving up music." As Benji loosened his grip, Max rocked back into his own sovereign space and said, "Maybe she changed her mind?"

"She'll be here. I wouldn't lie to you."

"I don't know. She didn't sound too happy about the whole thing. And by 'the whole thing' I mean me."

"Sounding happy has never been Claudia's strong suit. She gets it from our father. You can't take it personally."

"I don't. I read this book called *Birthright* about, you know, adopted people looking for their birth parents. I knew she might want nothing to do with me before I got into this." He held up a hand to stall Benji's interruption. "And you don't need to tell me everything's going to be fine."

"I wasn't."

"Yes, you were."

Benji zipped two fingers across his lips and let Max go on.

"Whatever happens with Claudia, even if she gets here and tells me to go away, I'm glad I came." His voice snagged on a need he couldn't name, deepened with emotion. "I'm glad I met you," he said. "And your mom. Though she doesn't know what to make of me either."

"Are you kidding? The closest she thought she'd ever get to having a grandchild is complaining she didn't have one. You're like Christmas to her."

"I don't think a twenty-two-year-old is what she had in mind."

"Give her time. Give them both time."

"You didn't need time."

Benji shrugged. "I'm like a dog: one sniff and my heart is yours."

"Your basic emotional whore?"

"Pretty much. Besides, being an uncle is easier than being a parent. Uncles buy cotton candy. Parents have to make sure you eat your peas."

"Those days are over."

"You're never too old for cotton candy. And you may not need to hear it, but it *is* going to be fine. Claudia's going to love you. I've known you less than twenty-four hours and I love you."

"You don't know me well enough to love me," Max said. "I could be a grifter for all you know."

"Are you a grifter?"

"No."

"Even if you were. She's your mother. How can she not love you?"

Max was awed and shaken as another self—one with a different parentage, a different provenance—began to take shape before him. He wanted to believe what his uncle said was that simple: mothers love their sons. Benji's philosophy on this point may have been as nuanced as a tenth-grade biology book, but Max hoped to throw a switch deep within Claudia, at the level of her genes, and watch maternal devotion blaze forth, unwavering and immediate. It should have been that simple, but darkness hung at the end of the path, a shadowy bend around which he could not see.

"Tell me more about her."

Benji began retreading the same ground they'd covered the night before when they crowded on the sofa with the old photo albums. For Max, a portrait of Claudia had come together, perceptibly, pointillistically, as Benji connected the dots between the third-grade field trip to Howe Caverns, the junior-year term abroad in Rome, the ribbon cutting celebrating her first building.

This morning, though, Max had his own agenda. "Am I the only one?" he suddenly wanted to know.

Benji stopped for a moment to take in his meaning. "Yes. God, yes."

"And I was a mistake?"

"You were—unplanned."

"She was my age?"

"Yes."

"Why didn't she just end it?"

Silence. "She tried."

Silence. "At least you're honest. What happened?"

"She couldn't do it."

"You told me she was tough."

"She is."

"What about Nick?"

"What about him?"

"Would they have gotten married, you think? If it wasn't for me?"

Benji shrugged. "What do you want to write?"

"An opera," Max offered. "I think."

"Opera's good. I've never seen an opera. But I know that everybody throws roses at the end." Benji crumpled a piece of paper into a mangled flower and tossed it at Max's feet. "Roses. Roses. More roses!"

Max pushed himself off the steps, a gust of exasperation that carried him into the wet grass. "Jesus, Benji. Give it a rest with the roses."

"Joke," Benji said soothingly. "I'm joking. Come on, sit back down."

But Max thrust his hands into the pockets of his hoodie and stood his ground. "Why are you being a dick? The concerts and the Grammys and the fucking king of Denmark. You've been up my ass with that shit since you woke up."

"There's an image." Benji tried lightening the mood. He picked up his makeshift rose, stuffing it, with a hangdog look, into the folds of his robe. "You're right. I'm a dick."

"What's your problem?" Max pleaded.

"Forget it."

"No. We're starting a—a thing here. I want it to be honest. I want it to be right. I hate weirdness."

"Okay. Okay." Benji held his hands up to show he had no intention of fighting as he fished in a pond of murky emotions. He found only two words sluggish enough to be caught. *"I'm jealous."* Max looked taken aback, and Benji rushed to say, "It's not you. It's me. It's all about me. But you're like this lens. You shouldn't be, I know. But I can't help it: I look at you, and it's like I see more clearly all the things I haven't done."

Max opened his mouth to answer, but Benji cut him off. "I keep thinking of this book my father gave me. Every year, on my birthday, Henry gives me a book. Gave me a book. He's way past remembering birthdays. But I used to think these books were his way of talking to me. He had so little to say, or so little I wanted to hear, I took each one like a message in a bottle. Like his only way of sending word across the shark-infested sea of his personality."

"Nice metaphor."

"Thanks. Took forever to come up with it. Anyway. Sometimes the message seemed clear enough. Like the year I left college, he gave me *Jude the Obscure.* Which is like the worst book for a college dropout.

But other years? I still don't know what he was trying to tell me with *Beloved*. He wished my mom had killed me in a woodshed? When I was thirty, he gave me *Oblomov*."

"Never heard of it."

"It's Russian. I forget who wrote it, but it's called *Oblomov*, and it's all about this guy."

"Oblomov?"

Benji winked. "This thirty-year-old guy who—wait for it—lays around in his robe all day thinking about all the great things he should be doing. Which of course he never does. He just gets fatter and lazier and more useless. And he knows it. That's the tragic part. He knows. 'He was painfully aware that entombed within him there was this precious radiant essence, moribund perhaps by now, like a gold deposit lying buried deep in the rock that should long ago have been minted into coin and put into circulation.'"

Max raised his hands in soft applause. "Impressive."

"Not really," Benji answered, giving his own robe a savage little flick. "Even bad actors can memorize. But that's how I feel. Like the best of myself is still down in the mines. Uncoined. And nobody's ever going to see it."

"That's not true. Cat sees it. I can tell by the way she looks at you that she sees something."

"Honestly, I don't know what Cat sees in me," Benji admitted, sadness softening his voice. "But you're right. I have Cat."

They were quiet a long time.

"What about Arvin?"

"Arnav," Max corrected. "What about him?"

"You didn't say much last night, which I've learned doesn't mean there isn't much to be said. Where did you meet?"

"We played in the Dallas Symphony together," Max answered. But the words had barely left his mouth before he started backtracking. "Wait. That's a lie." He cleared his throat. "No weirdness."

"No weirdness," Benji repeated, as if swearing to a pact.

"We met in the hospital."

Slightly thrown, Benji said, "I thought you were going to say online. Doesn't it seem like everybody meets online now? Especially gay guys. Did you know there's an app that shows you how far you are from other guys who are looking to hook up? Oh, look, there's a blow job, and it's only one hundred feet away. I know most of them say they're on there to network, but who networks with his shirt off?"

"What are you doing on Grindr?" Max laughed.

"That's it: Grindr!" Benji said with a snap. "My friend Marshall showed me. I'm telling you, the gays have got it figured out. What were you doing in the hospital?"

"Same thing as you," he said. He watched as his meaning sank in, as the weight of it dragged down the corners of Benji's mouth. "Not a bridge," he added, as if this detail somehow lessened the gravity of the act. "But. Yeah."

"What? What did you do? When? Why?"

Max returned to his spot by Benji on the stairs. He kept his eyes on his feet, occasionally pulling a piece of wet grass from between his toes as he spoke. "Some of those questions are easier to answer than others. When? Two years ago. I was in Dallas, which I tell Arnav is reason enough." Here, Max smiled, but his smile failed to smooth the creases that concern left on his uncle's face. He went back to grooming the grass from his feet and kept his voice low. "I flew down a few days before this big Haydn festival I was scheduled to play. It was a Monday. I remember because it was the Monday before Thanksgiving. I was supposed to rehearse with the symphony at, like, two o'clock, but as soon as I got to the hotel, I pulled the curtains and got into bed and knew I wasn't going anywhere. It was like the door disappeared as soon as I shut it: no way out. I'd been having a rough time for a while. A long while, but I kept going and going, traveling and playing, traveling and playing, doing it all like I was on a conveyor belt, but for whatever reason that day, the minute I laid down, I turned to lead."

"You were depressed?" Benji asked.

"Depression and I, we're on familiar terms, yes. When I was a kid, I didn't know it was depression. It usually looked more like anger than sadness. Does Claudia? Does she get depressed?"

Benji wondered at this. "Not more than your average overeducated city dweller. Sometimes, I guess. Claudia plays her emotional cards pretty close to the vest."

"Not me. I used to fly into these rages. Cursing my parents, throwing shit, wishing them dead."

"Claudia wished our mother dead every day when we were kids," Benji said, as if offering this genetic link might explain some aspect of Max's diagnosis. Then, with his nose crinkled, he whispered, "You threw shit?"

"Jesus, Benji, don't be so literal. I threw whatever I could get my hands on. My music stand. Plates. A ficus once, but no feces." Max took a moment to recover from the scatological digression before picking up where he left off. "My parents bore the brunt of it. Strangers were safe. I never went off on Phillip Glass." He laughed. "Or a fan or any of my mother's awful, stuffy friends who she made me serve drinks to, play *and* serve drinks, but whatever was left when I was done with my parents got aimed at me."

"What, like cutting?" Benji had seen a documentary.

"Except I wasn't a cutter. I can't stomach blood. I was a basher. I'd stand in front of the mirror and punch myself in the face until I had a black eye. I knocked a tooth loose once. Broke my ankle with a bat."

"When you were how old?"

"Eight."

"Your parents knew you were doing this?"

"I had excuses. I fell off my bike. I took a football in the face. But on some level they knew. I never played football in my life."

"And they didn't take you to a doctor?"

"Not right away. Amanda didn't put two and two together. Or didn't want to. Honestly, I think the tantrums thrilled her on some level. Convinced her I was the crazy genius she always wanted."

"Like Mozart."

Max made a gesture of concession. "My father used to say it takes a genius or a fool to pee in the punch bowl, but only the genius gets away with it. But then I started slamming my fingers in doors, and we couldn't have that. You can get by on the cello with a busted leg, but not with a broken finger. That's when she took me to the doctor."

"What did he do?"

"She. Dr. Haze. Seriously. I had a psychopharmacologist called Dr. Haze. She put me on lithium, which did wonders for my vibrato." Max simulated a severe tremor with his right hand. "I called her a few days before I flew to Dallas. Left a message that I felt like I was going to—you know." Here, Max held an invisible noose with one hand and let his head drop. "She never called me back. Said she never got the call. Right. Do you think she was trying to tell me something?"

"Why did you do it?"

"Why did you?" Max returned. "Why does anybody? You lose sight of the reasons not to, I guess."

They looked into the sky to see a thread of contrail unraveling in the wake of a jet, their eyes settling on the line of rooftops once it was gone.

"She's not coming, is she?"

"Okay, my friend. Let's put you out of your misery." Benji rose with a show of various aches and headed into the house. "I'm going to call her."

After he disappeared, Max opened his chat with Arnav and typed,

What if this was a mistake?

You can't put the genie back in the bottle.

It was a challenge, a distraction, a hand lovingly extended.
Max typed,

You can't unring a bell.

A watched pot never boils.

Easier said than done.

It's Christmas Eve. I walk through the door, blinded by a pyramid of packages, and call her name. The only response is the baby's cry. Claudia is there, not in her bassinet, but in the middle of the bed, packed round with pillows to keep her from falling. I say Jane's name. I walk through the rooms, saying her name in every one. I pick up the baby for a second pass. She quiets at the tree, jamming a fat little fist in her mouth at the sight of the twinkling lights, the mirrory pink balls on the silver boughs. She smells like pee. I smell like snow. The kitchen sink is full of broken eggshells, nesting measuring cups caked with flour paste, dishes skimmed with suds. I look out at George's house, thinking she's there. She must be with Evelyn, borrowing sugar, unburdening her heart. A bowl of vanilla-sweet batter sits on the kitchen table next to a greased cake pan. The oven light, but not the oven, is on. I dip my finger in the bowl and put it in Claudia's toothless mouth. Then I see it. Not the box, but the space where the box should be. The empty space on top of the refrigerator, between the Yellow Pages and the wall, a puzzle missing its piece. I go to the bedroom and put the baby down, making her cry all over again. The box. I storm the apartment looking for it. I dive under the bed, tear apart the closet, flip the couch cushions onto the floor before I see it, tossed in the folds of the tree skirt like a forgotten present. An army-green metal box with its latches sprung. I know before I open it. I know by the weight that the gun is gone. The gun with one round in the chamber is gone. The box of bullets, untouched. It is a joke between us: you only need one bullet, unless you plan to miss.

8.

The phone woke her. Benji's face, warped into its best imitation of Marlon Brando yelling "Stella!", lit up the screen. It was eleven o'clock, and Claudia was late. Unaccountably late. She offered a short secular prayer of thanks that the phone call came from Benji rather than her mother, whose four-minute, thirty-five-second reaction to this titanic news Claudia couldn't bring herself to listen to. It sat among her waiting voice mails, ready to sink her with glacial tides the second she pushed the "Play" button. But Claudia couldn't type *alive*—five lousy letters!—to allay Oliver's fears that she'd taken a deadly nap behind the wheel on the interstate. Who could expect her to open her mouth, let alone speak in sentences, let alone defend herself?

Did you get there?

Hello?

Just tried calling. Call me back.

Getting worried.

Officially worried.

???

Babe?

She tossed her phone onto the seat beside her and was about to start the car when, cued, it seemed, from on high, an enormous red SUV with windows smoky and chrome gleaming pulled up alongside. The engine idled for a moment before dying, leaving the parking lot in a quiet gray stupor under low-hanging clouds. When the driver's door slammed shut, Claudia closed her eyes, terrified that it was him, terrified that it wasn't, until the scuff of footsteps stopped at the rental car's side. A rap on the glass touched her like a live wire. She jumped. Nick leaned down and offered an apologetic wave. Time, in its ineluctable way, had transformed a familiar body into a strange one, replacing her lithe young love with this rugged and sturdier counterpart, no different than an Ovidian nymph turned into a towering and formidable tree. The blue of his eyes had softened toward gray. The self-consciousness that once stiffened his smile—she never did convince him that his crooked canine made him hotter—had been massaged away by time. He was as handsome as she remembered him, perhaps even more so with the signs of age ornamenting him like a patina: he now looked like he'd earned his beauty.

In Hollywood, Claudia would have rolled the window down for a game of cat and mouse, toying with him until he recognized her and his ancient grudges dissolved in a magical, amorous reunion—but Alluvia couldn't have been farther from Hollywood. And Claudia wasn't in a toying mood.

As soon as she was out of the car, standing before him, Nick took a polite step back, as if she worked in a department store and stood ready to spritz him with cologne. "If this is about my wife," he said, "you should really speak to my lawyers."

Claudia shifted under the weight of his scrutiny, willing him to recognize her, telepathically broadcasting her name like a distress signal tuned to his receiver. Eventually she said, "Nick."

Only then did the calm waters of his composure break. He stared. "Claude?"

She nodded.

"What? What are you doing here?"

A sudden tremor seized her throat, but she pushed the words out anyway. "Visiting Benji." She felt like glass, like her skin had gone translucent as a jellyfish, exposing her essential spinelessness, her secrets. She'd come all this way, it occurred to her, and she wasn't going to tell him why.

"I heard. How's he doing?"

"Better. Better. Word gets around."

"In a town of twenty-three people? Of course word gets around."

He invited her inside, listening to a version of Benji's recovery she'd broken into bullet points, and poured fresh water into the coffeepot.

"But enough about him," Claudia said. "My God, Nick. How are you?"

"I'm getting divorced. In case you didn't figure that out. I thought you were one of my wife's lawyers."

"I caught that. I'm sorry."

"Don't be. We aren't." He laughed in his easy, effortless way, as if Claudia was in on the joke.

"We don't have to talk about it."

"Yeah. Let's not." He set her coffee on one of four plastic folding tables arranged in the center of the room to make a larger one. "Milk? Sugar?"

Claudia shook her head.

"So," he said, taking a seat across from her. "Of all the people I expected to see."

"I know. Is this okay?"

"Sure. Yeah. You might have given a guy notice." Nick winked. "But sure."

"Believe it or not, I didn't know I was coming here."

"I believe it. I was in New York last week. I was this close to looking you up." He pinched two inches between forefinger and thumb. "Okay. Maybe this close," he added, doubling the space.

Claudia noticed his wedding ring. "How did you know I'm in New York?"

"How did you know I'm here?"

She clinked her coffee mug to his and took a sip.

They'd walked countless miles through deep, deeply intimate, conversational territory, having been confidants, confessors, striders with the same stride, up until the day they weren't, so it felt exceedingly strange to skitter along the safe path of small talk—Claudia's current commission for Selkirk and Sons Funeral Home, Nick's leaving a lucrative law practice to move back east and build things—when not far away, winding through the thorniest of thickets, ran the discussion they should have been having.

"And you don't miss it?"

"The law? Going on seven years and not a single tear."

"How could I not know you've been back for seven years? My mother—"

"How would she know?"

"In a town of twenty-three people."

"Not all of them follow local real estate development."

Casting a curious eye around the room, she surveyed the unfurled architectural plans spread out between them. If she looked interested enough, perhaps he wouldn't notice she'd run out of things to say.

"Hey, those aren't for show."

"I—I—" she stuttered.

"Claudia. Relax. I'm kidding. You don't need security clearance to be in here."

In actuality, the plans hadn't interested her, but now she felt obliged to give them more than their due. She stood to study them. "What is it?"

"Supermarket."

"The one they're building—" She pointed out the window, in the direction of the skeleton of steel and rebar she'd passed fifteen miles back, on the way into town.

"That's the one."

She'd gleaned enough about Amato & Sons on her previous night's web search to know that the company had long ago traded house painting for larger construction and contracting jobs across the Capital Region. Nick stood at the helm of the development of countless subdivisions, a college dance theater in Schenectady, a glittering glass office park in Troy, and, most recently, a shopping plaza on the outskirts of Alluvia that housed a dry cleaner, a tanning salon, a Chinese restaurant, and a gargantuan, all-purpose supermarket.

"Wow."

"Is that a good wow? Or a bad wow?"

"It's a wow wow. This is enormous."

"Forty thousand square feet." Looking up from the drawings, he stood and took in the room with mock pride. "I know what you're thinking."

"Oh?"

"He's building forty-thousand-square-foot supermarkets, and his office looks like the inside of the Elks Lodge."

She couldn't disagree. The stained industrial carpet, the Stars and Stripes fastened to blond pressboard paneling, the dusty plastic spider plants struck her as the original set piece of sadness, but her mind at the moment was far away, on her parents' porch, with the boy in the black hoodie.

"I wasn't."

"You're a lousy liar, Claudia."

Wrong. She silently corrected him. *I'm an excellent liar.*

"It's okay. I'd tear it down tomorrow if I didn't see my dad everywhere I look. For years he did all of his work out of our kitchen, so it was a big deal for him to have an office. A real office. Even if it is the ugliest place on earth."

"It's not the ugliest."

"It's close." He laughed.

"And you're preserving it in perpetuity."

"Carrying the torch of unsightliness."

"Generation to generation."

"Father to son."

Her laughter fell dead, as if he'd pulled out a gun and fired it. Claudia opened her mouth to say—what? What could she possibly say? But Nick raised his hand in beneficent appeal. "My bad. I told myself I wasn't going to bring it up. Which, I'm sure, is exactly why I found a way to bring it up. Pesky unconscious."

Claudia smiled uncertainly. She was aware of her hands, hanging heavily, stupidly at her sides. She suddenly felt the need for them to have something to do.

"Do you have kids?" Nick paused. "Other kids?"

"No. You?"

"No."

She cleared her throat and, twisting her engagement ring around so that the diamond dug into her palm, said, "How can you not hate me?"

"Who said I don't?" He stepped up and hugged her before she could respond, laughing mischievously, and held her close. "Don't get me wrong. I did. For a long, long time. But who wants to carry that around for a lifetime? We were babies."

When he let her go, she stayed close for a moment, waiting, as if he might reach out again. He breathed deeply then stepped away.

"I drove past this on the way into town," she said, returning to the table, the plans.

"You said."

"So much for Herrick's," she answered, aware that the little mom-and-pop venture where she and Nick used to buy paper bags full of Swedish Fish had closed long before the Amatos graduated from house painting. She espoused a theory of the world that would always favor Herrick's, the two-thousand-square-foot family-owned general store over the refrigerated, cheaply built goliath twenty times its size. In fact, it was precisely these "cathedrals of gluttony," as she'd called them in an article she'd soon inflict on a roomful of Barnard urban studies majors, that illustrated all that was wrong with Americans' sense of public space: 1) it was endless, 2) it was theirs for the taking, 3) anything and every-thing—rape of the land, depletion of natural resources, turning the planet into an unlivable oven—was excusable in the name of conve-nience. Give her a green market any day! She was an ardent, if not bullying, supporter of sustainable farming and found herself in Union Square twice a week filling her reusable canvas totes with a premium of local bounty. Preferring to patronize the sort of small bodegas and specialty shops that, shining like neighborhood beacons, made Jane Jacobs wax poetic, Claudia shared that vision of a well-functioning city and dreamed of designing dense, vital, suburban developments, with plenty of parks and pedestrian-friendly streets, that would lure the zeitgeist away from its isolating and egotistical fascination with the two-car garage and single-family home. She imagined building her own Winter Park or Seaside—though in no place as tacky or politically inept as Florida—and in this way hoped to make her mark by helping human beings make a smaller, less sprawling one.

"This is the problem with America." She tapped the tabletop, grate-ful for a digression to take them away from the past, away from even an hour into the future. "Here"—she indicated the Price Chopper with a perfectly polished nail—"you get ninety-five brands of toilet paper. But I don't need ninety-five brands of toilet paper. Nobody *needs* ninety-five brands of toilet paper. But we expect it. We're Americans: we're entitled to it! But we don't *need* it. But we think we *do* need it, so we build these, these behemoths—no offense—"

"Behemoth is better than a lot of other things you could have said."

"Like monstrosity."

"For example."

"These behemoths that are so big they have to be built where nobody lives. You have to drive ten, fifteen, twenty minutes to get to them. Then your family of four buys enough for four families because you drive a tank and live in a house the size of a tennis court. You have all this room, so why not fill it?" She could have cried for joy at the absurdity of the debate: not a word in twenty years, and within an hour, as intuitively as retired lab rats remembering their way through the old maze, they began the course of playful bickering. No matter the obstacles in their way.

"Claudia?"

"Hm?"

"Yoo-hoo. Where did you go?"

"Oh. Just that the carbon footprint of these kinds of construction is astonishing."

Nick, who'd stopped by the office merely to grab a set of plans on his way to the site of his newest monstrosity, admitted that the hundred-acre development he'd envisioned as a slam dunk—two hundred half-acre lots, two- to four-bedroom colonials each, yes, with a two-car garage—had become a burden, a blight.

"A behemoth," he said, "right up the ass."

It haunted his days, kept him up at night. The announcement hardly qualified as an invitation, but somehow not ten minutes later, Claudia found herself bouncing along beside him as the big red Escalade turned off the paved road and, like a needle lowered onto a record, followed a well-worn groove through the weeds.

The tall, dry grass that grew along the ruts brushed against the car with a drawn-out *shusssssh* as Nick talked excitedly about what he had in store. He asked if she'd heard of Compton's Mound. "Rust-eaten iron gates. Rubbled headstones. It's straight out of *Scooby-Doo*. All that's missing is a groundskeeper dressed like the Swamp Thing."

"I *have* heard of it. Benji's girlfriend is one of your rust-eaten iron-gate crashers."

"You mean those 'Save Compton's Mound' crazies?"

Tell him, Claudia ordered herself. *Tell him,* but shook off the idea like a shawl in the summer heat. "She thinks you're Hitler."

"Was she one of the ones who chained herself to the gravestones to keep the backhoes from leveling them?"

"I don't know if she's that devoted. She seems devoted. She has a T-shirt and everything."

"From the shit I've been getting, you'd think I was trying to tear up Arlington. This, by the way, was a family plot. For the most part."

"The qualifications."

"I don't need to make qualifications. It's private land. There are thirty graves here, total. A few of them soldiers who died in the Revolutionary War."

"And you want to dig them up? Maybe you are Hitler."

"Just because you fight in a war doesn't make you a hero. Even if it did—heroes get forgotten. *History* gets forgotten. The last burial here happened in 1860, and nobody's delivered a daisy since. Going in should have been." He bulldozed one palm across the other to illustrate the simple, satisfyingly boyish transaction he'd been denied.

"Haven't you seen *Poltergeist*?" Claudia couldn't refrain from asking. "Bad things happen when you build on a cemetery."

They passed fallen trees and little ponds gone acid green with algae.

"We don't want to build *over* the bodies. What kind of monstrosity-maker do you take me for? We're going to move them. To Glenlawn. My parents are buried in Glenlawn."

"That's where my parents are going," Claudia said, as if naming the destination of their next vacation.

"It has fountains. And weeping willows. It's lovely."

"So displacing the dead from their eternal resting ground really makes you a humanist."

"But then come the historical societies," said Nick, ignoring the jab. "Saratoga. Bemis Heights. Even Alluvia has one. They're all over this part of the state, protecting every last log George Washington ever peed on. 'There are soldiers buried there!'" His imitations were, as she remembered them, passionate but limited: everyone sounded like Jerry Lewis with a cold. "'This is hollow ground.' One of them actually said that to me. 'Hollow ground.' Maybe it was Benji's girlfriend. Is she dumb?"

"I don't think so."

"These people," he mused venomously. "The women would be happy churning their own butter while the men spend their weekends reenacting the Battle of Freeman's Farm. It's all spinsters and Second Amendment wackadoos."

"A humanist and a patriot," Claudia said, her hand finding its way to the console between them, her fingers, as if drawn by a magnet, tantalizingly close to his leg.

And Max, on the porch.

"Why do you care? If it's your property? It is your property, right?"

"It's mine. But contrary to popular belief, not all publicity is good publicity. The average resident of your high-end housing community wants to live outside the shadow of death and desecration." He changed tack and said, wounded, "You know what those T-shirts say? 'Amato & Sons Need to Develop . . . a Conscience.'" He shifted the Escalade into park and turned to face her. "I have a conscience."

"I know you do, but . . ."

"But. What? I *don't* have a conscience?"

"Not that. I was going to say the kind of developments you're talking about? If you think about it? They're the opposite of communities, Nick. People living like that wave to the neighbors across their half acre of lawn, and that's it. There's no interaction. Maybe a Halloween block party, but no public life to speak of. People are more likely to get in the car and drive to buy sugar than borrow a cup from the neighbor next door."

"Who still borrows sugar? You sound like you might like to churn some butter yourself."

"Are you calling me a spinster?"

He stared down at the rings on her left hand.

They turned to look out the window at the view afforded by the noonday sun: the clustered cemetery with headstones like broken teeth, the distant trees, a stretch of purplish mountain painted across the horizon.

"It's beautiful," said Claudia, "in a tumbledown sort of way."

He gave a quick, devilish smile and asked, "So what would you do, Madam Architect? You've got a hundred acres. No cemetery. No redcoats."

"No budget?"

"Let's not get crazy."

"You don't want cute little houses. What do you want?"

Nick bowed to her, as if ceding the floor. His eyelashes were as long and lovely as she remembered them.

"I'd build apartments."

"Apartments."

"Or row houses. Compact, sustainable residences surrounding a public lawn or garden. Pedestrian-friendly sidewalks. A community center. You know, a playground, a pool. Maybe some retail space. I know it's a sacrilege in these parts, but something to encourage people to get out and walk."

"Nobody likes to walk," Nick said with a philosophic shake of his head. "And nobody likes to rent."

"I rent."

"You live in the city. Up here, nobody lives in apartments."

Her face crumpled in amused disbelief.

"The poor and the elderly, okay. But no one else."

"And we wouldn't want them on our hands, would we?"

"People think it's a punishment to live in an apartment. They want the American dream. With a nice big lawn for their neighbors to keep off of."

They were twenty-two years old. How could he have expected more from her, at twenty-two?

"This is Alluvia," Claudia said with fresh focus. "You can't drive ten miles in any direction without hitting a trailer park or a meth lab. You talk about high end, but it's not exactly the Hamptons set."

"You're still a snob." Then: "The demographic is changing."

"Well then, so can what the demographic wants." Claudia willed a shift into lecture mode, tucked a strand of stray hair behind her ear, and began. "Nakagin Capsule Tower. Ever heard of it? It's one of the first buildings I ask my students to study. Not because it's flawless architecture. It's not. The apartments are straight-up Stanley Kubrick. Lacquered white walls, built-in reel-to-reels. Very Tokyo. Very *2001: A Space Odyssey*. But it's significant. It was built in the early seventies to house Japanese salarymen. Google it. You'll see, it points to a completely different concept of living. A completely different set of values. It says you can cook, sleep, eat, shower, even bop along to your reel-to-reel, and you don't need more than one hundred square feet to do it. You can live life in a—I called it an apartment, but really it's a pod, a, well, a capsule, an eight-by-twelve—"

"Eight by twelve." Nick exploded with a guttural laugh.

"See? It's unimaginable to us."

"It's not unimaginable. People do it all the time. In Attica. In Sing Sing."

"It was an experiment. A failed experiment," Claudia confessed. "But the idea is compelling."

"Among Japanese businessmen, maybe. You're insane, Claude."

"I'm not talking about building actual pods."

"Americans," Nick continued as if he hadn't heard her, "don't like identical. I don't want my pod to look like your pod. I know what you're going to say: then why do they live in cookie cutter subdivisions. True. But they like the illusion—"

"The myth."

"The myth." Nick nodded. "My house is different from yours. My house, my couch, my car—even if they're exactly the same—are better than yours. It's *why* we have ninety-five brands of toilet paper. I'm Charmin. You're Cottonelle. It's what makes me me."

"Ah, the Individual! Let Lady Gaga decide she wants to live in a pod, and you'll see how many people really want to be an individual. You wouldn't be able to make them fast enough."

"So you want me to build the Nagako?"

"Nakagin Capsule Tower."

"In Alluvia, New York?"

"No. But architecture that questions our use of space is possible. What are we leaving behind? Is it propitious or poisonous? We have the right— the duty, actually —to ask those things. Even here. Even in Alluvia."

The two of them, facing each other, struck a pose of serious consideration, both sober and unsmiling, until their eyes met and laughter, like water topping a levee, burst forth.

"Propitious," Nick said as soon as he'd caught his breath. *"Propitious!"*

"What's the matter with propitious?"

"All I'll say is people around here don't want their houses asking them questions."

She felt his hand before she saw it move. The heavy warmth of it on her cheek startled her, and before she could stop herself, she pulled away. Stung, Nick no sooner opened his mouth to apologize than Claudia, straining against her seat belt, leapt forward. She clasped his face, the satisfyingly rough plains of silver-flecked stubble, and pulled him into a crude but fervent kiss. Nick fumbled to free himself from his own seat belt without letting his lips leave hers. Loose, he shocked her again by squeezing improbably through the narrow space between the front seats, pawing, like a swimmer reaching for shore, toward the space he called the "way back." Tumbling over the backseat with a theatrical groan, he hurriedly lowered the seat backs, twice hitting his head, and crawled toward Claudia across the now flat expanse of coarse black carpet. Again, drawn like a magnet, she shot through the same soft leather chasm, pulling Nick with her as she inched her way toward the tailgate, flat on her back, staring into his eyes as he positioned himself over her, helping his fingers move from one button to the next.

Later, the world rushed back to her in the caw of a bird. They lay curled together in the back of the Escalade, slicked in cool sweat.

Claudia stared at the ceiling. Benji would be comforting him by now. Or perhaps Max, beyond comforting, had left. Perhaps he was gone for good.

The harsh, hoarse cry of the bird sounded again, offending her. She made a failing effort to rise to see where it came from. "What *is* that?" she asked.

"A crow."

"Awful."

Nick extended an arm under Claudia's head, making her a pillow of his sizeable biceps. She cozied up, ignoring the crow, which in most books had to be a bad omen, and breathed in the sweet drugstore spice of cheap soap and a musky something, something long forgotten but rushing back to her now, something fundamentally Nick, that crept (almost imperceptibly) beneath it. "Grab that blanket," he said.

"What is that?" she asked, not moving, except to bring her foot against the hard, oddly shaped form that the blanket covered. "A body?"

"Not quite."

"For a second I thought I was in for a threesome."

"Why? Would you be into that?" Nick asked sleepily. He squeezed her tighter, then said, "It's Stan."

Claudia sat up quickly, hitting her own head—"Motherfucker!"— and pulled the blanket from the guitar case. She popped the latches and opened the lid to reveal the battered, honey-brown dreadnought that had sung her to sleep many a night. "Stan."

They'd had a language all their own that was coming back to them. Shared sounds, tonic endearments, words laced with private meaning that returned to her after all these years.

"Sing me something."

Without so much as a raised eyebrow, Nick shifted obediently into sitting position, pulled the blanket round Claudia's shoulders, and took the guitar from her hands. "What's the lady's pleasure?" he asked, plucking a few notes to bring the instrument in tune.

"Do you have to ask?"

"Yusuf?" said Nick. "Always Yusuf." He played a teasing medley of the opening bars of a song that now seemed ineludible.

"Trouble," he sang.

❖ ❖ ❖

She was the worst person in the world, the absolute worst. She hadn't sold missiles to the Taliban or pushed through Tea Party legislation to slam shut the borders. She wasn't an assassin or serial killer or Ponzi schemer, but as she sat in the parking lot of the Guilderland Travel Plaza, she racked up a list of crimes that seemed to her comparable:

1. She'd driven three hours not to meet the son she'd never met before—as planned, as promised—but to crack open a chapter of ancient history and fuck his father.

2. She'd fled from Nick as fast as a coward could without so much as a word about said son.

3. She'd sliced her mother and perhaps, if he was lucid enough, her father with the knife of a decades-old decision she had always intended to keep sheathed.

4. And worst of all, she'd let down the boy who knew her only as the woman who'd let him down.

Her selfishness astounded her. After Nick dropped her at his office, she began the drive back to the city, rocketing along as if chasing a line that, if crossed, would return her to the time before she picked up the phone to find Max on the other end. She wanted normalcy. The world didn't need to be simple or happy, so long as it wasn't completely upside down.

Under a long, shadowing range of perfect cumulus clouds, Claudia made it safely through Mechanicville and Clifton Park, but by the time she reached Halfmoon, her hands started to shake. The more she drove, the more distance she tried to put between her and the problem twiddling his proverbial thumbs on her parents' front porch, the more she felt like she was wrestling another person for control of the wheel. One pair of hands fought to steer the car straight ahead, while another, with its equally implacable grip, struggled to turn it around. The warring led Claudia to drift between lanes, a deviation met with a wee but rousing horn blast from the tiny silver Smart car behind her. Shaking herself as if waking from a dream, she eased into the right lane and took the exit for the next rest stop.

She sat in the parking lot with the squeals of car-dodging, sugar-shocked children ricocheting around her. Listening to Benji's livid voice mails or responding to Oliver's backlog of frantic texts still proved beyond her, but she pulled her phone from her bag and put it on her lap. Of course it was only a matter of time before the thing rang, and when it did, Claudia kept her eyes shut against it. If asked, she couldn't point to the road that bypassed her maternal—*maternal?*—responsibilities so completely and led instead to the shabby cemetery where she stumbled out of Nick's Escalade with her panties in her hand. How, she wondered, did she get here?

The phone continued its trill, and Claudia opened her eyes to find her brother doing Stanley. *Hey! Claud-ia!* She knew that Benji would flay her for failing Max, turn the life preserver of her meeting with Nick into a sinking ship, but on the fourth ring, she broke down and answered anyway.

"Tell me you've been kidnapped," Benji whispered fiercely into the silence before she had a chance to say hello. "Tell me you're bound and gagged in some cabin in the woods and that's why you're not here right now."

"Why are you whispering," she asked with dread. "Is he there?"

"Of course he's here. He's where you're supposed to be. Here!"

"Can he hear you?"

"*Now* you care about his feelings? Where the fuck are you?"

She told him.

"What are you doing there?"

"Heading back."

"Wait."

"Benji."

"Here's what you do, Claudia. You put the key in the ignition. You've got the key, don't you? You turn the car on. Then you turn your ass around and get here. Turn around and get here now."

But she couldn't. She could no sooner find her way to Palmer Street—to Max and her mother and the fallout of a decision she'd made when she was barely old enough to order a drink—than she could transform her car into a plane and jet back to the city through the cloud-slung sky.

"Then I'm coming to you."

"Don't," Claudia pleaded. "Please don't."

"Those are your choices." His voice struck her, sharp as a hatchet and just as hard. "Stay where you are. Don't even *think* of leaving. I'll drive to the city if I have to, Claudia. I'll break my leg again, I swear I will, I'll kick down your door."

She sat in the car, the rolled-up windows turning it into a sweatbox, the discomfort of which she felt she deserved. As the minutes rolled by, twenty, thirty, forty, the chime of Oliver's incessant texts arrived, like the traffic report on New York 1, every ten minutes. Finally, feeling the next ding would be the hammer blow to the head that would end her, she dinged back with a text of telegrammatic brevity: Sorry! Case of nerves. Call later.

The echoing sound of yet another message stirred her to crack the window just enough to throw the phone out of it. It was from Benji. Inside, it read, @ McDonald's.

She made her way into the violently lit faux-timbered lodge where people peed and bought forty-ounce drinks in a mad cycle, wearing the enormous sunglasses of a Hollywood starlet in hiding. Wending her way through a herd of elastic-waistbanded feeders on a do-or-die hunt for pumpable ketchup, Claudia positioned herself at the mouth of the dining room, glancing from one sticky table to the next until her eyes stopped on her worst nightmare. There, at the back of the room, framed beneath a forged Bob Ross depicting the saccharine splendor of fall Adirondack foliage, sat Benji and Evelyn.

She took off her sunglasses as Benji's eyes met hers. To Claudia the two of them, sitting side by side with the grimmest of looks on their faces, resembled nothing so much as a twisted Oedipal take on *American Gothic*. She mouthed "Fuck you" to her brother, at which he turned to Evelyn, put a hand on her shoulder, and excused himself.

Evelyn could have used the sunglasses to hide her own red and swollen eyes, which, watching Benji as he went, soon came to rest on her daughter. She pulled one, two napkins from a tabletop dispenser and used them to blow her pink-tipped nose.

"Are you kidding me right now?"

"She made me bring her," Benji said as he approached, hands up in a posture of defending himself against a crazy lady.

"She's almost eighty, Benji. How can she make you do anything?"

"You're right. I should have knocked her down and driven over her."

"No. But what resolution do you think we're going to come to with her here? Why didn't you bring him too?"

"You mean Max? He has a name."

"Max," she said miserably.

"None of this is Mom's fault. Or Max's. You know that, right?"

She may have been the gladiator expected to lay down her sword and die, but self-defense came as reflexively as a hand pulling back from a flame. "So where is he? Why isn't he in your little vigilante party? You didn't leave him with Dad."

Benji rubbed his hands roughly over his face, as if to scour the anger that twisted his features. "Sandra's with Dad. Max went back to his hotel," he said with overly determined calm. "Seeing that you're suddenly interested in his whereabouts." He looked over his shoulder at his mother, at the impromptu interrogation chamber they'd set up in an orange plastic booth and said, "Come on." When Claudia didn't move, he grabbed her by the wrist and pulled. "Come. On."

She slid into the booth across from bad cop and crying cop and bowed her head. Evelyn, snuffling into her rough cardboard-colored napkins, said nothing, while Benji spoke in the fierce whisper he'd adopted for the day as his favorite tone. "Are you nuts?"

The room, loud and bright and beset with an oily smell that buried itself under Claudia's skin, was freezing, better suited to storing burgers than serving them, and Claudia, chilly in a tissue-thin cashmere sweater that showed the tank top she wore underneath, longed to pick up one of the two steaming cups of coffee that sat on the table in front of them. They hadn't thought to get her one. Or had thought *not* to get her one.

"Mom? What are you doing here?" she eventually asked.

"Oh," Evelyn said tearfully, as if speaking through a mourning veil. "Another right I don't have."

"I only meant that you and I have things to discuss. Things we might not want to discuss"—Claudia spoke softly—"here."

"I'm glad you think we have things to discuss," Evelyn shot back. If her voice had, with those first words, threatened to slip into a pit from which no sound escaped, it suddenly found a toehold and, climbing to firmer ground, said more loudly, "Because apparently we didn't have anything to discuss before."

"I don't know how to talk about this."

"Well then. Nothing's changed."

Claudia scanned the room helplessly. A contestant in a hidden camera show, she'd been set up and now waited for the host to come and put a stop to it, tell her it was only a joke.

Benji placed his hands on the table, avoiding the sticky soda rings and a gory smear of ketchup. "The point of this isn't to discuss this now. Here. The point is to get you home, Claudia. You need to do what's right."

She bucked at the words. "I don't know what you expect from me. Yesterday this kid blows my door off its hinges and walks into my life. I don't get time to adjust to that? I don't get to figure out what that means? I'm not ready—"

"Ready?" Evelyn snapped. "Was Benji ready to be stopped in the driveway? Was I ready to have a grandson I never knew *existed* up and march in? How could you? *Both* of you? How could you keep such a thing from me? For twenty-two years?"

Benji did his best to duck Evelyn's attack by marshaling his troops behind hers. "Mom's right. Your door wasn't the only one blown off its hinges yesterday. What about my door? What about Mom's?"

"What about that boy's?" Evelyn said. "We're sitting here thinking about ourselves." Evelyn pressed the wet, wadded paper mess to her tearing eyes. "I've never met two children so stupid. So thoughtless."

"You won't believe this, but I put a lot of thought into that decision. I agonized over it."

"You have no gratitude."

"Gratitude!" Claudia barked.

"We deserved that much. You don't think your father and I deserved that? To know what was happening? After raising you the way we did? After loving you? You don't think we could have *helped* you?"

"You would have made me keep it."

"Him," Benji fiercely corrected.

"And no," Evelyn went on without pausing, "we wouldn't have let you give him away."

Benji took stock of the surrounding tables, a seismograph reading the disturbances that their rising volume might be making, but no one looked their way. Whatever was happening with the crying old woman proved universally less interesting than a quarter pounder with cheese and fat fistfuls of fries.

"We would have raised him. I would have." Evelyn wept.

"He wasn't yours to raise. He was mine. And I did what I thought was best for him. I did what I thought was best for you."

"You did what you thought was best for *you.*"

"Yes. Mom. I did. I was twenty-two years old. Did I want to be stuck in Alluvia for the rest of my life? Did I want to marry Nick only to divorce him one or two or three years down the line? After we'd inflicted whatever damage we could on each other—and the baby—and Max—because all those years that passed were years we wanted to spend living other lives."

"There's nothing wrong with Alluvia. I'm tired of you carting out that song. You were raised there. You're perfectly fine."

"Am I? Because you're making me sound like a monster. Both of you."

"Can we *please* go home?" Benji asked.

"She's telling me she's too good to live where she grew up," Evelyn said, unable to surrender a bone still shredded with meat.

"You and Daddy decided where to live," Claudia answered. "You decided how many children you wanted. You decided how you wanted to raise them. Nobody made those decisions for you. Why should I have let you make them for me?"

"Nonsense," muttered Evelyn.

"It's not nonsense, Mother. It's not." Her resistance broken down, Claudia reached across the table and took a defiant swig of Benji's coffee, wishing it were something made from sour mash. "Benji and I were gone, grown up. You and Daddy were free. You'd been saddled with children for eighteen years—"

"Saddled," Evelyn broke in, "is your word."

"You know what I mean. With us out of the house, you could finally go out and live your own lives. You'd done your time. You *deserved* to live your own life. Doing what *you* wanted to do. Whether you took advantage of that—"

"Claudia," Benji warned.

"Let her finish."

"Nothing." Claudia retreated. "All I'm saying: I thought you'd be better off if you never knew."

"Do I look better off? And tell me. What did I want to do? Tell me, She Who Knows All. How do you know what I wanted to do?"

"I don't. But I thought there might be something other than raising children."

"I've never been ashamed of being a mother."

Claudia sighed. "I'm not saying you were. Or should be."

"Then what would you have me do?"

"I don't know." Claudia threw her hands up. "Travel?"

"Can we stop?" Benji broke in. He looked from his mother to his sister to the milling gluttons around them. "We need to go home and finish this," he said, eyes sharp and serious.

"I'm not going anywhere," Claudia answered. "He shouldn't have been able to find me. He would have been better off if he never did."

Benji leaned in. "You are so fucking selfish," he said. "And that's coming from me! If I find it selfish, think how selfish it must be."

She didn't have to play at being furious. Her blood, rising fast and hot into her pale cheeks, balked at the injustice of Benji's tone. Why did the whole of her family's sympathy rest with a boy they'd known for less than a day? Where was their love, their compassion for her? "Since when did you find the Manual for Good and Upright Living?" Claudia asked. "Share a page, Benji. Please. In your infinite wisdom, tell me, what am I supposed to do? Or is the best way to find some support in this family to find a bridge to jump off of?" Her voice cracked at the end of a sentence she regretted uttering as much as she relished it. She tore a stiff napkin of her own from its plastic dispenser and pressed it to her eyes.

"Claudia!" Evelyn gasped.

The tables had turned. Usually fuckups of such magnitude, with such gnarled, historical roots, belonged to Benji. Claudia wasn't prepared for the scrutiny of sitting in a chair especially reserved for him.

"What am I supposed to do?" Claudia asked.

"You're supposed to go see him."

"I was there." Claudia snuffled wretchedly. "I was there at seven o'clock this morning. Just sitting there, outside the house. I saw him. He was right there on the porch. But I couldn't."

"It's almost three." Benji tapped his empty wrist, as if a vestigial watch confirmed his calculation, and asked, "You weren't sitting there for eight hours. Where have you been?"

Like a deer that had wandered into an unexpected clearing, Claudia stood undeniably exposed.

"Claudia?"

"Nowhere."

"Nowhere? For eight hours?"

"I drove around."

"For eight hours?" Benji repeated. "Where did you go?"

"I told you. Nowhere."

"You didn't see anybody?"

She didn't like where this was going or that Benji, so quickly, knew how to get there. "Who would I see?"

He squared his shoulders, gazed long and hard into her eyes. "You tell me."

"Benji. Stop."

"Who did you see?" Evelyn asked.

"Claudia?"

"Stop!"

Benji pressed his palms to the table and leaned in. "You didn't!"

Evelyn dropped her napkin and narrowed her eyes. "What?"

"You don't know what you're talking about."

"Who else do you know?"

"Who?" Evelyn asked.

Benji put a hand on his mother's back to stifle her. "You hate everyone else in this town. Who else do you know?"

"I'm not on *trial* here."

"It would make sense," Benji reasoned. "I mean Max is his son too."

Claudia raised her hands to her ears as if he'd set off firecrackers next to them. "Can we not use that word right now?"

"Son?"

"Benji!"

"So you did see Nick?" A pause. "I thought he lived in Seattle."

"I can't listen to this," Evelyn cried, hiding behind fresh napkins.

"Well? What does he say?"

Claudia balled her napkin into a hard little wad and dropped it onto the table. She didn't answer.

"You didn't tell him, did you?"

Again, nothing.

"You saw him, and you didn't tell him? Your judgment is incredible. Unbelievable!" Benji said, "Not a word? I'm looking more level-headed and responsible the longer we sit here."

"How could I not think of him? But I didn't come here to see him, if that's what you mean. I didn't even know he was here. I thought he was three thousand miles away, but then I googled him."

"You googled him," he repeated flatly.

"I didn't plan it, Benji. I didn't. But then I saw Max, and I started driving, and the next thing I knew I was in front of the Anselmans' place." Benji's head fell into the palm of his hand as he muttered some unintelligible curse, but Claudia went on. "I wanted to tell him. I actually thought telling him would make it easier. That I'd be able to go back and meet, you know—"

"Max!" Benji shouted.

"What do you want me to say? I'm a coward? Fine, I'm a coward. But I thought maybe if we went to see him together, Nick and I, that I'd be able to get through it. But then we started talking."

"About what?" Benji pressed. "I'm dying to know."

"Ridiculous things. I don't even remember. The supermarket he's building. And Compton's Mound."

"Max is in tears because you're a no-show, and you're out there talking real estate development."

"It wasn't like that. He asked me what I'd do with the property and—."

"And?"

"He asked me to draw up some plans." She sounded like a little girl lost.

"Even better. It was a job interview."

"It was comforting, you ass. I may be in the wrong here, but I'm not beyond needing that."

Benji's eyes widened with disbelief as he grabbed her hand and hissed, "Did you fuck him?"

She pulled away to show the depth of the offense, but the prickle of heat dancing up her cheeks betrayed her.

"You did."

With that, Evelyn slapped Benji out of the booth, heaved herself up, and with an admonishment that she didn't have to listen to this anymore, limped away.

Claudia glanced with horror after her. She turned back to Benji. "Thank you for that."

"You *fucked* him?" Benji asked again, bringing the volume down to his inside voice.

Claudia leaned in close and whispered, "I didn't go there to fuck him. We were talking, and somehow—"

"It just happened."

"Somehow. Besides. It's none of your business who I fuck."

"You're right. It's not. It's not my business. Is it Oliver's? I'm pretty sure it is his business. Who, by the way, is convinced that you're dead in a ditch somewhere. Have you called him?"

Oliver. Certainly worse than any vow she'd broken was that she hadn't given him a serious second thought.

"I texted. He's fine."

"Oh? You found time to text your husband between fucking your ex boyfriend and your job interview?" Benji pinched the bridge of his nose and breathed a few steadying breaths. "Is this your plan?" he asked. "To go off the rails?"

"You, whose train hasn't seen a track in twenty years. Don't lecture me about going off the rails."

"But here's the thing: we're not talking about me right now. We're talking about you. And a kid, a *kid*, who is handling this situation with a level of maturity and grace that seems beyond you."

"I didn't ask for this, Benji. I never asked for him to find me." The conviction that she lived in a universe careless enough to send meteors crashing through the roof of her home unleashed a wild tremor in Claudia's voice. "He wasn't supposed to find me!"

Benji folded his arms across his chest, unmoved. "But he did. And now you have to deal with it. You're his mother."

Claudia stood.

"Mother. Son. What other words aren't you ready for?" After a moment, he wrestled his phone from his back pocket and, after a few swipes, handed over a picture of himself and Max, arms around each other on the Fishers' front porch.

Claudia looked at it for a long time.

Benji kept his mouth closed, watching to see if the mirrored eyes and mouth would work their magic.

"He's beautiful," she said, putting the phone on the table. Her eyes fell on her brother like he was a stranger, a salesman trying to sell her something she didn't need, couldn't afford.

"Then come home," he pleaded.

"I can't," she said, turned, and walked away.

I come home with sawdust in my hair and find the women sitting on the porch. Evelyn waves, but averts her eyes. Jane raises her cigarette and watches me through the twisting vines of smoke. They have sweating glasses of tea on the arms of their chairs, a bowl of cherries on the table between them. Jane presses the little black book she carries everywhere to her stomach, as if transmitting her poems through her skin, into the dark, solitary cell where the baby flutters and kicks. Flippy, she calls it. You want to take my hands. You want to take my tongue. *It is a topic between us: whether Flippy can hear these things, whether Flippy should hear these things, but asking the question again isn't worth the storm it would bring. Evelyn invited us for dinner, Jane says. Without Evelyn, all we would eat is SpaghettiOs. Jane writing, me writing, nothing more to wash than a saucepan and two plates. Evelyn says what she always says: It's no trouble. Jane stubs her cigarette on the bottom of her shoe. She fans herself with her little book, puts a cherry in her mouth, and chews.* You bloom and thorn. But I'm the one who bleeds

9.

Max made introductions. Evelyn. Benji. Arnav. Arnav's best friend (and Thanksgiving Day orphan), Paul. The group cinched together for handshakes, embraces, the passing of a foil-wrapped casserole from guests to hosts, then drifted apart on separate streams. The Fishers headed for the kitchen after directing Max and his friends into the living room, where Cat, looking cozy in a fawn-colored cowl-neck, offered them drinks. Paul announced his sobriety without footnotes or fuss, but Max and Arnav jumped at the chance for whatever amber concoction bathed the tinkling cubes and orange twist at the bottom of Cat's glass.

"Max," Arnav said. His head tilted warningly, judgmentally at the sight of the bourbon bottle.

Max pretended not to notice. He didn't want to be bothered about the medications Arnav insisted on bothering him about. Despite his boyfriend's doubts to the contrary, despite the drugs' ruinous effect on Max's creative impulses, Max continued to pop the complicated cocktail of antipsychotics and mood stabilizers twice a day, like a good boy, according to the rules. As he took the drink from Cat, he registered

Navi's concern as a stack of kindling registers a spark. He fumed but didn't, for the time being, flare.

Soon, the seven of them—Evelyn shepherding Henry into the mix—sat around the fragrant fire that danced in the fireplace as the rich scent of browning turkey crept in to overpower it.

"Mm!" Paul said. A dilettante makeup artist and taxidermy student, Paul made the better part of his living singing in New York City cabarets. His voice sounded like a Nina Simone song, honeyed and resonant. "Mrs. Fisher, that smells dee-vine."

Max had spent two of the last five weekends with what he called his "famiglia presto." Not including Claudia. How many withholding mothers did one boy need? But it mattered less that Claudia had given him the cold shoulder when his uncle, quite literally, had given him a warm one to cry on. And maybe this was all Max needed. All he had a right to ask for. Maybe Navi knew what he was talking about after all: maybe this was enough.

"You've gotten farther than most people ever get," Navi reasoned one night, head resting on Max's chest.

"You mean adopted people?"

"I mean people. In life. At some point, you have to be satisfied with what you have."

Max didn't agree. "You don't get to the top of the mountain if you're satisfied with life at base camp."

"You sound like one of those inspirational posters with an eagle on it." He kissed Max lightly then rolled onto his back, hands behind his head, staring up at the ceiling. "Base camp is pretty high. Not everyone is made to get to the top of the mountain."

"Exactly. Some people are meant to go higher."

Navi laughed. "My winged boy."

Evelyn had hosted two parties in Max's honor, intimate family affairs where she unholstered her bring-out-the-big-guns meals— slow-cooked short ribs, fish stew—dinners that required full days of preparation that she'd tired of making for her husband and children (thankless all), but for which she happily slaved away for the sake of her grandson. *My* grandson. *My* nephew. The possessives Max heard ringing through their sentences soothed him better than the benzos that had the maddening tendency to make the simplest of songs dry up the second his pen touched paper. (Of course, he was already someone else's grandson. Someone else's nephew. Someone else's son. But the Fishers held out the possibility of belonging in a way Max never felt he had. Benji and Evelyn and even the specter of Claudia, whose absence haunted their time together and united them as one, had Max saying more. *More!* Who—sorry, Navi—could really be happy with *enough?*) And so, the two words Max longed to hear, the two words he would not rest until Claudia spoke them: *my son.*

Nick had said as much. On his last trip to town, Max met Nick, whose arms had opened to him as wide as Benji's. They spent an after-noon tossing a football, despite the all-too-evident fact that neither of them especially enjoyed it, but hearing Nick utter that incantation? For whatever reason, it wasn't the same. Max wanted to hear Claudia say it. Needed (despite all his claims to the contrary) to hear it from her. But on the mother front all had been quiet: Amanda hadn't called; Claudia hadn't shown up. She did, however, concede to a longer, if no less awk-ward, phone call, during which she confessed her own shortcomings with a martyr's enthusiasm and said *I'm sorry* so many times he thought someone had left a Brenda Lee album skipping in the background. She asked for more time, and Max, who saw no other path to glory, told her to take as much as she needed.

"Max?" Evelyn roused him from his reverie and asked him to pass a plate of bacon-wrapped dates. She took a little jewel of glistening fat stabbed through with a toothpick and sank, satisfied, into her chair.

When the plate reached Henry, he regarded it as part of a custom he couldn't possibly participate in, as if Max had asked him to do a rain dance. He turned to Paul and said, "I have to go to the bathroom."

Tall, slender, with a skull-tight buzz cut and black almond-shaped eyes two shades darker than his skin, Paul cultivated a sleek androgyny not unlike Grace Jones and seemed no less unflappable.

Evelyn reached over to where Henry sat and shook his knee. "You're scaring people," she said, hipping out of her chair and leading Henry down the hall.

Cat offered to refresh drinks. Max held his glass aloft.

"Maybe that's not such a good idea," Arnav said. Here he sat, beating the same tired drum, louder, more boldly now that he had the buffer of an audience.

Cat, at the ready to pour more cocktails from a silver shaker, froze in midair until Max reached up with a light touch and tipped her hand.

Arnav turned from Max and addressed the group, bolder still. "Some of his medications," he said, "they don't mix well with drinks."

Max loved Arnav. Except on the occasions, like now, when he didn't. Looking across the room at his partner of three years, a blinding anger ignited in him with such speed he had to pour back his drink in a single gulp to extinguish it. What did Navi know? Thirty years old and second violin with the Dallas Symphony. Not that second violin of the Dallas Symphony was anything to sneeze at, but really, where did he get off telling Max anything about anything? Arnav was a first-generation Indian American from Plano, Texas. His parents, who, shortly after Arnav's graduation from conservatory, returned to Chandigarh, got him out of bed every Tuesday morning at a ridiculous hour for the family Skype session. Their good boy. Their *chhaila*. He woke at six each morning to submit to a punishing workout regimen, favored a tightly trimmed beard that he believed camouflaged an unflatteringly weak chin, and, in his button-down shirt and bright-blue V-neck sweater, dressed like a Southeast Asian Hardy boy. *Such a priss,* Max thought. *Such a prude.*

"I'm the youngest in the room, but I'm good without a babysitter."

"Ar-naaav," Paul sang under his breath. "Later," he mouthed. "La-ter."

When the red plastic thermometer popped on the turkey, Evelyn, as promptly as if a bell had rung, steered the group past these choppy waters and delivered them to the safe harbor of the table. Burgundy cloth. Gold-trimmed dishes. A small store of wine glasses that caught and shattered the light from two tiered candlesticks. They filled their plates from the mahogany sideboard—turkey, dressing, braised butternut squash, and Navi's scalloped potatoes with coriander and coconut milk, which soon had everyone asking how they could have lived with plain mashed potatoes for so long.

Paul said, "Wait." He stood over his plate with hands held like a conductor's, staying raised forks and open mouths, then ran to the foyer for his bag. A moment later, he reappeared very proudly with his contribution to the festivities.

"Paulina," Max marveled as Paul placed the strange centerpiece on the table. "You have outdone yourself."

"Paul," Evelyn said, bemused, "you shouldn't have."

"Know your strengths," he answered sagely. "Some people do a potato. I do this. Know your strengths."

Shifting in their seats, they each craned for a 360-degree view of the taxidermied tableaux. On a small wooden pedestal covered with hand-cut autumn leaves, miniature pinecones, and a painted, animal-hide tepee, a stuffed ash-gray squirrel stood on its hind legs. Its front legs were bent to its hips in a pose of diva-ish defiance, as if it meant to flaunt the fierceness of its outfit: an immaculately beaded white breast-plate; a leather-tasseled white loincloth and boots; and a headdress of flowing white feathers that trailed to its tiny clawed feet. "I'm very into taxidermy right now," Paul explained. "I just finished a tribute to Joan Crawford done entirely in mice. But this is my first squirrel. It's Walter Potter meets Cher's half-breed."

"Is this politically correct?" Arnav asked.

"What kind of gay man are you?" Paul answered. "Cher transcends."

"What she needs," Max said, "is a spread in *Vogue*. She's fabulous."

"Sacasquirrelea. What she really needs is her Captain John Smith."

"Sacagawea was Lewis and Clark," Arnav corrected.

Paul widened his eyes with queenly hauteur. "Are you sure?"

Henry forked a potato into his mouth and said, "Pocahontas was Captain John Smith."

The table looked to him, nonplussed.

"To Squirrelahontas, then."

Up went the glasses, clinking under the echoing cheer: "Squirrelahontas."

A delicious stream of Château Mont-Redon (thanks to Max) carried dinner nicely along, and everyone said a prayer of private thanks for the distraction provided by Squirrel Cher, who offered endless opportunity for conversation and occupied the place in the room where, otherwise, a giant elephant would have stood. The obvious and insistent topic that nobody wanted to face—Claudia's absence—a fact that Max more or less accepted, Benji ignored, and Evelyn fought the constant desire to apologize for fell into the shadow of Paul's discussion of the odd and unsettling triumphs of Victorian taxidermist Walter Potter and the methods by which one acquires enough dead mice to restage key scenes from *Mommie Dearest*.

"Is there a class for that?" Evelyn asked.

"There's a class for everything," Paul answered.

"Cat's going to teach a class," Benji offered. "Next semester. At the high school."

"Are you a taxidermist?" Paul joked.

Evelyn touched a napkin to the corner of her mouth with a look of happy surprise. "What kind of class?"

Benji nudged her. "Tell them."

"It's not really a class. And technically, I'm not a teacher. I'm more like a facilitator. They're dusting off the drama club—"

"She's being modest," Benji interrupted.

"I'm not. They haven't had a drama club in ten years. We're not sure there's going to be any interest is what I mean. It may be a very short job."

Benji drained the last of his lemon-wheeled water. "She's going to be great."

The group made their lively way through a conversational labyrinth; topics followed until they dead ended, from Squirrelahontas to Cat's teaching gig to Evelyn's painting (the merits of which Cat said Evelyn underestimated) to Paul's boyhood love of paint-by-numbers and his crazy love for his twin toddler nieces.

"Do you guys want kids?" Max asked Cat.

Now it was his turn for the nonplussed stares.

"We've been together three months," said Cat. She raised a hand to her throat, as if to keep herself from choking.

As they talked, a powerful grip of anxiety suddenly seized Max's heart. He couldn't point to its source, but felt a tightening fist grab hold of his insides. He tried talking, about anything, about whatever, to keep his mind from the pain of it. "I'd adopt a kid," he said. "We've talked about adopting a kid."

"Not at twenty-two, I hope," Evelyn said ominously.

"We're not quite ready to talk about babies yet," Cat assured the group. "Adopted or otherwise."

"Hold on a sec," said Benji.

"Hold on? You mean we *are* ready to talk about babies?"

"I'm not saying we're ready. I'm saying I understand the desire. To have a kid."

"I hear you," said Paul. "Men have their biological clocks too."

Max crossed his knife and fork on his plate and leaned back to rub his stomach. Let nausea look like gluttony. The more normal he acted, the more normal he'd feel. If only things worked that way.

"I couldn't adopt," Paul said. "Not that there's anything wrong with adoption." He tipped an invisible hat to Max. "But I'm too vain to settle for a stranger's genes. No, when I send little Antoinette to bed without supper, I want to see this face, in all its tragic beauty, staring back at me."

"Antoinette?" Evelyn asked.

"Paul thinks all children, boys or girls, should be named Antoinette."

"What else am I going to call them?" came Paul's dry response. "Joe?"

Before anyone could answer, the sound of the front door opening fell over the table like a cage. Everyone knew who it was. Everyone looked trapped. Even before the voice called out with a tentative "hello?"

In that moment, Max's body seemed especially prescient: his organs like a seismograph having traced some infinitesimal shift in the bedrock before the glasses and plates started to dance. According to Benji, neither he nor Evelyn had seen Claudia since she fled the rest stop, and the few subsequent conversations they'd had with her were as strained and useless as a clothesline trying to hoist a car. Max played the role of the more forgiving one. Perhaps because he had fewer expectations. She did strike him as a failure on some elemental level, but how, really, could he judge? He didn't know her. And though he seemed to be collecting samples of her limitations, those, while dispiriting, seemed utterly, utterly human.

After slipping a clerk two hundred dollars for his birth mother's address, Max had left the windowless records office with the knowledge that his search might end in a blind alley. He had readied himself to find the meth head. Or the rape victim. Or the woman too poor, too ill, too taxed, too privileged, too ambivalent, too ambitious, too pampered, too preoccupied to raise a child. What he'd found was a woman who was not much more than apologetic. Sorry she'd been too young. Sorry she'd wanted something else. Sorry she'd run from her first opportunity for reunion and flubbed every opportunity since. Sorry that the pace with which her acceptance moved was so very glacial. Sorry, so sorry for everything.

On another level, one deep below the surface of compassion and understanding, Claudia simply disappointed him. She pissed him off. She needed, he thought, to get over herself. But Max wasn't entirely paying lip service to his uncle when he said that Claudia's reaction was beside the point. His fledgling connections to Benji and Evelyn and even Henry, who more often than not had no idea who he was, sent his spirits soaring higher than anything he'd felt toward the Davises in a very long time.

Claudia. Evelyn sprang from her chair with the vigor of a much younger woman and rushed to intercept her in the front hall. Arnav reached across the table and took Max's hand, while Benji excused himself and followed his mother out of the room. Max heard the fierce whispering that rose to a crescendo then dissolved into silence. Into the troubling calm he felt himself fall. His face flushed. His heart felt ready to burst. And then she was there.

Claudia entered with exaggerated lightness, stifling the sound of her heels on the floor as if she were coming late to a concert and feared disturbing the players. Oliver, hanging behind her like a shadow, gave a tentative wave. Cat and Arnav and Paul rose to greet them, while Max, standing at the back of the group, might have been moving in a procession of mourners, waiting for a private audience with the woman in the stylish black dress, the last person in line who knows he has the most to say. They stood face to face. The room fell away and left the two of them together, alone. Not knowing what else to do, he extended his hand.

Claudia took it with the gentlest touch, as if any more pressure might set off an alarm. "Can I—" she began, but left the question unasked. With an uncertain step she closed the gap between them and hesitantly pulled him to her. Much as Max wanted to, he kept himself from falling into her embrace. He stood straight, spine rigid, for the few short seconds she held him, looking numb but feeling anything but.

He might sink into tears. He might break into laughter. A dark, manic wave with no outlet rolled about inside him, tossing his mind like a little boat with no lights to guide it. Oliver needled his way between them, embroidering his introduction with a sycophant's overstatement and praise, before Evelyn stepped sternly in and asked if they wanted something to eat.

"I'll get plates," Claudia said as Benji went for more chairs. "Max?" she asked from the doorway. "Maybe you can help me?"

He had the sensation of blacking out, a dark shroud draped over him in one room then pulled away to reveal him in another. How did he get there? She seemed magical to him. Standing not three feet away, speaking in a language he found beautiful but couldn't understand, she was the New Possibility—capital N, capital P—in a life that felt (for all its stunning and remarkable moments, since the day he could hold a cello bow) predictable, predestined, plodding. Amanda Davis had anticipated every step, and Max had puppied along. Violin at three, cello at six, eight hours a day, 365 days a year, music theory, composition, practice, practice, practice, Carnegie Hall at the age of twelve, the Eastman School, Juilliard, one step after the next.

Even with his illness, erratic and havoc wreaking as it could be, his life had seemed an utterly known quantity. Everything was anticipated, every day accounted for. He understood the cycle of it, the ups and downs, the highs and lows. He could tally the weight of all it contained, except the woman before him. The greatest unknown, the biggest unanswered question of his entire life stood just three feet away.

Max stayed where he was, watching as she took plates down from the cabinet and opened a drawer with a clatter of forks. She sat at the kitchen table and waited for him to take a seat across from her. When he did, she looked at him with a practically painted-on Mona Lisa smile, mesmerizing and unreadable. Three pies, an inordinate amount for nine people, lay atop the table. Pumpkin. Pecan. A lattice-topped apple. Claudia took up a knife and sliced, looking in the other room as if they might be caught making the transgression of this private, preemptory dessert, a risk that made the moment that much more precious. She served Max a piece, took one for herself, and raised her fork, waiting for Max to raise his and *clink*, like a toast of champagne. They ate their pie in silence, not comfortable but not entirely unlivable either, until Evelyn came and shooed them away.

By the time Claudia and Oliver had finished their meal, Max was beside himself. He wanted to be back in the kitchen with Claudia, in the quiet of that bright cocoon, patiently awaiting a dawning of wings, but the dining room and its chorus of voices insistently tugged him in other directions.

"Play," they said. "Play."

Offering an extemporaneous concert was the furthest thing from his mind, but Benji and Cat and poor, obsequious Oliver swirled into a vortex that slowly sucked him in. Like a prisoner who feels the rope tighten about his hands the more that he struggles, Max gave into the idea that some coveted moment with Claudia would come sooner if he simply gave in and did what they asked. She stood at the other end of a field crossable only by the coaxing of strings. He ran out into the freezing night for his cello.

❖ ❖ ❖

Claudia lay awake on the pullout couch in her father's study, Oliver breathing deeply beside her, dead to the world on even the thinnest of mattresses. She faced away from him, only their naked asses touching as was their habit, the closest to cuddling Claudia could bear, especially after their first month of dating when—honeymoon period over—she named her future husband and his body heat "The Furnace" and pushed him to the other side of the bed. That hump-to-hump contact acted as a security blanket of sorts and also a fail-safe GPS, broadcasting any movement Oliver might make that would require her to stow her

phone. Now, with him drugged with tryptophan and the soporific sat-
isfactions of star fucking, she could blanket herself in the moony light
of a tiny screen and type her texts to Nick with immunity.

Are you awake?

It was after one o'clock, but Nick's response popped up instantly, as
if he had simply been waiting to press "Send." Did u survive?

I'm typing, aren't I? Did you?

Nothing 2 survive at my brother's. Other than his wife's
cooking. Would rather have been w/ u 2.

Too tired to type your words?

All the kids are doing it.

I thought people our age were beyond that.

OMG. WTF? LMFAO!

No emoticons.

How did it go?

I'm a terrible person.

:-/

!!!!!

Why terrible?

Gutless.

You're there. That's not gutless.

All I do is hide. I hid from him. I hid him from you.

U keep beating urself up about that.

Then, before she could answer: You're there now.

Here and hiding!

Go easy.

I came to get my mother and brother off my back. And you.

That's not true. U wanted to see him.

I did.

He wanted to see u.

He needs something.

Who doesn't?

I don't know if I have it to give.

U don't even know what it is.

I'm like a mute around him.

It will get easier.

I wish I'd been better.

Ur expecting Mother of the Year?

No. Not up for that one.

U get to be nervous. And awkward. And confused.

Claudia didn't answer.

Ambivalent even.

You weren't. You played football! That's fatherhood 101. Textbook.

He doesn't want u 2 b textbook. He wants u 2 b u.

He told you this?

He doesn't have to.

I think he thinks I hate him, Claudia typed.

Why? Bc you didn't play football?

Because I'm hiding in my father's study.

Oh. When you said hiding . . .

I meant it. Something crazy?

Shoot.

I was thinking of us as a family.

Who family?

The three of us.

You have a family.

You know what I mean.

You have a husband.

Forget it.

We're not here to play house. Him or me.

Chastened, Claudia typed, I don't want to play house.

What do u want then?

A cry of floorboards from outside her door. Henry? But Henry had never had such a light footfall. He tended to stomp, especially now, raging around the house like an animal trying to get free from its own bafflement. Claudia left Nick's last question in the folds of the sheets and, pulling on a robe, crept to the door. She cracked it open the tiniest bit, careful of the double-crossing bleat of its hinges, and peered out. She feared finding Max stationed at the opposite end of the hall like a guard on duty, wanting some ineffable thing from her, but discovered Evelyn instead. Claudia had as much cause to fear meeting her mother, maybe even more considering that Evelyn refused to pretend that the cuts Claudia inflicted had healed. To reach out to Evelyn these days was to press an open wound that oozed hostility. Claudia wouldn't be forgiven until she'd done right, and doing right didn't include taking refuge in her father's study as soon as dinner was done, as if she had no other business with Max than the silent sharing of pie.

Regardless, something in Evelyn's posture concerned her. Her mother looked out the window in the way of people who shrink from being caught looking out of windows. Claudia opened the door, letting the hinges announce her. Evelyn turned and beckoned to her impatiently in a way that said whatever beef she had with her daughter had been put on ice for the time being. When she reached the window, Claudia saw on Evelyn's face a look of deep worry. A heavy crease trenched across her mother's forehead, and her eyes narrowed into a squint so troubled she seemed to see something vexing beyond the vexing thing she saw. With one hand Evelyn pushed Claudia behind her to shield her from sight, and the two, like aspiring PIs, looked down on Max (in a jacket far too light for the November night) as he walked in drifting circles across the lawn.

"What's he doing?" Claudia whispered, though there was no chance of her voice disturbing the party still going on below.

"He's been out there for an hour," Evelyn whispered back.

"An hour?! He'll freeze."

"Maybe not an hour. But Benji's been out. Arnav's been out. Trying to get him back inside."

Claudia saw what her mother saw. There was, in fact, something troubling in the way Max stalked the lawn: his pace, the flimsiness of his coat, his determination to suffer the cold. She knew better than to ask what she should do.

"You go," Evelyn said, needing no invitation to intervene. "Arnav is worried that he's sick."

"Sick?"

"With the bipolar."

"I don't know what that looks like," Claudia said. "Neither do you."

"Arnav certainly does. He says he can see Max ramping up."

"What does ramping up mean?"

Evelyn ignored the question, then asked, "Is it hereditary?"

"Manic depression? I have no idea." Claudia turned to go back to her room then turned back again. "I'm not bipolar, Mother. If that's what you mean."

"I'm not talking about you."

"And neither is Nick."

"I'm not talking about him either," Evelyn answered distractedly.

"Who then? You? Daddy? Are you telling me you're bipolar?"

"Is there anything you take seriously?" Evelyn asked, returning to her vigil. "Go and get your coat."

❖ ❖ ❖

He returned indoors with the sound of it. Max heard it playing, there, beneath all the other sounds. Beneath the cold that bit fiercely into his being and, even with a fire in the grate, refused to let go. Beneath the glee of the game going on around him. Despite the dizzying excitements and perpetual disappointments of the night. A song. A shred of song he'd needed the cold and the quiet to latch on to. Now he held it by a thread. He clung to it like a child holding a balloon in a strong wind. It threatened to whip away from him, irretrievable, at any second.

Crawling back onto the couch with the smell of the night on him, he sank drunkenly into Navi's warm arms and threw his legs over Benji's lap. He hummed.

They chastised him, trying to rub a little warmth into his bones, as they ran their last lap through a game of Celebrity. Paul, straining to act out a famous actor without benefit of words, gave his clues with imperious speed. On his knees, he touched a finger to his heart then held it in the air.

"ET!" Benji shouted.

Paul's encouraging nod quickly gave way to more clues. He jumped to his feet, pointing at the fireplace.

"Fireplace."

"ET in the fireplace?"

Paul shook his head vehemently. He mimed lighting a fire.

"Matches."

"People!" Paul clapped his hands, no nonsense. "How are matches a celebrity?!"

"No talking!" came the unanimous response.

"Start a fire."

Nodding, nodding, reeling in the answer as if it were a large fish, Paul practically jumped into Benji's lap.

"'We Didn't Start the Fire.' Billy Joel!"

"*Firestarter*," Claudia offered from the doorway. "Drew Barrymore."

"Praise Jesus!" Paul said as he plopped down, a show of utter exhaustion, into a chair.

Max closed his eyes. He had the sense that they were allied against passing time, against an evening that, no matter how they drank or sang or struggled to resist, was coming to its close. His moment with Claudia had come and gone. There would be others, there might be others, but this one he felt drifting inexorably away. He kept his eyes shut and listened to the party breaking up around him, the preludes to bedtime, Benji saying, "Does everyone know where they're sleeping?"

and "Fuck the mess. Leave it for tomorrow." They'd created a refuge of food and drink and friends and (Max said the word to himself) *family*, who were, even with their shortcomings, even though he barely knew them, unaccountably dear. He didn't want it to end. But it would. It was. He wanted more. More of his family. Yes, even more of Claudia, who had yet to convince him that she was anything more than (as Amanda Davis might say) a "royal pain in the hind end." And yet. There was something he wanted more, something that would only come to him once the others had gone. He heard his tune playing beneath the racket, those few precious notes that rose above the general din and announced themselves to his ears.

Max turned sleepily on his side, snuggling into the couch as Navi stood and tried to pull him to standing.

"You can't sleep here," Arnav said with a note of parental reproof.

If only Max could hold on to that delicate thread of sound, that shadow of a song that made a stitch under all the other noise.

Benji squeezed Max's foot. Then, seeing no movement, convincing Arnav to let him be, threw a blanket over him.

Max's mind moved heavily, slow with liquor, but suddenly there, with the music, was this:

> *With her foot on the threshold she waited a moment longer in a scene which was vanishing even as she looked, and then*—something, something—*it changed, it shaped itself differently; it had become, she knew, giving one last look at it over her shoulder, already the past.*

To the Lighthouse. Cat had given a copy to Benji when Benji was in the hospital, and Benji in turn had given it to Max. A book about an artist finding her vision, Benji explained, for an artist about to find his vision. Max had read it twice, devoured it on the plane ride home, committed passages to memory, so the words he wanted now, the sweet and pitiful lament of Mrs. Ramsay as her own party came to an end, came readily to hand.

His family moved around him, clicking off lamps, gathering bags from the front hall, the loud, communal march up the stairs. Max didn't move, trying to make out the sound that played below the roiling surface of their laughter. He lay as still as he could, trying to hear it. A few scattered notes. At first, he thought he recognized it as something they had sung earlier that evening, a snippet of Paul's tribute to Billie Holiday twisted into another shape, but the closer he listened, the more certain he was that the notes were new. The notes were his. He didn't know them. He wasn't hearing them again. They'd scattered through his mind like startled birds as he crunched over the frosted grass and now, finally—thanks to Cat's passing observation, thanks to his memory of Mrs. Ramsay bidding the night good night—they shaped themselves into a formation that sang out to him as it moved across the blank calm of the room. The phrase came to him for the first time, yet it was instantly familiar. It repeated itself. It formed like a silver-crested wave, swelling, swelling, before it folded in on itself and shattered, as on rocks, into silence. It was water moving against the shore. He kept his eyes closed and played the notes again. They were louder, more confident, drowning out the sound of footsteps overhead, over Benji's stage-whispered promise to see them all in the morning, over Claudia (still in the room) softly saying his name. Here, at last, she was. Too late. At least for the night, too late. He pretended she wasn't there.

"Max," she said, approaching, closer, closer, until he could smell the toothpaste on her breath. She touched his arm with the lightest touch. "Max?"

The wave crashed and ended, not with silence this time, but with another sequence. The sound twisted and surged and leapt. Before him, Max saw a light switch on in the darkness, a lighthouse whose beam illuminated a boy cutting images from an illustrated magazine. It was James. The notes were James, springing sprightly, the bounding leap he would make if only he could get to the lighthouse. If only the weather were fine. If only—and here the theme was interrupted by a dark, heavy throb of Mr. Ramsay's oppressive paternal shadow passing by.

Max heard the opening pages of the book. He was rewriting the opening pages of the book, translating them into the language of percussion and woodwinds and strings. He had to get up. He had to write it down. He had to be still so Claudia wouldn't disturb him, because Claudia would be there tomorrow and the music, perhaps, would not. He felt the blanket being tucked more tightly around his chin, the sound of her giving up and slowly climbing the stairs. He ordered his body off the couch. He had to write this down. How would he remember if he didn't write it down? But his muscles stayed beyond him. He called to her then, to Claudia, to Navi, but no voice came. *I have to write it down,* he cried as the song sank back into nothing. The silence of the house deafened him. He listened for the music's return. *I have to begin.*

The Sibyl at Cumae
for Henry

I said yes
to it and now it spites me.
Life! One year for every crumb
of sand on the beach. You
show me how to build castles
so I can spend the ages sweeping them out.

My cake is marble, shawled
with cobwebs, candlelit like a nebula.
Not even your song can make me eat it.
The knifepoints of flame, hammered long
by the owled night, are enough
to dress and dry a rack of meat.

I will never be young again.
I don't think I ever was.
Melt the silicate and wrap it round my husk.
I will fit. I grow smaller every year. I
belong on the shelf next to the lilac seeds,
a hull to rattle, a voice in a jar.

IO.

From: Claudia Fisher
Sent: November 24, 2012
To: Max Davis
Subject:

Dear Max:

Nothing I've said to you seems the right thing to say. Maybe there is no right thing. Or maybe there is, and here, hiding behind a computer screen, is the only way I can say it. I've started this message a hundred times and each time I delete it, thinking of another place to start. Maybe if I start here I'll find the way. But this is me starting over, and look where I am.

My only words to you cannot be I'm sorry. I'm sorry is another wall to hide behind, and I've hidden enough in my life. When it comes to you and me, I did what I did because I thought it was right. I still think it was right. No matter how much hurt it caused. No matter how much of a mess I've made, I can see worse pain, a bigger mess with such clarity that my heart skips.

I've failed people I care about. You most of all. And yes, I do care. And yes, I could have failed you more. You tell me that you would have taken your chances. I won't pretend to know your life with the Davises, but I look at you and do not see their fuck-ups, to borrow your phrase. You are a caring young man with a loving heart. You impress me deeply. There is your talent, but that is what the world sees. That's not what I'm talking about. Your arms have been open so wide to me when I know I do not deserve it.

Part of me wishes you were more angry. I might know what to do with that. But your love? Love, some-times, is the hardest to handle. It can bend us with its weight. I see giving you up through my mother's eyes, and I have a hard time seeing my love in it. Even the words, her words: "giving you up." In my mind, that's not what I did. In my mind, I was protecting you. Safeguarding you. Loving you. And not only you, if I'm being honest, but me and Nick too. None of which makes me a hero. None of which, I hope, makes me a villain either. Do I regret? Yes. Somehow know-ing that I did the right thing and feeling regret do not cancel each other out. Does any of this make sense? I feel like I've said nothing using all these words. They are a struggle to send.

Claudia

From: Max Davis
Sent: November 24, 2012
To: Claudia Fisher
Subject: Re:

Claudia—

I'm the age you were when you had me. If I had a kid today, what kind of parent would I be? Not a very good one, I guess. Navi & I talk about kids, but my dreams don't have a baby in them, not yet, just like your dreams didn't have a baby in them. Why would I blame you for that? I can't say why did you choose your work over me when work is all I know. I try to understand. Maybe that's why I'm not more angry. But I am angry. But I spent so much of my life feeling that way about everything —you & Amanda & being ground down by music when music was the one thing I could count on to lift me up. Anger isn't what I want anymore. Plus, it's harder to be angry when you understand. The more you look at a person, the more you understand them. Maybe I should be more understanding with my parents. What did they ever do to me that was so wrong? You said you were sure they did the best they could. Just like you did the best you could. But isn't that what everybody says? Except the ones putting cigarettes out on their kids' arms, but even they probably say they're doing the best they can, which only means that most people's best isn't good enough. I'm not talking about you or Amanda specifically. I'm just saying. Do you know Philip Larkin? He's a poet my boyfriend before Arnav introduced me to & he has this poem about how your parents fuck you up without even trying. Like it's a contract or something you sign when you have a baby, saying you're cool with basically wrecking another human being for life. I guess that's what therapy's for. Lol. Therapy & drugs & not the fun kind but the ones that screw with your mind until you can't think straight. Sounds like I'm screwed either way. But I'm glad to hear that's not the impression I make. I try to be a good person.

Max

From: Claudia Fisher
Sent: November 27, 2012
To: Max Davis
Subject: Re: Re:

Max:

Being a good person isn't easy. There are days it feels like a twenty-four-hour job. I wonder if work gets in the way of that. Of being good. For me. I think of Frank Lloyd Wright and Corbusier and Philip Johnson. Two philanderers. One Nazi sympathizer. Not the finest men you'd ever meet, but then you look at the work. Johnson atoned for his anti-Semitism, but even if he hadn't, who would remember it in the shadow of his Glass House, the Kunsthalle Bielefeld? They will stand longer than his stupidity. Not that adultery and bad politics are the province of men. Women, too, make terrible mistakes, but it's different for women. Men can have it all. Work. Love. Family. Or, if they can't, we forgive them the sins they commit while trying. The man can be flawed so long as the work is good. But women, we still expect to choose.

I sound like I'm getting ready to teach a gender studies seminar. When what I want to say is that I don't doubt your goodness. You have been kind and incredibly patient. And then there's *your* work. I have to trust what others say as I'm a complete idiot when it comes to music. Oliver has been tutoring me, though. Last night we listened to your recording of Philip Glass. Oliver says you capture the lyricism of Rostropovich. I wish I knew what he meant. Give me time. I'm a quick learner.

Claudia

P.S. I'm not comparing my work to Wright et al. So you know.

From: Max Davis
Sent: November 28, 2012
To: Claudia Fisher
Subject: Do you think . . .

. . . leaving our Subject lines blank means we have nothing to say?

It's officially been a week—8 days actually—since we met. Happy anniversary! Do you think it's odd that we had so little to say in person, but here we are talking like this on e-mail? Do you find it easier that way? I'm not complaining. I think I find it easier too. I'm not a huge fan of the phone. I hardly ever call people because I'm afraid I'm disturbing them & I NEVER leave voice mails because I hate the way my voice sounds. I'm text & e-mail all the way. I guess there are some relationships that work better when there's some sort of distance built into them. Speaking of work . . . I've been writing. Like a madman actually. I have this idea for an opera & now that I've started, my pen is moving faster than my mind. I'm having trouble keeping up. I feel like I'm coming out of a fog & I'm finally able to do the work I want to do. Amanda told me that I'd miss playing within a week of giving it up. Wrong. She says I'm turning my back on the audience that's been so good to me. I don't think I'm doing that, but I don't want to die knowing that all I did in life was play other people's music. I hate the idea of performing these days & recording is even worse. At least performances are honest. It's me, on stage, giving everything I've got. If I'm great, I'm grateful. If I suck, I'm happy I didn't buy a ticket. Lol. Playing is a moment between me & the conductor & the audience, you know? We come together to create this thing, something that's as alive as we are for the time it takes to make it & if I've done my job, the music doesn't die when the performance is over. It's gone. Like the moment, it can never come back, but it lives on in the people who heard it take shape. Without them, it's not music. It's practice. So they carry it with them as much as I carry it with me. It's funny you mention Rostropovich because he visited me when I was 12 & played for me in my dining room—like, who the fuck am I?!?—& that moment shaped the way I hear Bach's fourth suite. Forever. (Though tell Oliver I'm not him. I'm me!) Recording is a whole other story. When you're a musician, most people think that's your legacy, the record of your greatest achievements, but nope, I don't agree. You're in a studio for days on end, doing take after take after take, until a sound engineer steps in & stitches it all together like this quilt of the best parts & leaves you with a masterpiece you never actually played. It's a lie. If I'm going to be known, I'd rather have it be for the music I write than for the music I only sort of played.

M.

P.S. You're right not to compare yourself to FLW & company. Not because your work isn't as good, which I think is what you meant, but because your work is yours. Think Beethoven when he said, "There are & will be a thousand princes, but there is only one Beethoven."

From: Claudia Fisher
Sent: December 1, 2012
To: Max Davis
Subject: Something to say

M:

Happy anniversary to you too! May there be many more. And no, not always at such a distance.

I'm happy to hear work is going so well. What is the opera about? I know from my father that writing can feel a bit like making a soufflé, and though it's a different type of writing I imagine the same must hold true: the more noise you make about it, the more likely it is to fall.

I've been a bit buried myself. The end of the semester approaches and I'm readying to grade 30 papers about eco-responsible architecture. I just final- ized the designs for a space I've been working on, and I've started sketches for Nick's site at Compton's

Mound, which he tells me he took you to see. When is the next time you'll be in Alluvia? I know that Benji and my mother love your visits. I'm not sure when I'll be back. I've already been home more this year than in the previous two combined. Not under the best circumstances. I miss my father. I miss my mother, too, though she'd never believe I told you so. My father's illness has ruined him, but it's also ruined her in many ways. I don't think that had to be the case. If only she cared for herself as much as she cared for him.

It's odd that I still refer to my parents' house as "home" when I've lived away from them longer than I lived with them. Oliver and I rotate the holidays with our families, and this year we spend Christmas with his parents in Vermont. They have a lovely place in the mountains outside of Burlington, though whenever I stay anyplace more rural than 14th Street my fantasies about ax murderers kick in. I'll leave you, for now, with that.

C.

P.S. I wasn't exactly putting myself down by putting myself in the same sentence as FLW. I'm proud of my work. Though doesn't every artist compare herself to those who precede her? That seems inevitable. Besides, I don't feel bad that I'm not FLW or Eileen Gray or whoever. Benji is more the one who fears that History is going to sweep him under the rug. Not me so much. I understand his hunger for recognition. But I've never wanted it in the same way.

From: Max Davis
Sent: December 3, 2012
To: Claudia Fisher
Subject: Soufflé's in the oven

C—

Do you think it's odd how often I've been back to
Alluvia since September? My mom thinks it's way too
much. I know this because she & I have started talking again. I feel like we're hashing out the Treaty of
Versailles, taking it slow, but she's trying. Who knows?
I've spent most of the fall with Navi in Dallas, but
when I get homesick—or just sick of him, lol—I
seem to end up with your family. My family, too, I
guess I should say. I wish I'd known your dad before
he got sick. Most of the time he thinks I'm Benji,
which I don't mind but I think Benji does. Evelyn
offers me the big bedroom on the third floor, but I
prefer to stay in Henry's study & even with all the
stuff that's happening with your dad, it feels peace-
ful to me there. I get a glimpse of him. For whatever
reason, I work better there than anywhere else, which
makes me think maybe he left the place charmed.
Then there's Nick. He's so sweet & available. He offers
to fly me up pretty much every weekend like I'm in
college & have no money, but he always wants to do
these father/son things that I'm not sure actual fathers
& sons do—fishing, football. Last time he asked if I
wanted a PlayStation. It's like he has this checklist that
we're working our way through. He even mentioned
camping—talk about ax murderers!—but don't say
anything. I'm not sure he'd know I'm joking. Can I

ask you something? What's the deal with you two? You can tell me to mind my own business. Navi's always telling me how nosy I am. He says if I didn't stick my nose in other people's shit, I'd have nothing to smell. Except he doesn't say shit, because he's Navi.

    M.

From: Max Davis
Sent: December 9, 2012
To: Claudia Fisher
Subject: Did I offend?

Claudia:

Haven't heard from you in a while, so I wanted to check in. I know you're super busy, so don't feel like you have to write back, but I'm afraid I may have pissed you off with my last message. Forget I asked about you & Nick. It really is none of my business.

    Still your friend,

    Max

From: Claudia Fisher
Sent: December 10, 2012
To: Max Davis
Subject: Honeybear:

A brief story: my father, as I'm guessing you've gathered from what Benji has told you, could be—let's say—cantankerous. Not all the time. But he *was* a man used to having his way, and he didn't like more people than he did because he thought most of them were silly and inconsequential and getting in the way.

Those are his words, and it's always astounded me that a man who wrote with such understanding would ever think of anyone as inconsequential. In other words, it was difficult to imagine him calling anyone "honeybear." But once in a while, when he was feeling tender (or maybe when he was simply tired and his defenses were down) you'd hear him come out with it. I got a C in algebra. Benji fell off his bike. Actually, I think he said it more often to Benji, though Benji would never admit to that. It adds too much shading to the stick monster he's made Daddy out to be. But that's a story for another day. I tell you all of this to say that I am my father's daughter and that the word "honeybear" comes no easier to me than it did to him. I think I've said it one time, to Oliver, maybe, after he stubbed his toe. So know that you didn't piss me off. I have, in fact, been busy. (And I'm only half-way through those exams!) But that's no excuse to go MIA. I'll do better.

XO,

C.

From: Max Davis
Sent: December 13, 2012
To: Claudia Fisher
Subject: Save me!

Navi is working all this week because the DSO is doing a 5-day marathon of Handel's *Messiah*. Blah. So rather than having the apartment to myself all day & really getting down to work, I decided to spend the week visiting my parents. Seal the peace deal, I thought. It's been one day! One day & I've pulled half my hair out. Give her a topic, any topic, it's like her arrows are aimed at it before I open my mouth. I'm living in Dallas. I'm living with Navi. I'm gay. I'm broke (which, by the way, I'm not). I'm a walking target. Why didn't I go to Alluvia? Or to visit you? It's my own fault for coming here. I've made my bed, now I pluck myself bald in it. Hope the papers are off your desk—or on their way . . .

    Love,

    Max

From: Claudia Fisher
Sent: December 16, 2012
To: Max Davis
Subject: It's complicated

Max:

I never did answer your question about Nick. You probably thought not answering was my answer. If I'm going to be honest with you—and I want to be honest with you—I'll say that things between Nick and me are complicated. I know better than to burden you with too many details. Barriers exist between parents and their children—at least they should—and though I can't claim I know where they are, I do know that I want to respect them. Nick is my client. He's paying me to do a job for him. But Nick was my first love. We were together for 7 years, which at the time seemed like forever. But forever means one thing when you're 15, and something else entirely when you're 42. For all I know Nick's already told you this and more while you were out riding ATVs . . . the birds and the bees talk must be on the checklist.

    Claudia

From: Max Davis
Sent: December 18, 2012
To: Claudia Fisher
Subject: Do you realize . . .

. . . in your last message you referred to yourself as my parent for the first time? I'm writing from Plano, Texas. Navi & I decided to make a quick visit to his parents, who just moved back to the States to be closer to him. They're good parents. Plano has one of the largest populations of Indians in the country, though don't ask me why they picked Plano. I've seen more of Texas than I ever wanted to. I tell Navi why don't we pack up & go to New York. We could have an apartment there & I could write & we'd be close to so much music. Think of the music! It would be a world better than being stuck in Dallas, but then he says that's fine for me, but what would he do, he can't transfer into the philharmonic like he's switching offices at AT&T. I've nearly finished the first act of my opera—I told you I was moving fast. I worry maybe too fast, but I'm not about to stop to see if I'm right. Another thing Beethoven said: "Don't only practice your art, but force your way into its secrets." All I want to do is wall up with a case of Red Bull & write, write, write—you know that feeling when everything & everyone that's not your work is a bother? But you can't say fuck off, especially at Xmas, no matter how much you want to. Oh & before I forget, don't worry about Nick—it's too cold to ride ATVs & he doesn't really talk about you. Much.

    Your son,

    Max

From: Claudia Fisher

Sent: December 20, 2012

To: Max Davis

Subject: Keep working!

Max:

That's too bad about Plano. But I know what you mean. We're at Oliver's parents, and, yes, I understand the compulsion to tell them all to fuck off so I can get back to my work. The thing is they absolutely would fuck off if I told them to. Oliver's not exactly a doormat, but if you mistake him for one, sometimes you don't have to look far to see where he gets it from. His parents are warm, harmless people, but what does it say when the nicest thing you can say about someone is that she's harmless? They treat me like I'm queen of the castle, but even the queen gets sick of being the queen.

    I'm sorry this is so short today. But the troops are off shopping and I have a rare moment to work uninterrupted. I don't have a crystal ball, but I can see a pair of flannel pajamas in my future.

    XO,

    Claudia

From: Max Davis
Sent: December 22, 2012
To: Claudia Fisher
Subject: Alive in VT?

Happy (almost) Xmas to you & Oliver & Mr. & Mrs.
Harmless. I talked to Benji yesterday. I'm sure he did,
but did he tell you that he passed up the chance for
an audition? I was, like, what about your career & he
said what career? Do you think he's okay? He's going
to stay with Cat & help her with her teaching. I probably shouldn't say it, but I have this fantasy that one
day you & Benji & I will live in NYC together. Don't
worry. Not in the same apartment. Lol.

From: Claudia Davis
Sent: December 25, 2012
To: Max Davis
Subject: Merry, merry

Here I am—alive—in my Land's End pajamas, thinking of you. Merry, merry, sweet boy. And a wonderful
new year.

She's lovely, Jane says. Her father was always good to me. George. He paid twice what other contractors were willing to for the same work. Gave me a place to stay. All I had to do, he used to tell me, is dedicate a novel to him. A single star, livid as a shard of glass, bites down as Jane and I stroll across the grass. It is Jane's first night in the little apartment on the side of the garage. I take her hand and kiss it. He was a little conservative, though. He wouldn't have liked us "living in sin" in his own backyard. He wouldn't have liked it? Jane laughs. What about her? Evelyn? I ask what she means. What happened to the seer of everything? Jane asks. She takes her hand back and, though it is a warm July night, hugs herself as if she has a chill. I never said I was the seer of everything. You are. A writer like you sees everything. Everything except this. Jesus, Henry, the girl's in love. Girl? She's ten years older than you. That's beside the point. She barely looks at me, I say. And what does that prove? She'd do anything you asked her. I don't plan on asking for anything, except maybe supper from time to time, the woman knows how to cook. I'm serious, Jane says, staring up at the star. You have to be careful with people who can't say no. You should never ask too much.

II.

B ut what does he want?" Benji asked. He slung an elbow over the back of his seat and looked expectantly at the ball-capped boy slouched in the row of seats behind him. Brandon, who had received his learner's permit the week before, was, by his own admission, prone to taking an occasional detour from considering Macbeth's desires in order to imagine a well-plotted course over country roads in his father's Celica. He stared dreamily at the front of the auditorium, but his focus seemed farther off than Cat, who sat cross-legged under the floodlights of the stage, or any of the eleven cast members who surrounded her. Benji waved a hand in front of Brandon's eyes, a flagman at the finish line effectively bringing the race to an end.

"Yo, Mario Andretti. Where'd you go?"

"Have you ever spun donuts?"

"Your father's going to want you to parallel park before he teaches you to spin donuts."

A sheepish, "Right."

"So tell me: What does he want?"

"He wants to be king."

"Is that all?"

Brandon's heavy-lidded blue eyes narrowed as they met Benji's. He was a smart kid, but he didn't appreciate trick questions. If a trick question it was. "That's pretty much what he wants."

"But if being king were all he wanted, the play would be over in act three, wouldn't it?"

This line of argument piqued the boy's interest. He took in Alluvia High's musty little auditorium, with a stage too small to accommodate its marching band, and closed his eyes, considering the character he'd been charged with breathing life into. Benji and Cat had gone so far as to suggest that everyone treat his or her character, from the bloody but guilt-wracked queen to poor, taciturn Fleance, like a body he or she'd discovered on the beach. Limp. Lifeless. What did the body need to be revived?

On the first day of rehearsals, Ashley DiPetro, the mayor's daughter, whose general sense of entitlement Cat believed would serve her well as Lady Macbeth, raised her hand and, as if pointing out for the benefit of everyone that she, Ashley DiPetro, was sitting on a floor in a room in Alluvia High School in Alluvia, New York, in the United States of America in the Western Hemisphere of the planet Earth, stated the obvious: "Um. The script? You say the words in the script?" The fact that her tone bent her sentences into questions did nothing to diminish her confidence in them as answers.

"But reviving a character from the page," Cat explained, "isn't about recitation. It's about *resuscitation*." The fourteen students looked at her as if she'd grown a second head, but eleven stalwarts returned the next day (undeterred by the doubts that Ashley voiced on the way out of the auditorium: "They're not even real teachers. They're like my grandmother teaching prisoners how to read. They're not even being paid!"), and it was with these eleven that Cat and Benji began to unpack the "Scottish play."

Those first weeks of rehearsal were a time of challenge and (unexpected) joy for Benji. At first, he thought he'd made a mistake rejecting his agent's plea to take an audition for a new corticosteroid—a *national* commercial, she stressed, that could lead to bigger, better things—but pretending he had plaque psoriasis, much to his surprise, didn't outweigh his desire to be with Cat or to help her where she needed help, even if it involved a dozen teens who sometimes made him itch as badly as the fake ailment he'd turned down. Not knowing how to redirect their more annoying habits, Benji allowed the trains of their pubescent scandals, their brittle and silly love affairs, to barrel through the middle of their two-hour rehearsals. He tolerated their tears, their shrill and hormonal voices, their labored decisions over the best way to respond to an unfollowed friend's libelous tweets. He bit his tongue against the profanities he sometimes longed to hurl at them. He expected all of this, the mortification, the grandstanding, the giggling, the endless interruptions for *selfies*! What he hadn't foreseen was the satisfaction, an unheralded but trumpeting sense of accomplishment that came, say, when Josh Cooper's drunken Porter, taking Benji's note, stumbled onstage with his pants around his ankles. *#whowouldhaveguessedit?*

Agreeing to join Cat in the enterprise that she and the superintendent of schools had hatched at a protest at Compton's Mound, Benji quickly found himself moving from observer to line reader to mentor. Once he and Cat had walked the cast through the basic fundamentals of plot, after they relaxed into a drum circle where they sat pounding out the complexities of the script, Benji found himself accompanying Brandon Wright on strolls to the back of the auditorium, pacing up and down the deserted rows like counsel to the ambitious young thane.

Brandon's eyes, despite the heavy lids that always made them appear half closed, possessed an electrifying spark. At first glance he seemed little more than a solid B student, a second-string tight end for the Alluvia Warriors, an avid builder of model planes from World War II, who, outside of drama club, lived as a happy (or at least untormented) loner. But Brandon liked what he liked and took an exhilarating passion in it. His position on the football team earned him the currency a boy needed in a small-minded town to take up theater without being teased to death about it. He wasn't prone to bullying or easily swept away by the currents of adolescent fads. He didn't listen to Pitbull or Lil Wayne or really care for *Street Fighter IV*. In some respects, his classmates found him hopelessly out of touch. Who else but Brandon Wright came away from Mrs. Martin's ninth-grade English class actually liking Shakespeare?

"Think about the witches," Benji said. Lately, he found himself bringing the boy to the cave where the weird sisters brewed their brew, unveiling their apparitions, in the hopes that there, in the cauldron's steam, Brandon would see what made the brutal Scot's heart beat. "What do they show him?"

Brandon named the rival Macduff. And the bloody child. And the child holding the tree.

"Is he worried about Macduff?" Benji asked, taking them one at a time.

"Not really." Brandon ripped his cap from his head, as if it were a hindrance to thinking, and put it on his knee. "He just kills him."

"Then what does he see?"

Brandon described the next prophecies, the visions that Macbeth dismisses as impossibilities that circle back in the final act like snakes to deliver their deadly stings. This was where the boy got caught, where he, like most of the audience, became too entangled in Macbeth's comeuppance, in the satisfying fall of a rabid king. Macduff was *not* of woman born, Birnam Wood *did* march to Dunsinane, but Macbeth was undone by a desire that curled inside the heart of almost every man.

"What else does he see?"

The kings. Brandon always forgot the kings. Benji gave the boy his script and, tap, tap, tapping his finger on the page, told him to read. When the boy finished, Benji pointed down the aisle, as if the descendants of Banquo stood there in a line, gold-bound brows and treble scepters glinting terrifically in the light. *What, will the line stretch out to the crack of doom?*

Brandon pulled his hair back in studied thought, exposing a crop of small pink pimples on his forehead, while Benji, taking back the script, nudged him along. "Who are they?"

"Kings," Brandon answered.

"Past kings?"

"Future kings."

"'For the blood-boltered Banquo smiles upon me,'" Benji read, "'and points at them for his.' They're the children of Banquo. The sons of Banquo's sons. Macbeth has no sons. So who is going to survive?"

Behind them, Cat walked the three witches through the brewing of their potion, encouraging them not to cackle, to deliver the lines any way they wanted except with that awful, overused, Wicked Witch of the West cackle, bidding them softer rather than louder, until the room hissed with their chilling intent. Benji turned for a moment to watch her work, to see her dancing round the children who swayed round the pot. He smiled. He said to Brandon, "Did you ever read *Death of a Salesman*?"

"Last semester," answered Brandon, confused by but not averse to a random change of course. "In Ms. Arnold's."

"Ms. Arnold?" Benji's brows rose in amused disbelief. "She's still here?" By *here* he meant alive, though he kept his calculation of her improbable age to himself. "Do you know what Arthur Miller said Willy's masterpiece was?"

"What's this got to do with Macbeth?"

"Trust me."

Brandon guessed. "I don't know. His work?"

"You'd think so, right? But no, it's Biff. It's Willy's son, Biff. That's Willy's masterpiece." Benji remembered reading an interview years ago in which Miller said that his bedraggled salesman was writing his name in a cake of ice on a hot day. Not in stone, but in melting ice. Benji offered the thought to Brandon, but the boy was barely sixteen: he hadn't begun to worry whether monuments would be erected to him or if they'd stand or fall in the heat of the rising sun; he wasn't considering his own mortality or totaling the ledger that sooner or later every man felt tempted to total—the work he'd done, the children he'd fathered, all that he would leave behind—and coming up with zero. Benji said, "Do you know what I mean?"

Brandon gave a polite but half-hearted nod. Cat had released the other students for a ten-minute break, and Brandon, looking like a caged bird that watched his brothers and sisters fly free, marked their escape, rebel smokers filing out the stage door into the frosty March dusk, everyone else skipping off to the vending machines singing, *Fair is foul, and foul is fair.* Benji heard the rehearsal spiraling apart, the noise dissipating into the auditorium's eerie, canister-lit silence, but he couldn't let Brandon go. He didn't want to be alone with his ledger, with the roundly melancholy thoughts that waited for him at the bottom of so many columns. Zero, zero, zero.

One day he would have to accept it: he wasn't a king or a father to them. He wasn't Henry, whose eight published books already proved more resilient than their author. He wasn't Max, with his trumpeted recordings of Haydn and Bach and the finished first act of a promising new opera. He certainly wasn't Cat, who had no desire to live life on a throne of celebrity and acclaim, who seemed perfectly happy saving the graves of a few forgotten soldiers and directing a nothing school play that no one—no one, Benji couldn't help think, who mattered—would see. He shouldn't call it nothing; it wasn't nothing. After all, people who had neither fame nor recognition, men and women who made their sixty-, seventy-, eighty-year journeys from cradle to grave without rousing the attention of anyone but the few equally anonymous souls who marched by their side, filled the earth. But the notion of a common lot, Cat's annoying habit of reminding him that the good of the world depended on those who "lived faithfully a hidden life, and rest in unvisited tombs," offered Benji little comfort. Why couldn't he hold on to the thought that what he was doing here, now, with Cat and these kids, counted for something? It mattered. He tried to believe, even in some small way, that it mattered. But sooner or later, every happy bubble popped on the sharp, bristling quills of doubts that he should (at this very minute) be shilling a new topical cream for treating red patches of dead skin. He wanted more. Even if he tallied his involvement in the play as a positive, the new sum didn't erase the sadness that came from the old equations or the resentment Benji felt at having to feel that sadness alone. Brandon, who didn't have the first clue how or why they'd leapt from Scottish king to Brooklyn salesman, would leave Benji sitting with his failures by himself. Which was exactly what Benji couldn't let him do.

Benji picked up his script. He wanted—part of him needed—Brandon to see Macbeth's utterly understandable wish to be the spring from which his name would forever flow into the future. It was, of course, why the Scot lashed out so savagely at Macduff's children, but paradoxically, if you thought about it, it was also what saved Macbeth from being the simple monster everyone made him out to be. It's what made him human, Benji scanned the page for proof he could pull from it. He didn't want to live a hidden life. He didn't want to lie in an unvisited tomb. He hated to think that his only route away from such a fate involved an ointment called Humira. But before he could find a thread that his hostage might pick up and follow, Cat snuck up behind him. She unfolded a squeaky seat and kneeled facing the two of them.

"Guys," she said, "it isn't work camp. Take a break."

Brandon jolted to attention in his seat. "Can I, Mr. Fisher?"

Benji looked from his watch to the empty stage and laughed, as if he hadn't noticed the room emptying around them. "Yeah. Sure. Sorry, pal."

With the boy gone, Cat turned Benji's back to her and reached out to knead his neck. In her cowgirl work shirt and torn-at-the-knee jeans, she looked like the women he dated in college, the grunge chicks who swayed to Siouxsie and the Banshees and appreciated a good game of beer pong. Her fingers found a knot of corded muscle and pressed hard against it. "So tense."

Benji winced, grateful for the pain. He turned toward her, took her hand, and pulled her to him. She let her body go limp, leaning over the back of the seat as if she didn't mind him dragging her onto his lap, before she stiffened, snickered, pulled back. "What do you want?" She eyed his crotch openly, expecting to find a visible sign to explain his sudden need to hold her, but no, he wasn't asking for that.

"Come here," he said reassuringly.

Cat hesitated. Hard-ons aside, eleven twittering teenagers were due back at any moment. As she stood, Benji rose to release her hand. A flourish. She might have been his waltz partner, aimed at the end of one row, spinning gracefully into another.

"Come here," he repeated, reaching again for her hand.

She stood before him, slightly remote, until he repeated himself. With that she went, put a hand in his hair, and asked what was wrong. No answer came. What he wanted to say stood in the middle of a maze Benji had entered by way of Macbeth and theater's most fantastic failure of a salesman; it had something to do with his father and nephew, with his mother's disposable paintings and his sister's buildings, which Benji thought of as impermeable to time as the stone and steel that made them; it had something to do with Cat and with Benji himself. He tried pulling a single articulate thought from the ferment of his mind, but whatever he hoped to say about what is bound to last and what is doomed to fade, whatever distinction he meant to make between the two, slipped away. *The very stone one kicks with one's boot will outlast Shakespeare.*

Max, especially, agitated. Much as Benji loved him, he remained a cause of great confusion, at once the sting and the salve. For the kind of acclaim Benji hoped for, the accomplishments that bring us closest to some small reachable realm of immortality, already belonged to Max. What lit up Max's sky like a sun shone in Benji's as a mere star: forever distant, forever remote, a cold knifepoint of light (hardly enough to see by) in the nighttime sky. Funny: though Benji had spent a lifetime following fame, he stood as far away from it now as ever. Only recently, only since Cat and Max had come into his life (bright as beacons in their own right) had that original lodestar begun to fade. It was there, of course. It would always be there. But Benji no longer had to set his course by it, if he didn't want to. There were other destinations now, other ways. He was Max's uncle. He was Cat's lover. Six months ago, these places didn't exist, but suddenly they rose before him like warm, habitable planets in the inhospitable sea of space. They were home. Or becoming home. Some days, Benji wanted to give up trying to grab whatever crude, slippery tool would allow him to carve his name in a block more lasting than Willy's ice and instead do the things he told Cat he'd do as they curled on the couch and opened a second bottle of wine. He would finish his bachelor's degree, get a teaching certificate, join forces with Cat to lead Alluvia's thankless youth to that elevated plane where everyone speaks in iambs.

Benji turned and turned in the maze, but without a string to lead him out of it, all he could do was hold Cat closer. He placed a hand on her belly—a not entirely absent gesture—and thought, *Do I even want kids?* If his sister could turn into a halfway decent parent (or "parental figure"), couldn't he? He said nothing. He felt a wave of melancholy rise through him and crash into Cat, who registered it by clinging to him more tightly.

"What's wrong?" she asked, turning his face to hers so she could see into his eyes.

In their first days together, Benji spent the whole of his time hiding from her. Lying about his injuries and how he sustained them, it turned out, lifted him to new heights as an actor. Daily, he rehearsed a roundelay of depression and self-harm for her, for his doctor, for his sister and parents and Max, for himself, and thought, with more than a little self-satisfaction, that not only was all the world a stage, but that he, Benjamin Fisher—mocked, maligned, underestimated at every turn—was as good as any actor on it.

But time passed, and so, too, did Benji's feelings of fraudulence. The sharp outlines of his own mendacity softened and blurred as he himself began to believe the story he so carefully constructed for others. These days, when he listened to Max describe the harrowing hours leading up to his own hospitalization—testing the shower rod to see if it would hold his weight, cinching the belt around his neck, debating whether or not to answer housekeeping's terribly, miraculously, fatefully timed knock at the door—Benji felt a surge of empathy, of fraternity that nearly made him weep. Walking these last five months in the shoes of a desperate man who stumbled out of a theater one warm August night with every intention of jumping to his death no longer underscored the distance Benji measured between the reality of his experience and his fantastical account of it. It erased it. The mighty engine of the brain burned through his fabrications and falsehoods as though they were fuel and, by some marvelous neurometabolic process, produced a conviction with all the weight and carriage of unshakeable truth: we come to believe that Mother washed our mouths out with soap even when she wasn't there to hear us swear. To Benji's mind, he was no longer lying. No longer acting. He'd shown Cat a truth, and Cat stayed. He held Cat on his lap. She couldn't have been closer. And yet she hadn't the first clue that Benji wandered so much of the time wondering at his own desires, asking if he was satisfied, fearful that all they were in the process of building wasn't nearly enough.

"I—" he said, having no words to follow that one, when a swarm of freshly caffeinated students interrupted him. They could be such a nuisance, these kids, and, if he were being completely honest, such a relief. Jason Carmichael, the oldest and easily the most childish member of the cast, led the others in an uproarious catcall, a construction worker's whistle that echoed through the room. *First comes love, then comes marriage.* Both Cat and Benji hated him.

Cat stood, slow to let go of Benji's hand but ready to face her hecklers—especially Jason, her clueless King Duncan, on whom she lowered a sublimely regal stare. It took Benji a moment, but soon he joined her. Grabbing on to the seat in front of him, he stood, a nearly drowned body getting up on his feet, coming back to himself and delivering the only words he could possibly speak. "Okay, you clowns. Back to work."

Welcome to the governor's suite, George says. The rooms are stuffy and small, but nothing an open window won't fix. It's not the most deluxe accommodation, but it's yours if you want it. Thanks, Mr. Newland. And I'll pay whatever— He cuts me off with a sour face. Don't worry about that. I can keep a few dollars out of your pay, if it comes to that. But things aren't so bad yet. He looks at my little pile of things. That's all you've got? I travel light, sir. George, he says. A suitcase and a typewriter. And I'll bet the suitcase is filled with books, he says. Half filled, I laugh. Well, you won't need a suit for the work you'll be doing for me. He looks at my T-shirt and dungarees. Suppose what you've got on is just fine. But if you need something to wear to church. I don't tell him I don't go to church. If you need something for church, there's plenty at the back of my closet. No need, sir. He gives me a look. George. George, you've already done too much. In a world as mean as this one, he says philosophically, is there such a thing? Besides, no great kindness in giving a man a suit you don't wear. There's a rap at the door, and a woman comes in. She has gray eyes and smiles shyly. She puts a basket of sheets and blankets down on the floor. Her skirt whispers as she stands. Henry Fisher, George says, my daughter, Evelyn. She offers me her hand. Evie, you go on up and grab Henry here one of my old suits. Something he'll get a lot of wear out of. Black or blue. Yes, Daddy. George,

I try, but Evelyn breaks in. She is her father's daughter. It's no trouble, she says, meaning this to be the end of the conversation. No trouble at all.

12.

Since Oliver left, Claudia couldn't move fast enough. She woke an hour later than usual simply to drain the morning of its leisurely pace and stayed in her office, drafting plans for Compton's Mound over a carton of Chinese takeout, until she could barely keep her eyes open. Racing between the coffeepot and the shower, between the front door and the bed saved her from considering the giant hole in the closet where Oliver's stuff used to be. Or the beat-up Eames chair. Or the rug they'd gotten on that trip to Nepal. Or the gritty, black-and-white photo—in Claudia's opinion, his best—of a young Dominican boy leaping with balletic grace into the summery spray of an open hydrant. These newly bare places stressed her like thin spots on the ice: if she didn't skate over them as quickly as possible, she feared she'd fall in.

She had nobody to blame but herself. Making a monthly trek north to see Nick about "work," stealing an afternoon here or there to meet for "drinks" at the Bowery Hotel—all under the auspices of developing a hundred acres of land that weren't trivial so much as tangential—this was crime enough. But leaving evidence of their trysts on her phone, there, on the bedside table, where Oliver could do nothing but find it—how could she forgive herself that? She wanted to be caught—she accepted that—but she couldn't have devised a more cruel or cowardly way of announcing her betrayal than to let him stumble upon the photos that she and Nick exchanged with the hormonal indiscretion of the millennials she taught. Her breast here. His cock there. Some employing a well-draped sheet to artistic effect. Some with all the pretense of amateur porn.

Guilt bit into her viciously, but probably not as viciously as it should. Its grip lacked that grab-you-by-the-throat-and-shake-you-till-you're-dead quality of a pit bull attack, leaving her in the clutches of something closer to a cocker spaniel: pain latched on, but eventually, she knew, she'd shake it off. She'd live. Dare she think it: she'd thrive. Whenever her mind drifted toward the calm blue waters of freedom, of satisfaction, of newly refurbished love and the late-blooming family she always considered herself too ambivalent to embrace, Claudia felt a sudden stab of happiness against which she once thought herself impenetrable.

Nick, with no grander gesture than taking her hand, buttressed her change of mind. When she warned him that she'd sooner move to Staten Island than Alluvia, he replied that certain people depended on distance for the closeness in their relationships. She'd heard that somewhere before. But couldn't say whether it was true; for there was more than one type of distance, and Claudia charted figurative miles as well as literal ones. She and Oliver had lived in the same 1,200 square feet for the last ten years, and yet on some very real level their love seemed transatlantic: Oliver on one shore, she on the other. Occasionally they met for happy and passionate reunions, but those times of togetherness were brief and separated (at least for Claudia) by long weeks of ambivalence and abstemiousness and anemic wants that Oliver decided to accept. She withheld sex. She blunted her affections. He sat like a dog at the table, waiting for scraps; they lived as if this was the way life should be. But with the reappearance of Nick and their nomadic son, Claudia's compulsion for this sort of emotional distance collapsed under the weight of desires she used to think herself too evolved or too philosophically sophisticated to feel. She loved Nick. She loved Max. She wanted them. She wanted them near.

She graded papers on the train uptown. At 116th Street, she got off and had the handsome Armenian from the corner cart refill her thermos with strong black coffee before hurrying up Broadway to the main gates. In April, Barnard's campus radiated like a veritable oasis of green, the patina'd statue of the torchbearer, the yellow and green and blue banners flapping along the mullioned face of the library, the lovely expanse of lawn bordered with hedges and trees. As she made her way across the flagstone walk, Claudia took in the magnolia, its riotous blooms of dark and pale pink as beautiful as they were brief, an otherworldly confection balanced against a china-blue sky, whose petals were already letting go, tips curling with brown and wheeling through the air to make a shaggy carpet at the base of the trunk. She considered it for a moment, the sad beauty of the tree that proved if you looked at something long enough, you were bound to see its end in it, coiled, perhaps remote, but there. Amused by her own moroseness, she walked on, slipping into the steel-and-glass wedge named not only for the donor whose millions had made the building possible but also for the virgin goddess of the hunt, the Romans' protector of women. Her office nestled in the architecture department on the fifth floor.

She took the stairs, expecting perhaps to find her favorite grade grubber, the only student who turned Claudia's office hours into an occasion for weekly pilgrimage, who took up residence outside her door like it was the entrance to Lourdes, but Dylan (née Emily) Speck had yet to appear. In his place, sturdy and attractive as some particularly robust weed, stood Jennie Halvorsen, scribbling on a Post-it note she'd stuck to Claudia's door. Claudia, having no idea the frustration that co-chairing a committee with Jennie would cause, had agreed to oversee two other faculty members, a handful of students, and selected staff on the Campus Beautification Council. Because the primary task of the council—reviewing the design and installation of campus way finding—had stretched from a two- to four- to eight-month commitment, Claudia and company had been recruited to offer their opinion on a number of smaller (supposedly simpler) improvements, from the color and weave of rain mats meant to spruce up the lobby of campus buildings to the placement of a tree to commemorate the tenth anniversary of 9/11 (the planting of which now lagged eighteen months behind schedule), jobs that, in Claudia's opinion, required due consideration and a quick rubber stamp of approval, but that, thanks to the likes of Jennie, seemed doomed to languish in a swamp of academic inertia. Claudia had witnessed this phenomenon before. She'd seen the launch of the college's refreshed website, the adoption of its visual identity system, the delivery of stationery and business cards specially designed for faculty (because the suite of materials designed for administrators didn't quite pass muster) derailed by professors whose criticisms flowed as endlessly as the minutia they focused on. Ready with an angry tirade against a "childish" shade of blue or the Oxford comma, one could always rely on a Jennie Halvorsen or Jack Yu or Linda Garcia-Silvestre to steer a project into the bog.

Jennie, hearing the decelerating approach of Claudia's heels, looked up with a sour expression (her default) that immediately turned sweet. Her angular, deeply lined face brightened as she said, "Claudia! I was hoping to catch you."

"Jennie."

"Do you have a second?" she asked, not waiting for an answer but following Claudia into the cool white hush of her glass-fronted office. "I'd like to run something by you before tomorrow's meeting."

Claudia dropped her bag on the floor, shrugged out of her jacket, and, indicating a lime-green plastic chair for Jennie, sat herself.

"It's this tunnel project," Jennie began, digging into the folder in which she collected notes on the photo exhibition to be hung in the underground tunnel that ran from one end of campus to the other and allowed students to attend classes, even during the coldest months, in their pajamas. She pulled a photo from the stack of papers and slid it across Claudia's desk like some ominous classified document. "I think we need to revisit some of these images."

Claudia pried her attention away from Jennie's preferred hairdo, a thin, perpetually damp ponytail that made her look like a woman who'd just been pushed into a pool, and gave the printout a long, quizzical look. She couldn't immediately see why a photo of a slender Asian girl striding across the quad with a college tote bag under her arm had been condemned with a question mark scrawled on one of Jennie's infamous purple Post-its. Perhaps the girl's boots were too militaristic? Her blazer too businesslike? Claudia apologized, opening a desk drawer to find her reading glasses, but Jennie rushed in to provide a clue.

"It's the bag. Look at the bag."

Claudia did.

"It looks like a shopping bag, wouldn't you say?"

"Not really. It looks like a tote. It says Barnard on it."

"If you're looking closely, yes. But most people in a rush see only a bag. A bag that looks very much like a shopping bag, I think. It strikes me as somewhat classist. And, well, frivolous. As if our students came here simply to buy shoes." Jennie, an associate professor in the English department, who had signage consultants tearing their hair out to find a sans serif font with more "oomph," fed herself on lecturing more than debate. Claudia couldn't say how so many of her colleagues, whose minds were supposedly engaged with the highest concerns, with the most sophisticated and enduring questions, came to be so hopelessly humorless and petty. Just as she couldn't say how a woman who dressed in loafish brown flats and lumpy sweater sets felt so comfortable posing as an authority on questions of style, but here Jennie sat, outraged once again, ready to do battle in a cardigan the color of canned peas over the semiotics of a tote bag.

"But students selected these photos," argued Claudia. "It's their campus, Jennie. They should feel invested in the renovations being done on it."

Claudia's mind drifted as Jennie raised the rafters of a rebuttal—*vendability, elasticity, metaphoricalness:* she rattled off these and a half dozen other nominalizations and set to weaving her languorous intellectual web between them. With great effort, as if turning a car without power steering, Jennie drove the conversation toward Marcuse and the dehumanizing effects of capitalism (all from a shopping bag that wasn't one!), when out of the corner of her eye, Claudia noticed an approaching shadow slide across the outside wall. At first, she thought the shade moving like a piece of charcoal smudged across paper announced Dylan's approach, but the charcoal turned out not to be her FTM overachiever but her brother.

Benji looked good. Surprisingly good. With his eight-month-old sobriety, his new work going well enough for Alluvia High to consider paying him for it, and his commitment to a four-days-a-week running schedule, he looked fifteen pounds lighter, several years younger, and walked perhaps a little taller. His arrival came a day before she expected it. The visit, something of a mystery, involved a bit of uncharacteristically vague "business" to attend to, after which he'd promised, very uncharacteristically, to take her to dinner.

Not noticing Claudia's distraction or the happy journey her eyes made to Benji on the other side of the door, Jennie kept driving square pegs into round holes, until Claudia raised a hand like a traffic cop and brought her to a stop. "Jennie," she broke in, "I hate to cut you short, but my brother is here." She nodded at Benji, whom Jennie turned to scrutinize with all the enthusiasm of Inspector No. 25 stamping her approval on a cheap pair of underwear. "I need to speak with him."

Jennie rolled over the interruption like a tire hitting a nail. Deflated, she nevertheless insisted on finishing an untenably long sentence as she pulled a sheaf of problematic photos from her folder and pressed them to Claudia's desk. "Give these a look," she said portentously. "Get back to me." When she was gone, Claudia cocked her fingers like a gun and shot herself in the head before gesturing for Benji to come in.

He held open the door with a "hell-o!" so jovial it sounded more like a magician's "ta-da!"

"What are you doing here?" Claudia asked.

"It's nice to see you too."

"I didn't mean that," she said, standing. "I wasn't expecting you until tomorrow."

"I have a surprise that couldn't wait." Sticking his head into the hallway, he motioned his not entirely surprising surprise forward. Max. Claudia stood clear of her desk and held out her arms. The boy paused before moving past his uncle, taking stock of Claudia's reaction with a small, worried smile on his face. He may have triumphed on some of the world's biggest stages, but around Claudia he still tended to move like a kid caught in the spotlight at the high school talent show. Despite the easiness of their e-mails, even with a hug waiting for him, he looked like he wasn't sure how to begin or that he belonged here. Like he might, if he didn't take care, be met with a big, fat boo.

He and Claudia had met several times since January, but each time Claudia sensed the slightest apprehension in him. The visits themselves went fine, better than fine, she thought, with both of them eventually settling into a rhythm and harmony, but neither the rhythm nor the harmony seemed to last, so that seeing Max now left Claudia with the impression that she could register the smallest of irregularities in an otherwise strong pulse, an aberrant heartbeat that was probably nothing to be alarmed about but which alarmed her all the same.

Max stepped up for his hug and then, like a student delivered to the principal's office, slouched into a chair across from her. He'd taken to wearing black nail polish on his thumbs, which he proceeded to peel. Benji sat down next to him.

"This is a nice surprise," Claudia said, returning to her own chair and folding her hands on the repurposed lumber she'd turned into a desk. "Though someone looks unhappy." Could she be more passive? Could she sound more like her mother? *Someone looks unhappy?!*

Benji waited for Max to answer. "Max?" Then, to Claudia: "He's nervous."

"I'm not nervous," said Max petulantly.

"Nervous about what?"

Benji nudged gently with his elbow. "Show her."

With an actorly display of exasperation, Max pulled a battered post-card from the pocket of his hoodie and handed it over. Claudia looked. On the front, the image of a turbulent blue-black sea and, in fat white letters (just the sort in which Jennie might find the "oomph" she'd been looking for), the word LIGHTHOUSE. On the back, an invitation to a workshop concert of Max's opera, tomorrow night at eight. "It isn't a real performance," Max rushed to explain, his fingers moving from his nails to the silver barbell stabbed through his ear. He pulled on it with an intensity that made Claudia squirm. "It's not finished. The first and third parts basically are, but the second is still a sketch. A mess. But I need to hear what it sounds like so I know, you know, what works. I shouldn't have even told you about it." He reached across the desk and snatched the postcard back.

"Stop it," Claudia said. "Can I see, please?"

When Max didn't move, Benji took the card from him. He handed it back to Claudia, who pored over the words more closely.

If she submitted herself to the same eagle-eyed study she made of Max, she could admit that his arrhythmic heart wasn't alone. She recognized that initial pinprick of uneasiness. She felt it too. No matter how close their relationship became, part of her still sat in that Guilderland rest stop, hard and refusing, unable to imagine a *son* entering her life. Like *husband* or *wife*, the word wasn't, even after ten years of marriage, part of her vocabulary. (She referred to Oliver as her "legally wedded boyfriend" until the day he left.) And although she and Nick and Max lived in a very different place now—on banks separated by a stream rather than a wide, uncrossable sea—she still worried whether they could ever completely close the distance between them. Would she ever truly make amends?

She placed the postcard down on her desk and turned to Benji. "Is this the work you had to be in the city for?"

He winked.

"Well, what better reason?"

"What does that mean?" Max asked.

"It means I can't wait to see it."

"There's nothing to see," he said. "I told you: it isn't staged. It's just a concert. It's not even that. It's a workshop. Seriously, neither of you have to come."

"We want to come," Benji and Claudia said in unison.

"What if it sucks?" the boy said miserably.

"Since when has anything you've done sucked?" Benji asked.

"Benji," said Max warningly. He slouched deeper into his chair and attacked his piercing with renewed vigor.

"Are you okay?" Claudia asked. Uncertain whether the ground before her was allied or enemy land, she moved as if she might at any minute snag a tripwire.

"I'm fine."

"Because you seem—"

"What?"

"Not yourself."

"Who do I seem like?"

Claudia took a breath and tried again. "You seem—bothered."

"Bothered?"

"Bothered."

"Don't give me a hard time."

"I'm not."

"You sound like Navi."

"Well, Navi cares about you. So do I."

No response.

Benji extended a hand to rub Max's back. The boy bristled but bore it. "You don't get to sweep onto the scene," he announced hotly, looking not at Claudia but past her, to the immaculate shelves of oversized architecture books, the wall-sized corkboard on which she kept a rotating gallery of interests and inspiration, "and tell me I'm crazy."

"I didn't say crazy," Claudia answered. "Do you hear me? I care."

"We all do," Benji echoed. "And you know it."

Max relented with a sigh. He brushed a hand through the thick fall of his hair and apologized.

"Are you sure you're okay?" Claudia asked.

"You mean am I taking my meds?"

Claudia, suddenly surrounded by tripwires, stopped.

"It's okay. It's what everybody means when they ask if I'm okay." He laughed. "Did Navi call you?"

"No."

"Because that's, like, his favorite song." He strummed an electric air guitar and briefly rocked out. "Are you takin' your meds? Are you takin' your meds?"

"Are you?"

"That's the whole problem. It's why the second act is such a pile of—I can't think right. I can't write right. It's like I'm walking around with a fishbowl over my head. I can't hear the way any of it is supposed to sound."

"You feel that way now," Claudia ventured.

"I feel like that all the time. It's like I'm betraying my work so I can sleep at night. I'm twenty-two. What do I need to sleep for?"

"You feel like you're betraying your work, but you're doing the best thing for it. You're protecting—"

"I got it," Max broke in. "Arnav is a broken record with that shit. No offense."

Claudia smiled.

"Anyway, it doesn't feel like I'm protecting it."

Knowing how hollow any comfort she might speak would sound, she held out her hand to him. It waited in the air, waited the long minute while Max decided whether to take it. Lowering his eyes to his lap, he reached for Claudia's hand and squeezed it.

"Honeybear," she said.

Jane? Yes. Marry me. I'll never marry you. Why not? I'll never marry anyone. Never is a very long time. What do you want to get married for anyway? To dominate and oppress you, naturally. Forever? Forever. Forever is a very long time, but since you put it that way, fine, yes, I'll marry you. Say it then. I just did. Say it again. Is this the beginning of my oppression? Say when, when will you marry me? Tomorrow. You always say tomorrow. And I mean it, but then we wake up, and tomorrow's always today. There are words for girls like you. It's true, and I'll bet you know every one.

13.

It rose before her eyes like a city bearing her name. A vibrant, bustling hub stood at the center, the dense central ring of pedestrian-friendly shops, the drugstore, two restaurants, a community center, a nondenominational meeting house, a playground and swimming pool and gymnasium, from which lines of row houses—livably but not intimidatingly modern—extended outward like the spokes of a wheel. Alluvia had never seen the likes. Claudia imagined the streets humming and alive, neighbors strolling at dusk under the soft lamplight, gathering for concerts on the distant green. The dream cradled her for a moment, shielding her from the angry summer sun, from the irritants of the real bustling crowd building up around her, before the screech of a hot mike grabbed her by the shoulders and shook her hard. She came to in the middle of the desolate field. A thick of dark, bark-stripped trees standing where the village center one day would. A pond in place of her pool. She slapped a mosquito about to land on her neck.

The field at Compton's Mound, surrounded by slumbering backhoes and bulldozers, remained (for the moment) untouched. Nick might have set their heavy jaws in motion long ago, but Goliath of area business though he was, the slightest breeze of negative publicity threatened to topple him faster than David's slingshot. The only indication of the changes to come were the dozen large-scale renderings that stood on easels lining the front of the modest stage. Claudia stood before one of them, holding out her smartphone for a photo she'd been too distracted to snap. She hit the shutter and, with a few efficient stabs at the smooth glass screen, sped the image off to Max. *Wish you were here.* Cat stood a few feet away.

"Thank you," she said.

"For what?"

"For leaving the cemetery where it is."

Cat, who, to Claudia and Nick's great relief, had surrendered her incendiary Save Compton's Mound T-shirt in order to cross enemy lines and participate in the groundbreaking ceremony, lifted her sunglasses to study a rendering of the cemetery. Its shattered graves, enclosed by a refurbished iron fence, gathered around a new marble obelisk, carved with the names of the ancient veterans whose commemoration Cat and her not-always-merry band of protesters had fought so hard to secure.

"I'm glad you're saying a few words," Claudia responded.

"I'm not sure how I feel about the pet cemetery." She looped her arm through Claudia's—lightly, briefly; it was too hot for skin-to-skin—and strolled along to the next set of posters. "But I'll keep that to myself. It's the idea of sharing space with the neighbor's corgi. It doesn't exactly say sacred ground."

There's no such thing, Claudia thought. By this time, after all the spinning the earth had done, there were bones under every last boot sole. The only option for building, for walking, for moving on was to do so on top of them.

"Nick thought the owners might be less creeped out. You know, by the dead in their backyards."

"Compromise."

"Compromise."

Claudia's decision to leave the scraggly little gravesites more or less alone had as much to do with Nick's directives as it did with her budding affection for Benji's future wife. If he asked her, that is. If she said yes. But these things, to Claudia, seemed as inevitable as Benji putting his ducks in a row and asking his sister for help buying the ring.

A month ago, Cat and her sister, Molly, made their annual pilgrimage to the Iowan field where, twenty-four years earlier, American Flight 782 crashed to the ground. There was no finely etched slab to memorialize their parents' names. A couple who, like the 182 others who died that day, had no claim on the land, no say in whether nature would be allowed to erase so completely the tragic end of their tale. In time, the scarred earth did exactly that, reverting back to a lush, silky green sea of corn. If it weren't for the kindness of a sympathetic farmer, who set a giant white boulder in the nearby clearing behind his barn, the site would have gone completely unmarked. No place for the mourners to go. Nowhere to point to and say, *There. It happened there.*

When Cat was a girl, in the first years after the accident, she traveled to Mason City with her aunt and uncle, who provided the three McCarthy children with bouquets of daisies to lay among the carpeting flowers, the plush animals, the candles. Each year, the number of visitors diminished. Each year, the number of offerings thinned. The story worked on Claudia's sympathies, which seemed so much more workable these days. *You're like a brick,* Benji observed, *that's turning back to clay.*

The insult—who wanted to be called a brick or, for that matter, clay?—infuriated her, but the truth was she had so few girlfriends—so few truly close friends, period—that her softening self welcomed the chance for deeper intimacy. Plus, she liked Cat. She didn't spend too much time mulling over why. Perhaps her affections overflowed from her outpouring for Max. Or Nick. Or the bracing sense of accomplishment that came with the largest single project ever entrusted to her. Each had the effect of a stone dropped in water. Each rippled outward into an indecipherable complex of overlapping rings.

"Where's Benji?" Claudia asked.

"He's meeting us. He wanted to run."

"Literally?"

Cat nodded.

"That man has *changed*."

"That's what I try telling my sister."

"She's not having it?"

"Every boyfriend I've ever had she turns into one of her ex-husbands. Benji is Walter."

"And what is Walter's claim to fame?"

"Loser. Run-of-the-mill loser."

"Benji's sober. Going on a year."

"People turn their lives around."

"It does happen."

"She says, 'How do you know a year from now he's not going to be back to his old tricks?' So I have to wait until he's dead to see if he stays sober. Then I can date him?"

A bearded sound tech with a bandana took to the stage and rapped a finger on the microphone. "One, two. Testing, testing."

Cat stopped at a mounted view of the green, the Village hub rising, pale and violet, in the background, while computer-generated residents gathered around picnic baskets, threw Frisbees. "It's Eden."

Claudia laughed. "Secular, maybe."

"I'm not kidding. I would live here."

"In three years you can."

"Three years." Cat spoke the words like a fortune-teller whose vision had disappeared in a confounding mist.

"You say that like it's thirty years away."

"It might as well be. You know where you'll be three years from now?"

"Right here, I hope. Cutting a ribbon. Are you going to be standing beside me?"

Cat flushed. "Who knows? Some of that depends on your brother."

"The fact that Benji sees a future beyond the weekend is kind of remarkable."

"He's all about a five-year plan these days. It's part of his step program."

"Five-year plan? He never said. He probably thinks I'd make fun of him."

"You probably would."

Claudia raised her eyebrows, as if Cat had her there. "Independent of Benji—you have no idea?"

"So many things. I like teaching. And I'd like to get back to acting. Did I tell you I got a call for an audition?"

"Congrats."

"Yeah. It's only the Saratoga Rep, but—"

"No buts."

"And kids. Maybe. At some point, kids."

"With my brother?" Claudia burst out.

"You can't see him as a father?"

"I think he'd be a good father. If he could stay out of his own way."

They rubbed their eyes against a rolling wave of barbecue smoke, the char of burgers, and, beneath it, the druggy, satisfying singe of lighter fluid.

"So you'll be here." Cat coughed. "Cutting your ribbon."

Claudia waited.

"With Nick?"

"I used to think I was too much of a feminist to have a family."

"Whatever," Cat countered with a roll of the eyes. "Feminists can't have families? It's not the seventies."

"Maybe it's too late. I chose my work."

"Again: whatever."

❖ ❖ ❖

Benji stayed a fair distance from the crowd that lined up on the far side of the field waiting for free lemonade and hotdogs. He'd come straight from a four-mile run and walked up and down the patch of scrubby grass designated for parking, rewardingly wet in his wicking gear, looking for Cat's car. In the course of the last year, he'd dropped fifteen pounds. He felt firmer, stronger, more capable than he could remember feeling, and he nursed a fledgling fantasy of entering the lottery for next November's marathon. But Benji's plans for self-improvement didn't end with Alluvia High's drama club or the abs he was just beginning to coax into view. No less than Cat or Claudia, he had committed himself to unveiling a creation of substance and pride. He meant to redesign himself, to focus less on the glittering Vegas hotel he'd always thought he wanted to be and more on something truly habitable. If this meant trading lights and the promise of a gaudy but scintillating existence for life on a humbler, more human scale, then that's what he would do. He had Cat. He had Max. He had his students. He had his no-longer-quite-so-shaky sobriety. But there was more. More than racing Cat from their shaggy gray dock to the diving platform in the middle of the lake. More than continuing to shave seconds off his nine-minute-mile pace.

Finding Cat's black Volvo, the rear window decoupaged with stickers from Greenpeace and Planned Parenthood and Obama 2012, Benji opened the passenger's side door to retrieve the glossy college folder he'd left on the seat. He stood sixty credits shy of a bachelor's degree, two short years, and then a door he thought forever shut would swing open on a teaching certificate, on a classroom of his very own. SUNY Albany was not Princeton or Yale; it wasn't even Skidmore, where he'd started out, but he was learning to look at life with a lower wattage bulb, less glitz, less glamour. *It's enough,* he had to keep telling himself. *It's enough.*

He leaned against the sunbaked side of the car and flipped open the course catalog to pages Cat had helped him dog-ear the night before. He leapt between this description and that—Topics in Contemporary Drama. Play Analysis. Acting III (for certainly he could bypass I and

II)—as the festivities, in their official capacity, got under way. Someone from Nick's office tapped on a microphone and tentatively began, "Hello? Ladies and gentlemen? Hello?" while a man who looked like he rode a Harley made adjustments to the sound.

As Nick took the stage to scattered applause, the crowd still more intent on free barbecue than canned speeches, Benji scanned the mob for Cat. Separated from the few remaining protesters who stood on the unsociable side of a single sawhorse police barricade, who looked about as revved up now as a shed full of unplugged power tools, Cat stood at the foot of the stage, awaiting her moment. When Benji looked at her, his mind, like a leashed dog racing round a tree, tended to make tighter and tighter circles around thoughts of diamond rings (how could he afford one?) and proposals (what would he say?), but he willfully pushed his attentions in another direction, turning back to his catalog to read a description of Shakespeare after 1600.

"Excuse me. Sorry to bother you, but you're Benji Fisher."

Benji looked up to find a man of medium build with a trim waist and a salesman's smile. He had a formal, old-fashioned style of casual dress, as if he'd come straight from the set of *Mad Men*: white polo, tan slacks, navy blazer, tasseled shoes. His short blond hair thinned at the crown. And the heat of the day splashed large pink roses on his pale white cheeks. Sweating indecorously, he mopped his forehead and neck with a patterned pocket square and said, "You're a hard man to find."

Autograph? Gun? Benji's mind no longer stayed there very long. "Sorry. Have we—? Who are you?"

The man reached into his blazer pocket and produced a thin silver case from which he pulled a business card of considerable tooth. "Sam Palin. Bravo TV."

"Palin?" Benji repeated, dubious.

"No relation." Sam laughed heartily, a show of hands in surrender mode. "I can't see Alaska from my backyard."

From the stage, Nick's voice came deep and resonant as he explained to the crowd the experiment that was the Village, a new model of sustainable suburban living, a true community, words Benji heard echoing across the huge wooded lot without truly listening to them. For all he knew Nick was up there selling toxic waste, transfixed as he was by the logo on Sam's card, blue letters bold in a black talk bubble.

"I'm in a field in the middle of nowhere," Benji mused. "How did you find me?"

Sam held up his hands again with the same hearty laugh. "I'm not a stalker, I swear. I got your address from Nina Schweitzer. You remember her—your agent."

Benji let go a laugh of his own. He didn't need to be told who Nina Schweitzer was, though he did feel obliged to correct Sam and point out that Nina was no longer his agent.

"I don't know about that. She seemed very interested in the two of us talking."

"She didn't think to give you my phone number?"

"Oh, she did," Sam said, indicating Benji's pocketless attire, "but it doesn't look like you have your phone on you."

"And you—what? Just happened to be passing by?"

"Actually, I am. I try to make it to Saratoga two, three times a summer. What can I say? I like the horsies."

"Great, but how did you know I'd be *here?*"

"Nina gave me your number, but I thought it better if we talk in person. So I wound up at your parents'. That's the address Nina had for you. And your mother said you'd be out here for the day. The rest is GPS."

This, Benji thought, explained the recent, still-unlistened-to voice mails from Nina, who shortly after he turned down the lucrative offer to sell itch cream had told him in no uncertain terms that he didn't have what it took to make it in this business. As difficult as it was, Benji took pride in not listening to what she had to say. The last big opportunity to which Nina paved the way had landed him in the toolshed of the director of a piddling regional rep. Through silence Benji meant to transmit the message: Fuck off. Not interested. He wanted her to have proof that, professionally speaking, he had turned a corner. Moved on. He no longer lived to be a joke for hire. He lived, quite literally now, in a different zip code.

"So you must be what Nina keeps calling about?"

"She said you never got back to her, but I didn't want you to miss out on an opportunity."

"A big opportunity," said Benji. He'd heard it all before.

"You know what they say: it's not the size of the opportunity." Sam winked. "I kid. I kid. But yes. Hell, yes, I have a big opportunity." He clapped his hands together like a vacuum cleaner salesman revealing his latest wonder.

"I'm not looking for an opportunity. I like what I'm doing here," Benji answered without elaborating.

"I can appreciate that," Sam said, his eyes roving the grounds as if taking in the landscape of an inferior planet. The predominance of domestic cars and elastic pants. "Five minutes. That's all I'm asking for. Just give me that."

Benji looked over his shoulder, locating Cat as though touching a talisman, then returned the newsprint catalog to its folder and placed it on the red-hot roof of the car. "Go for it."

"Okay. No beating around the bush. I'm just going to throw it out there." He spoke with the smooth, smug arrogance of a world-class chef serving up his pièce de résistance, as if no one (not even those dismal vegans) could possibly turn down the prime cut of steak on offer. "We want you to do a show with us."

The word exploded in Benji's ears. Show? Show! He watched Sam's mouth move, but he could no longer hear the words coming out of it. His ears rang as motes of bright light floated down from heaven.

"Hear me out," Sam rushed to say. "It's called *The Comeback Kid*. We originally wanted to go with just *The Comeback*. It's cleaner, simpler. But Lisa Kudrow beat us to it. The cunt. I kid. I love Lisa. I do. But *The Comeback Kid* isn't bad either. It may even be better because you were, you know, a kid when you were a star."

"You want to do a show about me?"

"*About* you. *Starring* you. You *are* the show." Sam bulldozed Benji with his pitch. In a field ranged with heavy earth-moving equipment, he was the only one in action at the moment, moving ahead as if the only resistance in sight were a man-size bag of marshmallows. "You're not afraid of being the show. You've been the show before. 'That's what *you* think': that was all you. Let's face it: you did it so well, you basically fucked yourself for life. Nobody could see you doing anything else. Happens all the time to child stars. The machine chews them up and spits them out. I don't have to tell you. You've been hanging on to that horse for dear life since. Am I right? You're a talented guy, Benji. And I'm not just blowing sunshine up your ass. Your comic timing. But what have you been doing for the last twenty years? *I Love the Eighties*."

Benji grimaced. "Flatterer."

Sam pulled the pocket square from his blazer and wiped his face vigorously. His smile was less shepherd than wolf. "I'm not trying to flatter you. I'm talking straight with you. Can we put the bullshit aside? I don't know you, Benji. I don't know what makes you tick, or what's on your bucket list, but I'll bet money you didn't want to be doing Hamlet's dad in a hundred-seat house that, if I had to guess, was never more than half full. You want something bigger. Am I right?" Sam spread his arms like an offering. "Well, it's Christmas, my man. I'm here to give it to you. You just have to be smart enough to say yes."

He reminded Benji that just because someone is out of the scene doesn't mean someone is beyond the grapevine. Sam had heard about the drinking, about the drugs, about the dive from the bridge—"When you fall off a horse, you really fall off a horse!"—but that was the beauty of it. That was the comeback.

"I'm over those things. I'm sober now. Going on a year. So this one-man *Celebrity Rehab* is about eleven months too late." Benji didn't like this man. He hated the prep school blazer, the blotchy cheeks, the clear rivulets of sweat running to drip off the end of his pointy chin. But resistance was an act. If Sam had turned and walked away, Benji would have chased him down.

"First of all, no one's really ever over those things, am I right? I know. I'm in recovery myself. Four years now." Sam pumped a fist in the air and cheered, "Serenity now. But seriously, let me tell you, not a day goes by I wouldn't kill my own mother for a dirty martini. But. You go on. It's what we do. We go on. And we'd like to see you on that journey. Watch you, you know, climb out of that hole."

"But I'm not in a hole."

"You didn't let me finish. We want to see you climb out of that hole and move on to the next great thing. Get back on that horse, so to speak. That's what I'm talking about, Benji. We don't just want to see where you've been. Although that's definitely part of it. And we may want to re-create some of that stuff. The bridge, the drinking. Whatever. You know, to get the dramatic arc, but really we want to see where you're going. What's next. That's the whole thrust of the show. Your next move. Your comeback!"

Benji hadn't the wherewithal to admit that his next project sat on the roof of the car right behind him: sixty course credits heated to 120 degrees.

"We want to pave the way to that."

"To what?"

"To your name in lights. We want to follow you on auditions. Land you a commercial that doesn't make everybody think you're one itchy bastard. Maybe a little stage work. We want to see you in rehearsals, see the process. A real insider's view. But really it's about setting you up for an audition with a major director on a major project. The comeback."

"The comeback." As Benji repeated it, the lights of the abandoned hotel started flickering back to life, one by one. Welcome to Vegas. "When you say major project? Like a movie?"

"Like a movie. Which is still up in the air. All of this is up in the air until we have you, of course. But—and you didn't hear this from me—we're approaching Darren Aronofsky." Sam paused to let the name sink in, nodding in his smug, self-satisfied way. "Think about what he did for Mickey Rourke. Am I right? He picked him up out of a swamp"—here Sam's eyes swept the surroundings, widening at the aptness of the metaphor—"and set him down in the Dolby Theatre. P.S., I love Sean Penn. The asshole. I do. But Mickey should have won that Oscar." He leaned forward and slapped Benji on the shoulder. "Here's hoping they won't make that same mistake with you."

Just then, as if in cosmic agreement with everything Sam had said, the crowd broke into energetic applause. With Cat having praised the obelisk, Claudia laying out the dream of the Village, three hundred hot-dogs crammed into three hundred mouths, the people themselves were stuffed, spirited, satisfied. A few hoots and whistles greeted Nick, who, waving victoriously, stepped off the stage into a tiny throng of well-wishers. On cue, the same woman who'd set the festivities in motion untied an enormous plastic bag of red, white, and blue balloons and released them into the hot August sky. They swam upward through the air, this way and that, streaming ribbons beating after them like the tails of sperm as ABBA burst suddenly, joyfully, from a flank of enormous speakers.

"Benj?" Cat, as if teleported to his side, startled him. She rubbed his arm, smiling through a veil that wasn't entirely victorious.

"Babe," Benji said. He flashed a cat-that-ate-the-canary smile, needing a minute to orient himself before making introductions. "Cat McCarthy. This is."

"Sam. Sam Palin. No relation. I can't see Alaska from my backyard."

"Sam's an old friend," Benji said, jumping in to explain, "from high school."

Sam grinned his grin. "Benji and I go way back. Mr. Hume's history class, wasn't it? The times we had."

Benji, suspecting just how quickly and ecstatically a man like Sam could get carried away with lying, turned back to Cat. "You ready?"

"Whenever you are."

"Sure." He smiled, leaning over to kiss her. *Marry me.* To Sam he said, "Good talking to you. Give me a few days to think about it?"

"Absolutely. Absolutely." He took Benji's hand and pumped it vigorously. "You've got my card. Let me know. Let me know, or I'll hunt you down." He pointed his fingers at Benji like two revolvers—*Pow! Pow!*—and walked off into the fray.

"Think about what?" Cat asked, watching him go.

"Oh. Nothing. I told him I was thinking about getting my certification, and he said I might think about doing something with this—"

"With what?"

"Hunh? Oh. This, this summer camp he runs in Lake George."

"That guy's from Lake George?" Cat asked, going around to her side of the car. "What kind of camp?"

Benji opened his door, ducked to get in. "Theater camp. What do you think?"

Before climbing into her seat, Cat stood on it, reaching across the roof to retrieve Benji's folder. "Forgetting something?" she asked, a trace of the schoolmarm tinting her voice as she dropped the hot folder into his lap and started the car. When she turned onto the main road, Compton's Mound receding in the rearview, she said, "I don't know any theater camps in Lake George."

Benji tried to wring the strain of defensiveness from his laugh. "Do you know every theater camp in existence?"

"Um. No, Mr. Attitude, I don't. What's the matter? It sounds exciting."

Benji gave her thigh an apologetic squeeze. He unrolled his window before the gust from the air conditioner finished its climb into the cold and said, "You have no idea."

Are you going to sit there all day watching us or are you going to help? She isn't the prettiest girl on the beach, but she's the one I've been watching. I have two choices. Go back to my book, pretend I don't know what she's taking about. Or stuff the book in my bag and take the shovel she's offering me. I get up, brush the sand off my legs. What's your name? Jane, she says. Then, pointing to her friend, That's Mary. Mary could sell suntan lotion, but Jane sparks, the dark hair, the fiery-red swimsuit, the barely there tits and overcompensating nose. You need to get the sand wet; that's why it keeps falling down. Mary, bored, pulls a pack of cigarettes from her rolled towel and lies back to smoke. Jane walks with me to the water's edge, a bucket between us. You build a castle with this stuff here, the thing won't ever come down. I hike back up to dry land and turn the bucket over to show her. See how strong? Now you. No, you do it, she says, but not in a helpless, prin-cessy way. I fill the buckets and bring them back. I build up a pyramid of tightly packed sand that Jane, using the stem of her sunglasses, starts to carve A turret. A window. A curving wall with stairs. Not bad, I say when we're done. With two fingers, she slices her signature in the sand. Sign it, she says. That's stupid, I say. You did it, didn't you? You said yourself it'll stand forever, so sign it. Your masterpiece. I kneel, my leg hot against hers, and write my name.

14.

Act two was finished. Act two would stand. The trouble was, it stood alone. The foundation of the first act stood squarely under the roof of the third, but the act between didn't align with either, giving the entire structure the precarious feel of a Jenga puzzle. Not only would Max have to circle back to the beginning to shift act one so it supported all that followed, he'd have to smooth the transition between the second and third acts, the passage that led from Lily Briscoe's return to the Ramsays' shuttered summer house to her sitting in their dining room ten years after that first failed trip to the lighthouse, where everything was changed, where so much time had passed, where Mrs. Ramsay was dead, where Prue and Andrew were dead, and Lily with her paintbrushes and canvas asked, "What does it mean then, what can it all mean?"

Max heard those notes carried by the strings. Sweeping the silence like a beam from the lighthouse would sweep the dark, they came and went. Came and went. A first step, but where to go with it? What next? He hummed the few fledgling bars as he stepped from the shower and toweled dry, his body a darting shadow in the steamed mirror, but none of it seemed right. He brushed his teeth, swiped on his deodorant, and massaged a dollop of moisturizer onto his face, dropping the tubes and creams into his Dopp kit as he finished with them. Next: the pills. Opening the bottles one by one, humming *ba da dum*—no, that wasn't right either—he placed a colorful array of capsules in his open palm and quickly, before his reflection fully returned (he didn't like to see himself do it), washed them down the drain.

He opened the door with the stealth of a cat burglar to find Arnav sitting up in bed, waiting. Always a bad sign. Arnav awake in the middle of the night—Arnav, who had proven he could sleep through their westerly neighbor's porn-star-like attempts to pound his headboard through the wall, who failed to wake to anything but the shrillest, most obnoxious alarms—meant trouble of the sort Max usually (and with pride) thought himself crafty enough to avoid.

"Nav," Max whispered. A note of atonement sweetened his voice. "I woke you." He tiptoed forward, as though it wasn't too late for tiptoes, and dropped his toiletry bag into his suitcase.

"It's four in the morning," answered Arnav hoarsely.

Here was the darker side of love, pretending the person who knew you best—the person who brought you aspirin before you said you had a headache, who could sit down at a diner before you arrived and order your eggs just the way you liked them—didn't know you at all, that he was daft or dumb or had to be reminded of the simplest things. "I don't like to rush before a flight," Max said.

"Your flight isn't for another four hours."

Max felt himself moving on a conveyor belt, steadily drawn toward an argument he didn't want to have. The battle was coming. It had been coming for weeks. And it was coming now. Now that Max had one foot out the door, they could lob their respective grenades without having to live with the fallout.

Max dropped his towel, already hard. Sex was the wrench he most enjoyed throwing into the conveyor belt, certainly the most gratifying way of cutting off a confrontation, of jamming the proverbial works.

It was hardly fail proof, but that didn't mean he couldn't try. "Which means we have time to say good-bye." He crawled across the bed, into the warm yellow blanket of light cast by the bedside lamp, and knelt by Navi's side. Stroking himself with one hand, he ran the other through the fur on Arnav's chest. He tugged first one nipple, then the other, then traveled south, to the thick, musky nest between Navi's legs, his fingers combing through the hair, tugging, before wrapping themselves around the stubby shaft of his boyfriend's slumbering cock. "We have time to say good-bye, like, two or three times."

Arnav retrieved Max's hand from under the sheet and said flatly, "Tell me I'm wrong."

Max collapsed like a puppet on snipped strings. "You're wrong." His head lolled to the side in a show of theatric frustration. He gazed at Navi with innocent eyes and said, this time with an air of great solemnity, "Will you stop! Do you want to draw blood and check my lithium levels? Everything's fine."

Throwing the covers to one side, Arnav bounded out of bed, stormed into the bathroom, and shut the door. Max wanted to call out, but the loud gush of pee made the silence between them deeper, more rigid and impassable. When Navi emerged, he stood, naked, hands on hips, waiting. "Everything is not fine. You're averaging three, four hours of sleep a night. Your mood is all over the place. You were a complete jerk to that waiter last night."

"And I apologized to him."

"You don't think I know you by now? You're swinging like a mad-man from tree to tree. I'm just waiting for the vine to break."

"I'm working," Max explained. With the carnal detour he'd hoped to travel blocked, he sensed that sincerity was the only route open to him. Or rage. He certainly had it in him to throw a tantrum, especially now, with three weeks' worth of psychotropic drugs dissolving in the drain, but he tried for the gentler, more reasonable path. Hugging his knees to his chest, he went on. "I'm finally working again."

"What are you talking about *finally*? You've been working since you started."

"Yeah, but now I'm in a groove. I'm almost done. And it's *good*." Work: here was his first defense for all misbehavior—insomnia, over-sleeping, overeating, forgetting to eat entirely, brooding, neediness, acting like a jerk, jerking off five times a day. The only defense that mattered. "You'd rather have me where I was when the radio wouldn't tune? When once every third day I might grab a snippet I could work with. Something I could barely hear. Some faint little melody I had to chase down before it sunk back into static or broke into noise. Noise. Or would you rather have me here, where I am now? Where the station's been playing twenty-four hours a day for—"

"Three weeks. I know how long."

"You say that like it's a bad thing. Nearly a month of solid work! I'm supposed to apologize or something? I finished the second act, Navi. That's a good thing. That impossible fucking act. Why aren't you excited about that?"

"It's not a good thing," Navi countered, "sleeping three hours a night."

"When music is the first thing I hear in the morning and the last thing I hear at night, and everything else, everything that's not it, is a fucking distraction, that *is* a good thing."

Arnav may have been stung, but Max knew he wasn't fragile enough to crack at being called a distraction. He also knew Arnav wasn't crazy, though he wasn't above trying to make him appear so.

"You know I'm happy that you're working. But what kind of work are you doing on three hours of sleep?"

"Stop saying that. I'm sleeping more than three hours," answered Max more coolly. He aimed for poise, for the kind of imperturbability that might throw Arnav off his scent, but Arnav's jaws were locked, and he wasn't letting go.

Navi walked to his dresser and put on his little oblong spectacles, staring, blinking, as though Max were an exhibit meant to stir up curiosity and concern. "We went to bed at one."

"And I woke up at four. Fine. Three hours. You know I can't sleep when I travel," Max said lamely. Then, with rising heat: "I don't need you counting sheep for me. Or giving me etiquette lessons. Or anything. I'm fine. Just like I fucking am."

Arnav returned to his side of the bed. His granny distaste for profanity tightened his mouth into a thin, straight line, but he folded his legs under him and took Max's hand in his. "You're flying solo."

Now it was Max's turn to bound off the bed. He went to his dresser, retrieved a few more T-shirts (though he'd already packed more than he would possibly need), and dropped them in his bag. "You say I'm not taking my pills. I say I am. Are you counting them?"

"You wouldn't leave them in the bottles. You're too smart for that. You'd flush them down the toilet."

Wrong, Max thought, diving through the loophole of his lie with this slightest of technicalities. "So you are counting them?"

"I'm worried about you!" It wasn't often that Max saw anyone as even-keeled as Arnav abandon equanimity. He seldom heard the deep, mellow voice that supported him like bedrock quake with such high emotion. Ready for it (for anything!) as Max thought he was, the sound of Navi approaching tears left him undone. But he could not, would not concede. Now that his mind had a taste of clear, fluid, creative freedom, he refused to slip back into the thick, jellylike waters of lithium and Depakote, where his mood might have been stable but his brain refused to swim at its quickest pace, where the stream was perfectly calm but also silted and slow, and a beach full of radios (there for no other reason than to torture him) refused to tune. Max had music now, and now was the only thing that mattered, no matter the harm, no matter the price.

"I know you," Arnav finished dismally. "I know when you're working out of a good place. And I know when you're high as a kite."

Max leveled his eyes and, meeting his own dare, said, "You can't stand it when I'm successful."

Arnav lifted his glasses and rubbed the weariness from his eyes. "That's it, Max. You got me. Because up until now I've been holding you back. Watching you wither away in obscurity."

"It's good that I'm going," Max answered. Stuffed as his bag now was, he had to lie on top of it to wrestle the zipper shut. "It's good I'm getting out of here."

"Because Evelyn is so much more supportive than I am. You honestly think you're going to write there with everything that's going on?"

Max did. He may have been kidding himself, but he did. In fact, it sounded to him like the perfect plan. Later that afternoon, he and Benji, Cat, and Claudia would descend on the house on Palmer Street, filling it one last weekend before they admitted his grandfather to Saratoga's best geriatric nursing facility and Evelyn began her search for a smaller, more manageable home.

By Monday, after delivering Henry to St. Anthony's Home for the Aged, after his mother and uncle (and, by all accounts, almost aunt) had returned to their lives, he would find himself with two precious weeks of writing time in an undisturbed room. A room of his own, where he could rest assured that Evelyn wouldn't come poking at him in the middle of the night with maddening accusations. She had no designs on shoving even a single, solitary, dulling pill down his throat. Instead, she'd offered him time, a room, nothing more (what else was there?), all in exchange for keeping her company over dinner. "Evelyn's excited about my writing," Max said as he stepped into a pair of underwear, pulled a striped purple tank top over his head. "She didn't invite me there so she could sit at my bedside with a notebook. She invited me there to work."

"She invited you there because she's going to be lonely. Understandably lonely, rattling around in that house all by herself. She's going to want you to sit in her lap all day."

"She married a porcupine. You don't think she learned how to step away from Henry when he was working? How to give him space?"

"I think she doesn't know you well enough to know when *not* to step away. That's the problem."

"I don't need a social worker, Arnav. Or a sleep therapist. Or another fucking psychopharmacologist. The only thing I need right now is a cheerleader."

"And the Fishers are going to do that for you?"

"Better than you, looks like."

"You've known these people for less than a year, and suddenly they're your family. They're the de Medicis. They're the patrons of your art, not those of us who have lived with your bull—"

"Bullshit," Max practically spit the word out for him. "Stop being so churchy! You can't even say 'bullshit,' for fuck's sake." Max wheeled his suitcase to the door and stopped. "And they're not my *patrons*. I don't need their money. Unless you're talking about their love and support."

Navi let this pass with a roll of the eyes.

"And what does knowing them for a year—"

"Less than a year."

"Have to do with it? I knew you four months before we moved in together."

"And you probably agreed to that because you were manic."

Max turned off the light. Two dark silhouettes stared across the cold blue of a shadowy, starlit space. "They *are* supportive and loving," he said to break the impasse. "And if you can't be? Do me a favor: stay out of my way."

❖ ❖ ❖

Four banged-up baggage carousels spread across the lower level of the airport. The digital display signs that hung over each to indicate the arriving flight numbers were uniformly dark, which left Benji to guess which whining silver daisy wheel serviced Flight 2732 from Dallas/ Fort Worth. He'd chosen the fourth, based entirely on a towering hulk who reminded him of Johnny Cash, a face carved, he imagined, by the unforgiving Texas sun, dressed from head to toe in black, a Stetson tipped down over his eyes. Trying to locate Max according to the costumes of potential copassengers was uncertain business. There was no telling where these people hailed from. But Max, who twenty minutes ago had sent a text that simply read *Landed!*, had been unresponsive since. Johnny Cash seemed the best bet.

A sizeable crowd formed around carousel no. 4. Women in overly snug, jelly bean–colored sweatpants claimed their animal print suitcases and rolled them through the shushing automatic doors, and still no sign of Max. Benji texted him again, and a moment later, as if in answer, from the opposite end of the terminal, he heard the deep, sonorous cry of a cello. He walked toward the sound, toward a small group of people who had suspended their hurrying and gathered around the tip of carousel no. 1 to watch Max, sitting on its edge, bent over his instrument as if caught in the most intimate of conversations with it. Eyes closed, head sawing from side to side, Max's entire body moved as the bow cut across the strings to sound a phrase that repeated and repeated and then ever so slightly changed, deepening, shifting onto another plane before continuing its stately march.

Benji worked his way to the front of the crowd. He wanted to be the first person Max saw. But then, before Max could lift the bow from those fine, final, attenuated notes, the boy jumped up as if an electric charge had touched the metal ledge on which he sat. He let go of his cello, which Benji, leaping forward, saved from clattering to the ground, and with lightning speed picked up two coins that had fallen to his feet. He parted the crowed with two bounding steps after the man who'd tossed them and, reeling his arm back like a major league pitcher, sent them flying at the back of the man's head.

Flinching, the man turned. When he realized what had happened, it took only a second for confusion to boil over into anger. "What's the matter with you?" The man was well into his fifties, thickly built with a mad scientist shock of untamed white hair. This appreciative (if stingy) patron of the arts took a menacing step toward Max and asked the question again.

"Do I look like I'm begging for change?" Max yelled. "Do you know who I am? I don't need your fucking fifty cents."

The man, muttering loudly about ungrateful assholes, let himself be led away by his more quietly unnerved wife, though the well-being of his manhood required him to turn several times during his retreat and, like a dog jerking its chain, demonstrate his continued willingness to fight.

Benji didn't know what to do. He laid the cello in its case and, stepping cautiously forward, put his hands on his nephew's shoulders. Max spun around, ready for further battle, but shifted with disquieting ease into a mode of joyful reunion. He threw his arms around Benji's neck, ignoring the crowd lingering awkwardly around them, including a little girl with tight, ribboned pigtails and a missing front tooth who asked her mother, "What's wrong with that man?"

"How's it going, champ?" Benji spoke softly into Max's ear. "You okay?"

Max pulled back and laughed. "Great. Great. I'm great. Why do you ask?"

❖ ❖ ❖

He let Evelyn set him up in Henry's study. The pullout couch wasn't nearly as comfortable as a proper bed, but Max preferred the study. He wanted to be planted in ground made fertile by his grandfather's work. As she always did, Evelyn mentioned that the master bedroom, quiet on the unused third floor, would make for a better studio, but she also wanted him to see that she took his work seriously, that she respected it and would let him wring from Henry's old workspace whatever artistic miracles might be left there. After all, it was, as Henry used to call it, the "Cave of Making." "So make," she said to Max as she left him to unpack his bag. "Make."

But there was, even with his radio playing nonstop, only so much he could make in a day. He had worked on orchestrations on both legs of his flight (from takeoff to landing), stolen a few hours in between lunch and dinner, stolen a few more before bed. He was exhausted. Not tired, nowhere near ready for sleep, but exhausted all the same. It was eleven o'clock. Max retired with Evelyn, thinking he might stumble upon the melody he needed for act three, a phrase mined from act one, but timeworn, changed, the sound whereby Lily returned to the Ramsays' summer home, set her easel down on the grass, and made ready to finish the painting she'd started ten years before.

Max captured something close to it on a scrap of paper and, alone in his room, played it on the rollaway keyboard connected to his computer. It was rough as a block of clay hauled up from the earth; he was happy to have it, but lacked the energy to trim it or shape it or make it flow like the rhythm of Lily's brush as it danced across the canvas with its flashes of blue and green. He played the notes again but preferred to write on paper, the intimacy of penciling the notes on neatly inked staffs, and turned now to the tidy sheaf of 213 pages that comprised his almost finished opera. He leafed through act two, the section called "Time Passes," and reviewed the closing bars. It really was sturdy. It really would stand. It played in his head, a cord of intertwined themes that unraveled and, one by one, like the characters themselves, died out. Silence encroached upon the music, washed over it like waves swallowing an island, until silence was all there was.

A knock at the door. Max was cross but also, somewhere beneath the irritation, relieved.

Claudia stood at the threshold. Benji would have twisted the knob and barged in like a golden retriever, but not Claudia. She waited in the hallway, patient, uncertain, softly saying his name.

He slid the papers aside and answered the door.

She smiled tentatively, looking lovely changed into the drapey cotton clothes she slept in; her long brown hair fell lightly over her shoulders, her face scrubbed pink. "Care for a nightcap? Well, I'm having a nightcap. Benji's having tea."

He turned back into the room and picked up his score to show her.

"Is this it?" she said, placing a reverent hand on it.

"This is it."

"And you're almost done?"

"I'm working on the transitions between acts."

"We should leave you alone then."

"No." He grabbed her sleeve as she turned to leave and asked her to sit down. "I could use a break."

Claudia took a seat on the couch, considering the hieroglyphics on the pages Max had left with her. "I always wished I'd learned how to read music."

"It's not too late. I could teach you."

"You have better things to do. Like working on your transitions." She looked around the room, the ghost of her father battering away at his Olivetti, ransacking his bookshelves for the one and only epigraph that made sense.

"What's wrong?" Max asked.

Claudia shook her head. "A little sad. My dad's study."

"It brings me luck to work in here." Max collected the sheets from her and, adding them to his half of the score, tapped the edges into one neat sheaf, which he carefully laid on Henry's desk. "He wrote eight books in here. At this desk. I figure if I can pick up a little of that magic."

"Don't let him hear you say that." A look of sorrow landed on her face, which she quickly shooed away, half amused, as if to say it didn't matter now what Henry heard. "He always said writing was work. Not magic. He hated when other writers said they were channeling voices from another realm. He said writing had more in common with ditch digging than sitting around like a clairvoyant waiting for Aunt Gladys to tell you a story. You show up every day and you work."

"He's right. But there's always a little magic, I think."

"And it's not eight books. It's nine."

"*Nuisance, Open Ground, The Skirmishes, Nostomania*—that's my favorite." Max ticked off the titles he'd read since last September on his fingers. Five. Six. Seven. "I'm forgetting the essays."

"*Imponderable Needs.*"

"Right. Eight."

"See that safe right behind you? That's nine."

"What is it?"

"I don't know. No one's read it. Except my uncle Roger, and he has reservations about publishing it."

"Why? Isn't it any good?"

"Roger says it's his best. But he thinks publishing it could be—messy."

"What does that mean?"

Claudia shrugged. "He won't say."

"And you haven't read it?"

"Nope."

Max turned to look at the safe. "He keeps it in there?"

"He's never written on a computer."

"I get that," Max said.

"I don't," Claudia answered. "It's dumb."

They went downstairs, and two hours later, after three neat pours of bourbon (after which, Claudia, with an uneasy sense of parental duty, cut him off), he returned. The room, with all its lamps burning, seemed violently lit. He turned off all but the task lamp on Henry's desk. It threw barely enough light to see by, but Max wasn't deterred from taking a slow, bobbing stroll around the room. Swaying lightly, he studied the spines of Henry's books, pulled one volume and then another from the tightly packed shelves. His fingers found the collection of Henry's awards, feeling them like a blind man, trailing over the smooth etched crystal, the cool etched bronze. He examined the trinkets that had little value, he supposed, to anyone but Henry—and now that Henry had forgotten them? What was the worth of this toy soldier? Of that heavy brass urn and whatever was inside it? Sooner or later it would all be swept away. Everything, everything goes. Finally, he came to sit at Henry's tank of a desk, a large gray metal antique with silver-handled drawers buffed by a thousand openings. Max peeked into these, disappointed to find a pack of unopened cigarettes and a box of large wooden matches, dusty manila folders stuffed with ancient contracts, a faded photo of Benji and Claudia, thrilled and frightened, being locked in the shiny red seat of a Ferris wheel.

He spun round in the chair. He spun round and round like a game show wheel, not knowing where he'd land. As the room slowed, the objects in it separated from the smear that speed and drink had made of them. Here was the desk lamp. The couch. The fancy flat-screen computer shagged like a bulletin board with taped notes and newspaper clippings. The score. The safe sitting atop a waist-high bookcase. When he stopped, his eyes were level with the squat cube of black metal with a combination lock fitted into its hefty handle. He rapped his knuckles on the top, waiting, as if something inside might rap back, then tested the door. It swung open heavily on its hinges. Max looked around like an amateur thief who expects the hand of the law to clamp down on him. He angled the desk lamp so he could see the fat stack of typed pages tied with a length of butcher's twine inside. The last book. The messy one. The only copy of whatever it was in the world. With care, Max removed the bundle and placed it on the desk. He slipped the knot from the string and, boosted by a vaguely stimulating sense of criminality, started to read.

The title page: EVERY WAND'RING BARK.

Max wasn't 100 percent sure he liked that, but he turned the page and read what followed: *I am minutes away from meeting the woman I think I'll be with for the rest of my life and years and years away from the one who will make the rest of my life livable.*

In the morning, he woke to an old analog clock whose face glowed green. He sat humped in the chair. Stiff neck. Sore back. Head throbbing from three belts of Blanton's. The pages of Henry's book lay in a chaotic nest around his feet. What had he read? The realization hurt his head as much as the bourbon. He gathered the papers on the floor, determined to return them to the right order later, and stuffed the rumpled pile back into the safe, afraid he'd be caught and made to lock it away before he could return to it.

It was six o'clock. Soon Evelyn would rouse the troops with coffee and eggs. Max felt, in that moment, as if his legs had been swept out from under him, a churn of emotions pulling him out to sea, an unwanted knowledge threatening to take him under. What had Henry been thinking? And Evelyn? And was it true? His heart ached for them and for the ghost of the woman who had always stood between them and, most of all, for Claudia, who hadn't a clue that her mother had wandered into the woods so long ago and ended herself in a pile of snow. He felt love for his grandparents and their attempt to weave a web to protect their daughter as much as he felt contempt for their duplicity. How could they do it? How could they think they'd get away with it? And they were getting away with it were it not for the four-hundred-page confession Henry planned on dropping only after he'd escaped from the fallout. They were saints, sparing Claudia the cross of a painful secret, and they were cowards, protecting themselves for keeping it.

The question was: now that Max knew, what would he do? To continue to hide the secret from Claudia was, in effect, to relegate her to the same realm of ignorance from which he himself had fought to break free. Sure, she was blissfully ignorant of her ignorance, but did that excuse confining her to the dark? Wouldn't she want to know her place, her origin? She was strong: if he exposed to her the cracks in her foundation, who better than she to fix them? Then again, what if he brought the entire house down? His mind slowed at this thought as if he'd drilled past all the dirt and muck and finally hit bedrock. Did he *want* to bring her house down? If his immediate impulse was to rescue Claudia from a lifelong lie, to deliver her closer to the truth of her own story, he had to admit that beneath this lay the obdurate wish to see her suffer as he had. Tit for motherfucking tat.

He meant to stay quiet, to mull over his options as he ate his toast and eggs and, like a true Fisher, pretend that nothing was wrong. But the quiet of the kitchen struck him like a fist, and instinctively he struck back. No sooner had Evelyn ushered him to the table and poured his coffee than he said wincingly, "How's your eye?"

Earlier that week, Henry, lost in some waking nightmare where everyone before him was a stranger, had slammed Evelyn in the face. She wore the result, a swollen mask of purple and green, with soldierly stoicism, brushing past Max's question with a pat on his back.

"Where is everybody?" he tried.

"Asleep. I'm surprised you're up."

He watched her fuss over the coffeemaker, holding the brown-laden filter like a dirty diaper before dropping it into the trash. "Will you sit?"

She looked as if he'd asked her to dance. "What is it, honey?" She took the seat beside him, her smile brightening but looking even more puzzled as he touched her arm.

"Did you read Henry's book? The new one?"

"Nobody's read that. Except for Roger."

"Did Roger say anything?"

"About the book? Not to me. He and Henry did have a fight. Or I don't know if I'd call it a fight. They're old friends. Friends disagree."

"Why did they fight?"

Evelyn laughed. "I feel like I'm on *Law & Order*."

Max smiled nervously, took a sip from his mug.

"I don't know what about," Evelyn went on. "Roger liked it from what I gathered. It wasn't that. But for whatever reason he didn't think Henry should publish it."

"And neither of them told you?"

"Oh, I let those two do their thing. I learned a long time ago not to ask questions."

He might have stopped there. He told himself to stop there. But he'd pushed a rock down the hill, and forward it went.

"Because I read it."

Evelyn cocked her head to one side, as if she'd misheard. "You read it?"

"Last night. He must have left the safe open, so I read it."

"Oh. Oh now. We better keep that to ourselves." She patted his hands and got up to go to the cupboard. The container of flour. The clatter of muffin tins. "I think muffins this morning."

"Did you hear what I said, Gam?"

"I heard."

"Henry never told you what it was about?"

Evelyn shook her head.

"All those years he spent working on it?"

"Your grandfather is a very private man. He kept his work to himself." She paused. "You want to tell me what it's about."

"It's about you." The rock, gathering mud and sticks and size all the way, rolled on. He couldn't stop it now if he tried. "About you and Claudia and Henry." An impossible silence. "And Jane."

Evelyn set the measuring cup on the counter and stared out the window.

"Gam? Did you hear?"

"I heard you."

"Is it true?" he asked. Then, when she didn't answer: "I *know*." He shaped the word as if he could cram all his meaning into a syllable that would spare her from hearing more, but the word wouldn't expand to fit it.

"Jane," she said. "He wrote about her?"

Max waited a moment to see what she would do. Would she cry? Scream? Fall to the floor and tell him to get out? All she did was stare. He stood up and slowly went to her. Flour dusted her hands, which were clenched into what seemed the frailest fists.

"He said he never would." Evelyn sighed. "He hated memoirs. He said they were tacky." She exhaled, a pale, disbelieving laugh. "He breaks the dish. I get to clean it up."

"Maybe that's why Roger said what he did."

"Roger loves Claudia." She looked into Max's eyes then, pleading, "This would crush her."

"You don't think she deserves to know?"

Returning to Max, snatching up his hands, Evelyn said, "We've gone all this time. We've lived all this time fearing this—this curtain was going to be pulled back and show her, but it hasn't. It never was. And now. She doesn't need to know."

"Where would I be," he asked, "if I never knew? If I didn't know you all existed, where would I be?"

At this, Evelyn bit her lip. Max pulled her to him and held her tight. "You have to tell her," he whispered in her ear.

"What good would it do?" she cried. "Jane's gone. Henry's gone."

"You have to. You can't not tell her, Gam. You have to. You have to. Or I will."

❖ ❖ ❖

Max commandeered the picnic table, looking over a great pile of papers (held down by a can of Diet Pepsi and a bottle of charcoal fluid) that

fluttered in the barely there breeze. He wore the bottoms of his preferred uniform, black camouflage cutoffs, with the tank top he'd worn
the day before, and, although the day's heat felt like an attack, the gray
knit cap Evelyn made him for Christmas. He looked, Benji thought as
he stared out the kitchen window, like a member of a punk band. Or
homeless.

"Do you think he's all right?" he asked.

Claudia stopped chopping celery and stepped up beside him for a
worried glimpse. "No."

"What are we going to do about it?"

"I called Arnav last night. After we went to bed."

"You shouldn't have done that." Then: "What did he say?"

"What I thought he'd say."

"So this isn't all—" Benji's hand spiraled into the air, a gesture of
some ineffable creative power that Max possessed (or that possessed
Max).

"Inspiration? No."

Benji hadn't told her, hadn't told any of them, about the previous
day at the airport. Why, he reasoned, make a big deal? Or a bigger one.
Max was working. Benji didn't want to interfere. To raise the alarm and
bring the whole family running held the appeal of derailing a train,
and he didn't want that on his conscience. But his confidence in the
wisdom of his omission began to waver. He could no sooner erase from
his mind the sight of his sweet, humble nephew hurling pocket change
at a stranger's head than he could scrub a blot of ink from a white shirt.
"He's looking a little ragged," Benji said.

"I looked up the symptoms last night."

So had Benji, but if anyone had to assume responsibility for knocking the train from its tracks, shouldn't it be Claudia?

"What did it say?"

"Pretty much what we're looking at. Driven behavior, insomnia,
self-medication, an inflated sense of self."

Evelyn, loudly hipping her way down the hall, entered the kitchen with, "Whatever's happening, it's not good." She wore a pink polo shirt and flowered culottes and kept her face angled so the children couldn't see her black eye, which, of course, Claudia did.

"Oh, Mom," she said. "That eye."

"Oh, Claudia. If either of you say one more thing about 'that eye.' Enough already."

Claudia shook her head and frowned. "I told you something like this was going to happen. We should have found a place for Daddy months ago. If not last year."

"Would you like me to travel back in time? He's going tomorrow." She stepped up to the window and took a look, three visitors at the aquarium considering a strange, possibly dangerous fish.

"What's wrong with you?" Benji asked, appraising the expression on his mother's face. "You look like you've seen a ghost."

Evelyn went to the counter, took up the knife to continue what Claudia had started. "What do you think is wrong?" she snapped. "I'm worried about him."

"So what would you propose we do?" Claudia asked her brother.

"Leave him alone. For now." How Benji had fumed at their mother's talent for denial, which had, much to his and Claudia's told-you-so dismay, earned Evelyn a sucker punch. But here he was doing the same thing.

"Leaving him alone isn't an option," Claudia said pointedly.

"I'm not saying leave him alone," Benji said testily, even though he just had. "I'm not saying *ignore* him. We need to keep a close eye. But if you try to rein him in, you're going to get nothing but a fight. You might even lose him. And where would he go if not here?"

"When did you become an expert?" Claudia asked, but before Benji could answer, Evelyn broke in with, "What do you mean lose him?"

A shell of silence hardened around Benji. He may not be able to say it, but they all knew what he meant.

Claudia, a note of triumph in her voice, announced, "Navi will be here tonight."

"What is this going into?" Evelyn asked tightly. "Tuna fish?"

"Chicken salad. Chicken's in the fridge."

"He left to get away from Arnav," Benji reminded them.

"Did you ever stop to think he may not be making decisions from the best place right now? Arnav's been through this before. He'll know what to do."

"Or he'll chase Max away, and then we'll be outside instead of inside, and then there will be nothing we can do."

Cat, who had been sitting quietly at the table until this point pulling the ends from a pot of string beans she planned to make for dinner, said, "You did the right thing, Claudia."

"Catman," Benji said, the sweet in his voice mixed with caution. "Put on some music?"

Cat abandoned the beans and held out a hand. "Give me your phone."

"Use yours. You have better music."

"I don't have better music," she answered angrily. Things had been rough between them lately. His mind was constantly switched to Bravo TV and his phone a top secret conduit to Sam Palin's Realm of Promises.

"Use mine," Claudia offered, producing her phone as if waving a white flag. She set it on the table, then relieved Evelyn from chopping the chicken.

Cat rose. "Forget it. We'll use mine." She huffed as she plugged her phone into the little dock that sat on the counter and pushed "Play." An album Benji and she had listened to a hundred times before. "I'm so sick of *A Ghost Is Born*," she said.

Benji wanted to ask, "Then why did you play it?" but let the moment pass.

Evelyn, who had left the room to get Henry, returned holding his hand as he mumbled like a child, "I don't want to eat."

"You have to eat," Evelyn answered. "You'll die if you don't eat."

"I want to eat outside."

"It's so hot out," Benji complained.

"It's summer. It's not that hot out." Evelyn deposited Henry in the chair next to Cat and, taking a vote (only Benji voted for air-conditioning), asked Claudia to help Max clear the picnic table.

Benji watched his mother bustle around the room, suddenly stabbed in the heart by the increasingly pronounced drag of that arthritic hip. She hadn't had it easy. He turned to his father, too much of a wreck, too much of a ruin, to blame much anymore, but still Benji blamed him. And then there was Max. And Cat. A familiar rabbit hole opened up in front of him—how to do right by either of them?—but before he fell into it, his phone rang. A twinkling starshine of a ring that, lately, did nothing so much as set Cat's teeth on edge. He fished it out of his shorts' confusing array of cargo pockets and said, "Damn. I've gotta take this."

He disappeared out the back door, the screen slamming shut behind him, and slipped around the side of the house, shyly, guiltily, like a boy who needed to pee.

❖ ❖ ❖

"He's been getting a lot of those lately," Cat explained to Claudia.

"What's that?"

"Phone calls. Of the damn-I've-gotta-take-this variety."

Claudia dumped the chicken into the bowl with the celery and walnuts and quartered green grapes and went for the jar of mayonnaise.

"He doesn't say what they're about?"

Cat plunked her beans into the pot, two at a time.

"I want my mother?" Henry asked.

"Business. He says they're just business. This theater camp thing in Lake George with some guy he met at the ground breaking a few weeks ago. Or didn't meet. Reconnected. From high school. Do you know Sam Palin?"

"Doesn't ring a bell. And you don't believe him?"

"I don't not believe him, exactly. Did you ever read *Highlights* magazine when you were a kid?"

"Sure," Claudia said, fond of the memory of those cartoony pages. "I'm surprised you did. You're so young."

"Remember that game: the two pictures side by side, similar except for the smallest details, and you had to pick out the differences? Look! The stone disappeared! Or: there's a monkey in that tree! That's what it feels like with him. I know something's changed, but I can't put my finger on what it is."

"Have you talked to him about it?"

"I googled theater camps in Lake George." Cat's fingers moving through the beans, snapping off all evidence of the vine with impressive speed.

"It's come to that?" Claudia asked sympathetically. "Googling? I've been there."

Cat laughed. "I don't know. I feel like one day you're taking business calls, and the next you're packing your things and saying, 'Sorry for breaking your heart.'" Two beans missed the pot and tumbled to the floor. She stopped midway from picking them up. "Claudia," she began, flushing pink. "I didn't mean."

"Where's my mother?" Henry hammered his palm on the table until Claudia stepped to his side and asked, "What do you need, Daddy?"

"You're not my mother." He sounded small all of a sudden, broken and lost.

"She's not here. Is there anything I can get you? It's me, Daddy. Claudia, your daughter."

When Henry didn't answer, Claudia looked to Cat with a tolerant smile.

"Open mouth, insert foot," Cat went on.

Claudia raised a hand, a priest giving absolution, before returning to her salad. "He's not cheating. Take it from the woman wearing the scarlet letter."

"How do you know?"

"He's my brother. He'd tell me." She sounded sure, though her confidence on this front, in one's ability to say, yes, without doubt, I know this person well, better perhaps than he knows himself, had been brutally shaken over the last year.

"Take this," Claudia instructed, "and these." She handed Cat the cool bowl of chicken salad balanced on a stack of colorful plastic picnic plates. "I'll get my father."

Over lunch, they discussed their imminent outing. Evelyn had to go to a big-box store to pick up odds and ends for Henry's move: a hamper, a tiny television meant more to kill the nursing home's antiseptic silence than to entertain him, and packages of new undershirts on which she'd been instructed to write his name. They'd agreed that Benji would drive their mother, Claudia would stay with Max and Henry, and Cat would go for a long, mind-clearing run.

But as they finished lunch and cleared the table, Max, apparently immune to the heat as he spread out with his considerably dog-eared score, had a different idea. Cat and Benji could go on a run. Claudia could drive Evelyn. And he, Max, could keep an eye on Henry.

Everyone, especially Claudia, thought this a bad idea.

"But Henry naps after lunch. He'll nap. I'll work. Won't you, Henry? Besides," he said, turning an eye full of challenge toward Evelyn and Claudia, "you two should spend more time together."

Claudia sat on the wooden bench beside Max and put a hand on the pyretic pink of the back of his neck. He quickly ducked away. "You're getting burned," Claudia said.

Max slapped his sweaty cap onto the table and returned to the music sheets scattered in front of him. "We'll be fine."

"I don't think that's the best idea."

"Well, I think it's a great idea."

"Max."

"Claudia."

She wanted to scold and say, "I'm your mother," but she had promised herself she never would. She hadn't earned the right to play that card.

"Go!" Max shouted when it was clear that Claudia had no intention of moving. He waved off her lingering body as if ridding a garden of crows. Benji, Evelyn, and Cat watched as a jolt ran through Claudia's system. She stood. He lowered his voice. "When you needed space I gave it to you, you know? I gave you two months. *Two months.* I'm asking for two hours," he said with a stuttering laugh.

Nobody seemed to know what to say, but everyone, out of faint-heartedness or bewilderment or the paralyzing fear of pushing back, bent in the direction of Max's will.

"At least put on sunscreen," Claudia said before retreating into the house.

Inside the gelid laboratory of the kitchen, Benji and Cat hatched a second plan to set Claudia's mind at ease. Regardless of what Max wanted, regardless of what Max even had to know, they committed to camping out in the living room—unseen, unheard—until Evelyn and Claudia returned.

"Leave it to me," Benji assured them. "He'll be fine."

❖ ❖ ❖

When Max woke—fifteen, twenty minutes later—he jumped, startled at first by the unfamiliar surroundings, the shocking greenness of grass in need of trimming. He turned to see a ragged but fully functional beach umbrella stabbed into the ground behind him, casting him in benevolent shade, but ignored this as if it had always been there and snipped the thread connecting his mouth to a button of drool on his score. The midafternoon air, without a breeze to freshen it, rose thick and steamy. He didn't mind the heat: it reminded him of Dallas (not that he cared if he ever saw Dallas again) or, more accurately, of Arnav. The heat climbed like a steep but scalable slope. A challenge to be overcome and somehow a comfort, if only it didn't make him so sleepy.

He rubbed his eyes. He wanted to call Arnav, to apologize for what he'd said, to tell him all that he now knew, but a chain wrapped round his mind refused to let him stray. He picked up the page where he'd left off. Evelyn and Claudia and Jane would have to wait. He flipped to the beginning of act two. Here: the organizing theme, the faintest quote from Elgar's "Nimrod." Into this dawning melody, he twined the motifs of the characters, the reedy lilt of beautiful and grounded Mrs. Ramsay, the cello-heavy brooding of her philosopher husband, young James' tender despair, of everyone from capering Cam to solemn Andrew. Everyone and everything set in a losing race against time. Mrs. Ramsay's theme dying as she died. Andrew: lost to the war. Prue: lost in childbirth. Everyone else aging, tattering into something stiller, quieter, more spare and profound, but nevertheless redolent of their younger selves. The echo of them in them. Max picked up Woolf and found the passage he'd marked.

there rose that half-heard melody, that intermittent music
which the ear half catches but lets fall; a bark; a bleat; irregular,
intermittent, yet somehow related; the hum of an insect,
the tremor of cut grass, dissevered yet somehow belonging;
the jar of a dorbeetle, the squeak of a wheel, loud, low, but
mysteriously related; which the ear strains to bring together
and is always on the verge of harmonizing, but they are never
quite heard, never fully harmonized, and the sounds die out,
and the harmony falters, and silence falls.

This, he'd done. The sound of passing time, harmonies splintering into shards of dissonance and, one by one, being swept off the shore by silent waves, churned by the soft opening of act three into smooth shells of beach glass and Lily's first astonished words. *What does it mean then, what can it all mean?* He pushed his way past another stinging thought of Claudia—*would* she be crushed by such honesty?—and fought to stay on the lawn with Lily, the unrealized artist, alive with all of her self-doubt as she lifted her brush from her canvas and tried to stop Mr. Ramsay from striding across the lawn with some silly comment about his boots.

Max had days, whole months, when he doubted his music could genuinely touch another soul. Just as Lily couldn't reach Mr. Ramsay in any truly meaningful way: *There was no helping Mr. Ramsay on the journey he was going.* Was anyone to be helped? (And who would help Claudia?) Could music, Max's music, possibly be a lifeline? To someone? To anyone? If he let it, his mind could chase his doubts about his creation until he hadn't an hour left in which to create; he could wonder endlessly whether what he made had the power to reach a single person or whether everybody, in the end, like poor old Ramsay, was doomed to make the journey alone.

A call came from the house, faint but still loud enough to nick him from his concentration. He couldn't make out the words, but soon the sound resolved itself into Henry's voice and the embers of a barely there keening fanned into a bellowing shout. Max put his pencil down and listened. "Dead!" He tossed the only word he could make out into the pan, waiting to see how much it weighed. Could he ignore it? Did he have to go?

"Liar! You're a no-good liar!"

Trudgingly, Max loped to the screen door where Henry's complaint came clear as a bell: "She's not dead, you're a goddamned liar! Jane! Jane!"

Max called in, a sharp warning thrown at a barking dog. Immediately Henry ceased. Max called in again, softer this time, a question—*You okay?*—but again got no response. Torn but effectively deaf to anything but a strand of music waiting to be laid down on a staff, he hurried back to the table. He didn't have time for Jane. Understanding what needed to happen, he knew better where to place the notes, how to begin his graceful climb. He had to balance all things: light and dark, youth and age, vision and blindness, life and death, music and silence. Just like Virginia Woolf, he had to hold on to everything at the same time. He must, like Mr. Ramsay, sit in a little boat rocking beneath the lighthouse, both triumphant and defeated. He must think *I have reached it!* and *We perished, each alone.* He must make the music large enough to contain the despair and the hope, the failure and the goal, the truth and the lies. He must be large enough to contain both.

He started with the cellos in D minor. Cellos, with Max, always had a lot to say. The cellos provided the pulse whereby the heart beat. He heard the violins next, and a soft wind, barely a breath—what was it?—coming from the flutes. No, not flutes. In truth, he didn't much care for flutes. Oboes. Yes, oboes were better. Let the breath come from them with a somnolent air. He thought of writing, he once explained to Arnav, as being tuned to a transmission in another language from another place, another plane. The composer, the writer, any artist tried his best to catch what he could, but as with all translation, something inevitably was lost. He tried to capture what he heard as faithfully as possible, with as little loss, with as little distortion as possible. He looked down at the page, disappointed. Then he smelled smoke.

A pleasant smell at first, wood, a neighbor lighting a barbecue or burning branches in the yard. Max breathed it in greedily, but after a moment it grew into something else, becoming thicker, more complicated. He couldn't parse the scent, but something other than wood burned. He erased the notes he'd just written, cuffed the rubber shavings onto the grass, and poised his pencil to go at them again. The cellos, yes.

He wrote without stopping until, at last, the coming sound of it, the hiss, a gunfire *pop!* made him turn. His eye, still half-expecting a silvery scarf of smoke from a neighbor's lawn, the burning of dried branches in a heavy drum, trailed the fences and hedgerows. But no. As soon as he saw it, the radio switched off, and another sound overtook him as the music died. Everything drowned in the cloud of tar-black smoke mushrooming above his grandfather's house. It swelled through the air, climbing taller than the trees, tattering into thinner gray wisps only at its highest point. Max ran. He ran as fast as he could across the lawn and up the back steps to find the second floor roiling with smoke. Small fires, some growing, some curling and sputtering out, burned from one end of the house to the other. Scattered like a pile of burning leaves, index cards filled with cramped and tightly written words provided the glowing orange ember that turned the shower curtain into a scrim of flame or writhed in corners into harmless curls of ash.

He called Henry. He covered his mouth with his shirt and started toward the study, where the smoke thickened and singed. Fires of varying sizes danced erratically in every room, but the largest was here, in a furnace fed by a thousand books, some of which Henry had thrown to the floor in a madly budding bonfire.

"Henry!" Max called. He heard nothing. Then, to his left, from the couch, came a rough, hacking cough. Plume after plume of smoke moved past him like a row of soldiers with only the slightest space between. He tried to time his passage to the billowing march but missed and, swallowing a fiery mouthful of smoke, fell to his grandfather's side in a fit of jagged retching.

Henry easily outweighed him by thirty pounds, but Max was young, stoked with adrenaline, and, filling his lungs with clean air from under the sofa, capable of holding his breath for an impressive length of time. He heaved Henry, who was by this time mostly dead weight, into a standing position and dragged him forward. They nearly tripped over a tangle of books strewn across the floor, but fumbled into the hallway, where the smoke thinned and there was air to be had. They careened down the stairs. Both coughing violently, tears scorching their eyes, a rope of clear, pendulous snot dangling from Henry's nose as they crashed through the screen door and fell with a clatter onto the porch.

A band of neighbors, frozen on the lawn with looks of terror and amazement, snapped to life at the sight of them. Four men who were no longer made for running ran up the steps, two taking Henry, two taking Max, and pulled them onto the lawn, while a clucking cluster of women hovered above, unbuttoning Henry's collar, wiping Max's face, assuring them that the fire department was on the way. Henry, still rasping, face smeared with soot, whimpered, "She's not dead. She's not dead," while Max hung his head between his knees, heaving heavily, and, barely able to form the words, told him to shut up. Far away, the wail of a siren.

Between the smoke and the sleeplessness, a wrap of suffocatingly tight sheets wrapped around Max's mind. He could simply give over to the weight that pulled on him and curl back in a senseless cocoon onto the thick green lawn. But then, like a stroke of lightning, an urgent flash lit him up from the inside. His eyes snapped open. A light, brighter than the flames that lashed the upstairs windows, rent the cloth binding his limbs and made him jump to his feet. He wasn't exactly thinking of Claudia or the book, but the afterburn of both set him running for the house.

The assembled men, lungs already whistling from their labor, weren't quick enough to catch him, but one of the more spry women managed to snag his foot, which sent him crashing hard into the porch steps. He knocked his shin but hopped past the shocking pain of it and vaulted, in three Olympic strides, up to the study. The room was hotter than he'd left it, and the smoke came faster now, like filthy water flowing over a breached dam. Max stripped off his shirt and tied it tightly, bandit style, around his mouth and nose before dropping to the floor. Crawling forward with great care, he avoided the hills of burning books and groveled toward the desk.

At first, he didn't believe it: the safe had burned down. The history of Henry and Jane forever lost. But he felt farther along the bookcase, his sense of spatial positioning thrown off by a good three feet, until his panicked hands came to the hot metal box. His fingers jumped as if they'd found a live coal. He cursed, but again pushed past the pain. A sense of invincibility danced in a flash across his storm-riddled mind, a tonic, an opiate: nothing could hurt him, nothing could stop him. Holding his breath, he snatched off the shirt and used it to pry open the door.

The book was there, curled by the heat but unharmed, and he moved as if extracting it were a child's game, the steady hand needed to snatch it from its narrow opening without touching the hot surrounding walls, like a kid tweezing the patient's funny bone without inciting the cruel electrical *bzzzzzt* in Operation. With the shedding nest of pages in his grip, with every piston firing, he saw an exit route running like a white seam across the room's deadly black felt, as easy to follow as a runway, out of the smoke, out of danger, a mattress of soft, fragrant grass waiting for him on the other side.

Hugging the shaggy beast of his grandfather's book to his chest, he flew forward like a sprinter hearing the starting gun. The white trail led out of the room. His eyes didn't need to be open to see it—the trail, the green, the sky—but his body was a crucial foot off from where he thought it was, and his sneaker caught hard on the base of Henry's chair. Max snapped forward. His head, with all his momentum behind it, smashed into the corner of the desk. The pages scattered like birds through the room. The heat kited them up and away. They drifted down, falling into flames, feeding them or buckling into brittle shapes of ash.

Max groaned. He lifted his hand to his head, his hair already slick with blood. His eyes fluttered and closed. The smoke drifted above him but sent its tendrils down, knitting the billowing cloud to the fledging fires that thickened it. He coughed himself still then listened. The wood of the shelves popped and snapped. Paper scraps fizzing through the air like comets. The breath of the fire crawling closer to his ear. The closing approach of the sirens. The curtains, the books, the rugs, the walls. Everything falling beneath a roll of orange waves. Everything being swept away with a music all its own.

15.

Benji sat on a crowded lawn in a circle of fifteen students more than half his age. He'd lost track of how he'd gotten there—everything he did happened in a blear—but it wasn't longing for the programmatic cheer of new student orientation. He felt, as he had every day of the past month, as if a giant hand had picked him up and set him down, morning to night, moving him like a pawn in a game he had no wish to play.

Of course there was no hand. He wasn't caught in a dissociative fugue. He woke and dressed and ate and ran and shat and showered and slept, but he did it all without any sense of self-propulsion, driven to drama club, to the Cineplex, to Sperry's for a night with Cat, by the self-preserving sense that it was simply better to do these things than not. He didn't have to hide his grief, but if he didn't display proper evidence of coping with it, if he didn't demonstrate that he understood the word *accident* and had no cause to blame himself (but who else in the world could he possibly blame?) his mother and Cat would come for him. They'd interject themselves. They would, as if he were a man sinking into the sea, start throwing him lifelines, and their lifelines weighed as much as chains. The last thing Benji wanted was rescue.

The students finished up their lunches and settled into sharing, according to rules laid down with demented enthusiasm by a junior advisor, the details of their lives. Tammy, said advisor, exuded a blond, bland kind of commonplace beauty: her vacant smile would later make her a natural for real estate sales or fund-raising and development. She produced a big cellophane bag of M&M's and instructed the girl next to her to take a handful.

"Let's see. You took . . . five. Five? You can do better than that." Tammy demonstrated what constituted a proper handful and dumped them into her victim's waiting hand. "Count them. How many do you have? Sixteen? Now we're talking! Now you tell us sixteen things about yourself."

The second girl, an auburn giantess with an intriguing gap between her front teeth and unfortunate bangs, saluted the group. "Hi. My name is Vanessa Darby. I grew up in Glens Falls. I was captain of my varsity volleyball team. Go, Indians! My favorite color is magenta, though with this skin I've been told I shouldn't wear it. Is that the sort of thing I'm supposed to say?"

Tammy gave a thumbs-up.

"My favorite food is pizza. I have no idea what I want to major in. Journalism, maybe. Or maybe premed. Is that sixteen?"

"Six," shouted some sadistic stickler for rules.

After Vanessa had completed her struggling autobiography, she passed the bag of M&M's like it burned, and round they went with the sugar-amped sharing. It might have been a balm to Benji's mind to let Bob from Sleepy Hollow or Barb from Anaquassacook siphon some calm little current of thought where he could escape the waters that sooner or later spilled into that hospital waiting room, that bright linoleum box where he'd slept for two nights, where he and Cat and Claudia (who couldn't bear to look him in the eye) and Evelyn and Nick and Arnav joined Jim and Amanda Davis (who also couldn't bear to look at him—or any other Fisher, for that matter) on a diet of soggy sandwiches and vending machine coffee, hopeful, now that Henry had made it out of the woods, that Max would soon follow, leaning on the doctors' cautious optimism, on their *We have to wait and see*, on their *We have some promising news* until the winds changed and, like that, he was gone—*subdural hematoma* were the words they used—and nothing, nothing, nothing could ever be done to make it right.

But Benji found he could no sooner float in the calmest, most inconsequential pools of Bob's or Barbara's lives than he could pretend that he belonged where he was sitting. He heard voices, needling, implacable voices that had been building in volume since the memorial service that the Davises refused to let him or his family attend, a chorus of voices that positively screamed now with the inanity of his present situation and told him to go. It was wrong. Everything he was doing was wrong. Fake. Nothing but more ruin crouching on the road ahead.

When an impressively muscled boy with three freckles under each eye like a cartoon drawing placed the candy sack in Benji's lap, Benji took his handful with the enthusiasm of a machine, but found he couldn't speak. His eyes had fallen onto his zippered lunch sack, an orange nylon bag stuffed still with his uneaten lunch, which lay on the grass before him, bright as a coiled snake. He couldn't take his eyes off it.

Tammy, nearly preorgasmic with the biographical trove promised by his baker's dozen of M&M's, tried to get the ball rolling. "I love your T-shirt," she said. "Where'd you get it?" It was black, adorned with a picture of Harold Gray's loveable, empty-eyed Orphan Annie and the words "Tomorrow (and tomorrow and tomorrow)." A gift from Brandon Wright and the rest of the *Macbeth* cast.

She wanted thirteen things? Benji could have come up with thirteen things. He could have told her about the great, good success of the drama club, what he'd gotten from it, yes, but also what he'd given up for it. He could have said that, two hours before his parents' house burned down, he'd slipped into the side yard like a wounded animal and given Sam Palin a faint but final no. That Sam had said, "It's your life, buddy," as if he could see the end of it, and, "It's all good," as if it was anything but. Benji had chosen a path that afternoon. A life. The sort of life in which he'd build on the $600 he'd saved to buy Cat's ring or don a rented tux for the premiere of Max's opera. He chose this life, which changed on him in the blink of an eye, which left him falling without warning from the sky as life has a tendency to do.

Last year, on a desperate August night, he'd stood on the bridge and found no one separating him from the pitiless black gorge. Now he had Cat. He had his mother, his sister. He had the blessing that was Max, until that crucifying moment he no longer did. He'd spent the last year climbing up, out of that ravine, and this, in the end, is where the effort landed him. What role did he think he was playing? And where did he think it would lead? He was a fool strutting his disastrous time on the stage until, in the time it took to run a three-mile route he'd run a hundred times before, he destroyed everything.

Max was gone. Max was gone. And one day, no one knew when, no one knew how, the others would follow. He would lose Henry. He would lose Cat. He would be back where he started. Alone. All of these thoughts—was that thirteen, Tammy?—somehow fit into his little zippered pouch as snugly as a baggie full of carrots, a banana, a ham and cheese on rye. It was, at that moment, the saddest and most dangerous thing he'd ever seen. It was the rest of his life. If he let it, it would follow him through the years. It wasn't Cat and children and a two-car garage. It wasn't love or forgiveness or the possibility of being redeemed. It was 6,500 sandwiches before he stepped his way to a dusty death. It was 6,500 bags of baby carrots, 6,500 bananas. If he died today, he'd be worse than forgotten. It would be as if he'd never been born.

With that, Benji stood. Dropping his M&M's like empty seed husks into the grass, he left everything—lunch sack, orientation packet, campus map—where it lay and, ignoring Tammy's surly protest, started the long walk back to parking lot D.

❖ ❖ ❖

She sat on the edge of Henry's bed and read the letter aloud. She'd been working on it since the day Max died, since the day she watched her opportunity to tell Claudia the truth come and go on that endless drive to the store. Evelyn might have unburdened herself then, though she couldn't shake the notion that telling would do nothing but add to her load. And not only hers. Claudia, too, would bend with the weight; Evelyn's bold and upright girl brought to the ground by a forty-year-old lie.

Excepting the reverend who married her, never had Evelyn admitted to anyone that she had opened the door one day and took into her arms another woman's child. Never had she wanted to. Never had she seen the need. She and Henry had worried for a time that the secret they kept from Claudia would be exposed by nasty children or gossiping neighbors or the self-appointed scourges of a small upstate town. But the elderly neighbors who knew of Jane's disappearance had, miraculously, moved on or gone demented or died before her daughter reached the age that may have tempted them to disclosure. And the young families who took their place had never seen the woman named Jane They knew of no scandal, no secret, and so Claudia grew, as Henry and Evelyn intended, with a sense of belonging she had no cause to doubt.

Except, on some level, Evelyn knew, she did. As soon as Max appeared at her door, Evelyn couldn't avoid seeing just how much her daughter did. Why else would Claudia keep such an enormous and essential predicament from her? Why else would she turn from her mother's guidance? Her love? Why else would she leave buried the lie of her own child, year after year, decade after decade, until the child came crashing into their lives like an avalanche? Evelyn came to see Claudia's secret as retribution for her own. For now that Henry's mind had dissolved, and with it the oath he insisted they keep, the fault rested entirely on Evelyn's shoulders. Thus, the letter.

What started as a rambling six-page admission of and apology for burying the bones of her daughter's history—a truth Evelyn felt compelled to offer in a sort of tribute to Max—had swelled, in the weeks following his death, into an imprecation of her very own existence. It was her fault, she said, rejecting the comforting thought that Henry shared (and possibly deserved even more of) the blame. It was all her fault.

But who was her admission for? The further she read, the more she wondered who stood to benefit from what she had to say. Was it for Max, who was gone? Was it for Claudia, who had the rest of her life to live? By confessing her heart, Evelyn alone stood to feel lighter. Claudia had lost Max. Claudia had lost Henry. And now Evelyn stood ready to take away what was left. She read the letter through to the last words. *Love, your mother.* Your mother: what was left after that for Claudia to lose?

Evelyn gave no more thought to tearing up those pages than she would about pulling her hand away from a flame. She did it instinctively. She shredded the letter, bit by bit, her eyes spilling over at the sight of the awful confetti raining down into the trash. How could Max forgive her? Tired, she shifted her position on the bed until she was lying by Henry's side, her head pressed to Henry's head. He looked at her then, and she wondered who he thought he was looking at. If he realized he was looking at anyone at all. Maybe she was, in Henry's mind, his wife. Maybe she was Jane. Maybe she was a girl he never thought to mention, a girl who lived in his mind eons before she walked into that apartment off the garage and met the boy with the suitcase full of books. But no. Evelyn wasn't Jane. She wasn't even Evelyn. She was nobody, just as Henry now was nobody. She curled next to him and drew his arm around her. She closed her eyes and breathed deeply, as if readying for sleep. Now perhaps, at last, they could rest.

❖ ❖ ❖

By the time Benji arrived, his mother was gone. He stood in the doorway, stunned by a smell that made his stomach lurch every time: floor cleanser and beige food and, somewhere deep underneath, the dark offense of human shit. He closed his eyes and opened them again, as if this brief respite might make the yellowish light oozing from blister-like sconces less terrible and the man in the bed, nearly unrecognizable to him under his thin white sheet, more like his father. He'd spent his lifetime wishing his father would disappear, and now that Henry had, Benji wanted little more than to get him back. He didn't like coming here, so it surprised him to find that, lately, here was one of the only places he could stand to be.

Once Benji overcame his body's reflexive response to the indignities of dying in a leased room with lemon-colored linoleum, he found himself sitting sentinel over his father, in the vicinity of a precious calm. He stepped forward and peered down from Henry's side into a face washed clean of recognition. Gone, the disappointments. Gone, the wit. Gone, the sharp-toothed eminence. All the lasting things, it turned out, did not last. His father's mouth opened and closed, opened and closed, like a fish mouthing clear, silent bubbles into the air. Benji pulled up a chair and sat. This was the vigil he never dreamed of keeping. And this was the last.

Benji had, since the fire, set to rereading his father's books. From beginning to end, first to last. He'd never admitted to Henry that he'd made a first lap with the old man's oeuvre and now, a quarter of the way into the second, Henry couldn't understand him if he did. In his twenties, when the exchange of Henry's infamous birthday books struck his son as especially pointed, Benji secretly dipped into the pages of *Nuisance* and *The Skirmishes*; if Henry had corked a message in some bobbing literary bottle, Benji took his chances on finding it here, in the pages of *Nostomania* and *Derelict's Fee* rather than anatomies of postwar America or bloated Russian doorstoppers. Perhaps Benji, like the disinherited Dimitri Aster in *Nostomania*, had come to wait for his father's last words.

For 513 pages, for 212 days, Dimitri stands over his father's bed, patient for the bastard whose gambling partners have beaten him into a coma to open his eyes and say what he has to say. And then, 212 days after Dimitri's vigil begins, after 212 days of tortured reflection on Phelan Aster's paternal shortcomings, the father opens his eyes and says to his son, whose mouth is loaded with the gob of spit he's dreamt of launching into his failure of a father's face (no matter what the old man croaks), "And now what?"

Dimitri swallows his spit, sensing in the question the first signs of melting a glacier-size impasse, then looks up at the beeping heart monitor to see the thorny green vine of his father's sinus rhythm snake into a smooth, straight line. A 513-page joke. And now what? And now nothing. Some joke.

Benji, who'd spent more than 212 days of his life hawking up a final, Dimitri-ish send-off spritz of his own, regarded the absurdity. The more you remember, the more you've made up: this, from *The Skirmishes*. The father he'd grown up with differed from the father before him differed from the father as husband or artist or teacher or man. Benji had a death grip on a single part of Henry, a few lines he'd redacted from the whole of the text that made the whole more legible to him. He found it hard to fit that piece into the puzzle that lay before him, to complete the portrait of Phelan Aster or Henry Fisher or whatever enigmatic monster Benji had whittled down from a much longer, more complicated story: he saw no trace of that man in the figure before him (who wasn't, as Benji expected, raging against the dying of the light but slipping as gently, as slowly into it as one can).

"Pee," Henry said. The voice, hoarse but coming like a flock of birds bursting from the stillness of a tree, startled him.

"Dad?" he said.

"Pee," Henry repeated, his eyes not moving from the ceiling, as if aiming the appeal at a higher power. "Pee. Pee." The word burbled out like water from a fountain, a steady stream of monotonous sound.

Benji rose. He lifted the bed sheet to see the insult of a wet mark blooming along a leg of Henry's pajamas. He pushed the call button that summoned the duty nurse and went to the door to watch for his approach. But nobody came. Looking over his shoulder, Benji weighed his options. He called down the corridor but didn't dare jog the short distance to the end of it to find the nurse. Even if he could hear his father speaking the entire time, he could not bring himself to leave his post.

"Pee."

He turned back into the room as though he knew exactly what to do, stalking into the huge tiled square of the bathroom, where safety bars attached to the wall near the toilet and shower, and a drain (reminder that the entire operation could be hosed down when the time came for the next occupant) took up the center of the slightly sloped floor. Grabbing the round plastic pan that Evelyn used to soak Henry's calloused feet, he filled it with warm water and a soapy sponge and carried it to the side of the bed.

Benji's hand found its way to his father's forehead, and as though it belonged to someone else, he watched it smooth down Henry's hair. Sweat rose on Henry's skin from the strenuous work of saying that single word, and part of Benji looked on as another part of him—more present, more suitable, more unafraid—moved through its paces. He pulled the sheet over the end of the bed and undid the buttons of his father's pajama top. Henry no longer smelled like Henry, and his body had shriveled over the course of a year into a less familiar thing. He looked smaller than he actually was, childlike, as if the man he'd been had slipped inside this loosening skin to hide among the bones.

Benji, shushing Henry's demand into nothing more than a steady susurration of sound, carefully freed his father's arms and began sponging them down. The soap belonged to Evelyn, the sweet vegetal scent of lavender that trailed after her showers, which left Benji with the impression that both of his parents were there, his mother's hands perhaps guiding his. He lifted his father's arms to wash underneath them, then moved gently down the torso, the skin giving as though it were a suit one size too big, before coming to a stop at the elastic-banded pants where the maroon fabric darkened as the water touched it. These he tugged from Henry without pause, slipping into a rhythm, a pace no longer set by his mind. He rinsed the legs next and then the feet, the pale, smooth skin from which the hair had somehow disappeared, before his fingers moved to the adhesive strips that closed Henry's diaper. He unstuck the flaps of tape and used them to seal the leaden, urine-soaked pad into an innocuous white ball.

Over the course of a year, Henry's condition had raced from moderately severe to severely severe like a NASCAR driver shifting into his final laps. Benji paused to take in the whole of his father's body, the daunting decline made unavoidably real, but he carried on, washing the shrunken gray privates with stoic competence before rolling Henry onto his side and running the sponge up and down his back. He found a fresh diaper in the closet, fresh pajamas in the drawer. His hands smelled like lavender. He pulled the blanket to his father's chest, leaving barely a trace that he'd been there. Henry stared at the same spot on the ceiling, mouth moving softly, speaking a language nobody but Henry could hear. Once again Benji smoothed his father's hair. He looked down, wanting his father's eyes to turn toward his, which they would not do.

And now what?

❖ ❖ ❖

Claudia stood at the gates of campus, hearing the taxis zip by, and waited for something to move her. A force, a charge to send her coursing through the branching circuits of the city. She walked its length from Barnard to her apartment on Fourteenth Street, passing the dirty-looking dry cleaning shops, the proliferating Duane Reades and flower-fronted bodegas, the uninspired restaurants and bland brand clothing stores, letting the crowd carry her along at its own graceless pace until it delivered her (sore, exhausted, ready to pass out) into Nick's arms. The route could neither be long enough nor short enough. She found satisfaction in the stab of being alone, in wandering into the used bookshop on Eightieth Street and sitting with a copy of the Mary Jo Bang poem she left on Max's grave like a Jewish mourner might leave a stone, in looking for a look-alike among the skateboarders gathered in Riverside Park. She wanted to avoid the comforts of Nick and his shared grief and suffer, as much as she wanted him to curl on his side and let her hold onto the trunk of him as she plummeted into a sleep that had yet to give her a glimpse of her son. She dreamt of dogs chasing her through a Home Depot that sold nothing but chandeliers but no Max. No matter how many times she said his name before two Klonopin carried her off to a place she could no longer get to by herself: No Max.

Today, having wrapped up office hours during which she dismissed a doe-eyed sophomore's project with a few sentences of streamlined imperiousness, Claudia returned to watching the video that played on her screen for the better part of the day. Max wasn't in the video, but Max was there, in the room, the music his, the concert his, the first concert of a work he thought too shaky and unrealized to share but after which he stood for the briefest of bows. So unnerved he'd been, inviting her to it. So worried, sitting across the desk in that green plastic chair, fiddling with the shiny silver bar that pierced his ear. Of course there were other videos online, a trove of his lionized feats, but Claudia found this the most personal. As if it had been recorded especially for her. She felt the beat of Max's heart in it, and finally, as he appeared with a mixture of embarrassment and pride at that small gale of applause, she felt hers too. She hit "Play" and, before it could come to an end, stepped out of the office and locked the door.

It was hard, nearly impossible, for her now to make the trek to the Village's building site without passing by the burned-out shell of the house. With its roof open to the sky, it looked like a great ship, hull rent by a rock, turned belly up on the land. Work felt beyond her; waking to the sun or rain or clouds that insulted her every morning with the start of a new day should have been beyond her. But it wasn't. She woke. She got out of bed. She worked. She felt broken but not beyond being put back together, even by this, a fact that only broke her more. And yet she moved. Like it or not, she was moving. Were there no emotions—no happiness, no disappointment, no shattering loss—that time would not wash away? Was there no life? It felt like a betrayal—not merely to Max, but to some larger, more fundamental idea of being human.

Once, she stood at the gates until the sky turned purple and a security guard emerged from his little roofed box to ask if she needed help. No, she said. And stepping into the stream of pedestrians, she started on her way.

❖ ❖ ❖

On the drive back to Cat's house—already he thought of it as Cat's house, as someplace foreign to him, as someplace he didn't belong— Benji snapped their *we* into a *you* and an *I*. It came apart with heart-breaking ease. There was Benji. There was Cat. He let himself into the kitchen, still pungent with garlic from last night's meal, knowing that she wasn't home. She was at the gym or dropping boxes by the post office or wherever she had to be before reporting, in another two hours, to the high school auditorium for a student orientation of her own. That morning, he'd sat at the table shaking two packets of sweetener onto his cereal and said, "I'll see you there."

Now, he beelined for the hall closet, dragged his suitcase into the bedroom, and flung it open on the bed. If there was a benefit to having accomplished so little in life, certainly it was having so little to pack. His shirts and pants and shoes tumbled in. Sweaters and winter jackets he left behind. He doubted he'd need them, although the desert, he knew, could be cold at night. He walked through the entire house, from the dock she'd soon hire somebody else to draw up for the season, through the bedrooms and dining room and kitchen and baths. Ghosts everywhere. He closed his ears to them and, before leaving, stopped in the downstairs office where Cat paid their bills. It was a task she hated, and usually Benji stood in the kitchen making up pet names to distract her. *Can I call you Boobaker Soufflé? Can I call you McGee McGrutter?*

He stole a clean sheet of paper from the printer and wrote, *Cat*— His mind, working like a bellows for the last few weeks, tried to stoke the fire wherein an acceptable good-bye could be forged. A list of reasons, tight as a suit of armor, that Cat would have no choice but to find ironclad, unassailable, no matter how she battled against it. He was a murderer. He was a waste. He tried six times, his pen trembling so much the words looked more like Arabic than English, and wadded his failures into the wire basket beneath the desk. *C*— (he finally wrote) *I don't belong here. I never did. I love you.* —*B.* He left it on the counter with his key.

He called Sam Palin on the way to the airport, who laughingly reassured him that "no" and "yes" often lead to the same place. Sometimes you take La Cienega. Sometimes you take the 405. "A little LA humor," Sam joked. "Don't worry, you'll catch on."

Benji bought his ticket at the counter (and, with his credit card balance reset to zero and $600 calling to him from his new savings account, opted for the upgrade). Ubiquitous white buds planted firmly in his ears, he sat at the gate, stuffing noise into the cracks of every door that he had, in just the last few hours, slammed shut. He didn't want to see reason shining like a light through the crevices. He wanted oblivion and darkness and mind-blotting sound.

A jowly woman with thinning hair jabbed an angry finger in her ear, a gesture that carried with it an urgent need for a state closer to silence, as universally understood as a hand pressed to the throat means *I'm choking!* "It's not a library," he gruffed, turning the volume down as much as he dared. Radiohead sang of being crushed like a bug, of growing wings, and Benji mouthed the words with them. He boarded the plane not when the flight attendant called for first class but when the dwindling herd of passengers made it clear that the plane was leaving. He took his seat, pulled down his sunglasses, which Cat would have found unforgivable—Really? Are you that cool, Mr. Mover and Shaker?—and sank back into the unyielding cushions, the closest thing to an embrace he had allowed himself all day.

Eyes closed, music blaring, he felt gratitude for the slight movement of the plane beneath him, the extended foreplay of a long taxi before the climax (delayed once for traffic; delayed twice for a passenger in need of the restroom) of takeoff. His sigh of relief left him nauseous, as if he'd robbed a bank and the getaway car was actually getting away. A fine sheen of sweat glistened on his face. Then: the tap of a hand.

Benji ignored it at first, pretending to be asleep, but when it came again, insistent and unwelcome as room service when you're flat out and jerking off on the hotel bed, he ripped the Wayfarers from his face and turned to his seatmate like a lion ready to feed. The kid beside him— eighteen, twenty—smiled without apology. She was a California beauty who wore her looks loosely, as if she didn't even know they were there, with pale blue eyes that looked out on the world with casual interest, and a lax bun of sun-streaked hair knotted at the top of her head. She finished a sentence Benji couldn't hear. He plucked a bud out of his ear.

"You okay?" She laughed.

"Fine," Benji deadpanned.

"Because you've got ahold of the seat arms like you're trying to rip them off." Again no response. "Nervous flier?"

Benji loosened his grip, put his hands dumbly in his lap. "I guess."

"Want a drink?" The girl toggled her head at the flight attendant in the process of delivering a gin and tonic two rows ahead. "They're free."

"I'm fine."

"Cool."

He went back to his music, aware that denying himself a wee bottle of Tanqueray meant nothing with a small pill-shaped plastic case in his bag in which rattled three Percocets. The magic beans he'd kept all this time, in case the day came when he needed a stalk to climb away on. No, he told himself. No. But why then had he brought them? Why had he kept them? Why make a miserable day all the more miserable?

He hitched himself to the steely riff of Radiohead and let it carry him where it would. He stood on a bridge. The railing would either hold him or it wouldn't.

Sometimes you take La Cienega. Sometimes you take the 405.

EPILOGUE

The woman is five months along. The farthest she's ever been. The first, she lost at eight weeks; the second, at four. Fleetingly she thinks, *I'm thirty-eight. How many more chances do I get?* The old fear—familiar but still startling—tugs at her, but she finds she can hold on to it now. It's balanced against a strength rooted deep inside her, a sense of possibility, of—dare she even think it?—invincibility that comes with her swelling belly. She arrived early with her blanket, with her bag of cheese and crackers and grapes, a bottle of wine and two stemmed cups made from recyclable plastic. She is celebrating. They are celebrating. A promotion is cause to celebrate. A promotion is also, she realizes, cause to be late. She searches the crowd, looking across the dusky field of the Village for the bald black head she knows so well, held tall and (when heels are involved) high above the crowd, the white dress with the giant navy dots, the killer yellow shoes. (Who, she asked earlier that morning, wears pumps to the park?) She taps the face of her watch as though it's betraying her.

It is an uncommonly cool summer night on the outskirts of Alluvia, New York. The lawn is filled with couples, with families, with groups of gathering friends who've driven from Albany, Schenectady, Saratoga, beyond. They stretch out on tasseled blankets, batik tapestries, on grass-stained sheets set aside for such occasions. They talk. They argue over the news. They eat. The sky darkens like a glass of water in which someone's dipped an inky brush, from violet to blue to almost black. There are fireflies. There are, for a moment, birds diving to feast on them.

Everyone watches the birds until someone says those aren't birds, they're bats, and a ripple of panic and delight moves through the crowd. *Bats!* People flat on their backs, hands covering their faces, laughing and cringing and crying, *Bats!* But soon enough the bats are gone, and the musicians and singers take the stage, which rides above the grass like a barge of light, a radiant yellow boat with women in black gowns and men in tuxedos slowly taking their seats on deck. They tune their instruments. The crowd's attention, braided together for a single second by the strange tentative sounds, unravels again. They mistake it for the start, and a surge of enthusiasm, frayed at the edges with impatience, with uncertainty—*Should I be somewhere else? Doing something else?*—travels across the field as through a snapped elastic band.

Still, she looks for that head, that dress. Fearing it will soon be too dark to see, that they will miss each other, that she will be left alone with her cheddar and grapes, she feels a hot wind of anger blowing through her. It threatens to sweep her off the blanket, to carry her like a kite, up and out of the park, out of the day she's so carefully planned, but she manages to stay. She ties herself down with a string of faith, flimsy in the face of her lover's new ten-hour workdays, but still strong enough to hold. All this is for her. For her.

After all, it's her wife who insisted they come. It's she who loves opera. She who owns every CD of the boy who wrote it. Such a sad story. She pops a grape into her mouth and pulls what strands she can from a tale she's heard a handful of times in the thirteen years they've been together. It's an opera based on *Mrs. Dalloway.* No, that's not right. She always makes that mistake. It's not *Mrs. Dalloway* or *A Room of One's Own*—the only two she's read—but the other one. The one about the sea. Technically it's not an opera because it was never finished. Technically, though only a professional might hear its faults, it's a fragment. But this fragment, her wife believes, is better than most *opéras complets*. Its fragments written fifty years ago (a semicentennial concert, the event listing said) by a boy, or not a boy, but someone who died very young (how did he die, again?), who was twenty? Twenty-one? She forgets how old—if her memory is this bad now!—but it was something terrible. Something sad. Maybe cancer or something about a boat?

She squints her eyes and sweeps the crowd like a lamp from a lighthouse. That's it! Not the sea, but a lighthouse. She chastises herself: It's called *Lighthouse*, stupid. And there it is: the dress. She raises her phone, turning on the app that sends color-coded pulses of light, a Morse code of their own making for exactly this purpose, finding one another in a crowd. The music begins just as the two of them settle in. There is no time for talk. No time to ask about the other's day. The crowd quiets. They kiss quickly as her wife smooths the dotted dress and she herself peels the foil top from the wine, as if nothing were amiss, as if the night wasn't nearly ruined.

Eight weeks. Four weeks. Twenty-some years. If she thinks about it, it's all so sad. So terribly heavy, if you let it be. It can leave you stripped and naked and utterly alone. The thoughts dance in her mind, tiny threads hanging from a sweater that she has to choose, deliberately choose, *not* to pull. Satisfying as unraveling can be. Sad as the world sometimes is, she also knows its beauty, its rare and occasionally breathtaking charms. There are days it leaves her helpless, paralyzed with happiness, afraid to move lest she set the clock ticking again and bring it all closer to its end.

She touches her belly. They clink plastic glasses. Five months. Five months. The cello rises in a wave that crashes into silence. Then the violins. Then a boy, barely visible to her, so tiny at this distance under his yellow veil of light, sings in a clear, liquid soprano, "Tomorrow."

They own everything he ever recorded, but this is the only thing he lived to write. Who knows what he might have done?

"If it's fine—tomorrow."

He certainly would have finished his opera, she thinks. He was so close. She feels sure of this. But. But. She wants to say something to him, to speak privately, as if in prayer, to thank him for this moment, this night. She puts one hand on her wife's leg, on the soft silk of the spotted dress. She eats another grape. Everything seems possible. Everything seems right. She closes her eyes and tries. She tries, but it feels so silly. The words won't come. But if she does this, she feels the need to do it right. To call his attention, if his attention is there (somewhere out there) for the calling. (There are days she doesn't know what to believe.) But how to begin? *Her memory!* she laments. How to begin, how to do it right, how to thank him for one incandescent moment, when she cannot, for the life of her, remember his name?

ACKNOWLEDGMENTS

The following people have my deepest gratitude:

My editor, Carmen Johnson, and my agent, Kate Garrick, both of whom so generously helped me discover a new and better book in the one I'd written;

My friends and family, some of whom read earlier drafts and provided me with encouragement and tremendously insightful critiques, all of whom have offered their love, support, humor, free psychological consults, career counseling, and never-ending wisdom: Adesh Brasse, Liz Budnitz, David Cafiero, Ken Corbett, Christina Crosby, Michael Cunningham, Matt Feldman, Meg Giles, Michelle Hand, Lyle Ashton Harris, Beverly Hopson, Kevin Hopson, Tara Hopson, Janet Jakobsen, Daniel Kaiser, James Lecesne, Leyden Lewis, Debie Lowe, Christian McCulloch, Adam Moss, Christopher Potter, Dave Purcell, Seth Pybas, Sal Randolph, and photographer extraordinaire Matthew Sandager;

Ian Holloway, for whom I don't have enough endearments;

Tyler and Grace Hopson, Bird and Mila Giles-Purcell, and Sofía Holloway Osorno, who are too young to read this book at the moment but belong in this list;

Matthew Rottnek and Joan Swanson, for patching a sometimes leaky ship and keeping it afloat;

And Melvin Galloway. For everything.

ABOUT THE AUTHOR

Photo © 2015 Matthew Sandager

David Hopson earned an MA in American and English literature from Washington University in St. Louis and an MFA in fiction from Columbia University. He lives in Brooklyn. *All the Lasting Things* is his first novel.